Also available as an ebook:

Era 1 of *The Happening Man*

The
Happening
Man

Vic Chamberlain

Matador
9 Priory Business Park,
Wistow Road, Kibworth Beauchamp,
Leicestershire. LE8 0RX
Tel: 0116 279 2299
Email: books@troubador.co.uk
Web: www.troubador.co.uk/matador
Twitter: @matadorbooks

ISBN 978 1788037 242

British Library Cataloguing in Publication Data.
A catalogue record for this book is available from the British Library.

Printed and bound in the UK by TJ International, Padstow, Cornwall
Typeset in 11pt Minion Pro by Troubador Publishing Ltd, Leicester, UK

Matador is an imprint of Troubador Publishing Ltd

Stephen Cheshire's help with the computerisation whilst aboard SS Arcadia in the middle of the South Atlantic.

And most of all to my darling Jenny Ormesher for her patience, tact and unwavering assistance and enthusiasm in enabling me to get the book done.

THE HAPPENING MAN

SEASON TWO

Major Trigg Hemmyng's planning for the establishment of the NY Ranch had been accurate and had been achieved within the financial budget that they had set themselves, but one aspect of the plan was proving to be much underestimated. The consequences of the rustling attacks on the livestock were proving an embarrassment of riches simply due to the number of captured horses that were now in Sammy Wheeler's corrals. The 'problem', added to the urgency in getting organised to manage Nancy Wheeler's rapidly growing output of dairy products, was concentrating Trigg and Roger's thinking and the need to revise the plan, and quick.

What Trigg and Roger had seen as a steady line of business producing a steady input of cash, was, due to Beattie's enthusiastic selling efforts, proving to be an even better business than either of them thought it could eventually become. Now they had a corral full of 'captured' horses where the majority of their previous owners considered that their only remaining use would be to pull a hearse. The horses could stay in the corral, a rest would do them no harm, and be bulked up some into better looking animals after being over-ridden by their now departed previous owners, but if these rustlers kept coming at the same rate, then what was now a benefit could soon become a nuisance. Trigg Hemmyng was not minded to sell them off cheaply, to be rid of them, because that would only devalue the local market and cause resentment among the other horse dealers and he had no intention of doing that. While they were out on the ranch, they were no problem, but he needed to get organised and get the market price for these horses.

The deal with Beattie Smithers was that she would sell the goods, the NY Ranch would deliver the goods to her place and she would organise the delivery to the shopkeepers, this being a trade-only operation.

Jake and Beattie had a place on the east side of the town, where they could, were they interested in becoming horse dealers, take, say, take six horses at a time. Only one way to find out – go and ask them.

Trigg and Roger sat and surveyed their site. Neither had seen it before and it was not in a prime spot but if Beattie could sell horses as well as she sold dairy produce, maybe that wouldn't matter. The place was reasonably close to the rail station, and Main Street, so it was not out of the way and a good business could easily be worked from there.

Trigg and Roger talked through a deal with Jimmy Hansom and a deal was formulated. The bank had been busting a gut to lend money to Major Hemmyng, but Trigg had quietly rebuffed their offers; he was not interested in anyone having a hold on the NY Ranch. It was theirs and theirs alone, and any children that they may be lucky enough to beget. But then this took a different turn. It transpired that Jake and Beattie were only renting this place. The fella that owned the place, and the empty lot next to it, had been killed in a business feud and his widow was keen to sell and go back East.

The deal that Trigg proposed was that they would form a new company where he and Roger would own 45% each of the shares, Jake and Beattie 10%, and the bank would provide a mortgage to cover the cost of purchasing the freehold of the land. Any buildings erected would be paid for by the company as and when needed. The company's business would be that of a hardware and horse traders. His only conditions were that Jake would continue to haul the 'scrap timber' out of Herbie's yard and that Beattie would continue to find business for the dairy products, both these conditions being a simple agreement and should either find a suitable replacement, then he would not disagree.

The bank hummed and aahhed over the finance, but when shown the livestock he already had, that would be 'fed' into the business, they readily complied.

Tommy Brennan and his men arrived on site, and when Jake and Beattie's battered and poorly built cottage was adjudged to be in the wrong place on this larger site, a new one was quickly constructed. The lumber from the old cottage was used to enlarge the barn and stables, and a hardware store, with an office above, was constructed from the 'scrap' timber. Roger and Trigg now had a town office for the NY Ranch.

Jake and Beattie were delighted; no more stairs for Jake to lug his damaged hip up and down every day and Beattie had a brand new home for the first time in her life. She couldn't hold back her tears of joy; there was a god and they were working for him. It was the answer to many of her fears of the future, particularly for Jake with his injured hip.

Trigg had gone out on a limb as regards Jake. He was basing his faith in Jake on Will Lawton's regard for his old sergeant. If Will rated him highly as a man, that was good enough for him. Honesty and reliability were the basic values he sought in a man, and with a 10% interest in this new venture as well, that had to be a proposition that both Jake and Beattie would grasp with both hands and work diligently to protect. There was nothing for nothing, especially out here in the West. It would take hard persistent endeavour to reap the rewards but he was pleased to be able to give them the chance. If Beattie's progress in garnering business for the NY Dairy Goods was anything to go by, the future looked rosy.

But the rustlers kept on coming although most perished under the ever-watchful eyes of Scobie, GG, Clikka and a new addition that had arrived, young Pony Chaser, the result of a heartfelt plea from his father to Scobie. The youngster was a good-hearted lad but prone to being headstrong; 'Please take him under your wing and educate him; if not he will surely be dead within the year.' The father had said. Scobie and GG knew the father well, and that he was the only son.

Trigg was agreeable, the papers were signed and the youth, renamed Chas, was brought onto the NY. and, under Scobie's tutelage, soon became a valued member of Scobie's team. He took to the work and quickly learnt to become a member of the team and to be patient and contain his aggression until instructed to do otherwise. He also took to the bronc-busting for Sammy Wheeler, his youth enabling him to bounce well when he was 'dumped' off. It was Chas working with GG who spotted the gang that made its way onto NY's land from the Pine Bluff's direction, taking pot-shots at the signboard informing them that they were moving onto private land. They were observed as they continued west, until they descended into a gully and stashed their saddlebags and checked that their firearms were fully loaded. Then they began to move west again, splitting into two groups, four in the lead group, the other five following on half a mile to the rear. GG kept his telescope trained on the leading group and sent Chas galloping into the ranch to raise the alarm. These trespassers were well away from the cattle, but to GG they still looked bad trouble.

When Trigg and Will edged over the crest and saw them, they felt the same way as well. As he focussed his glass on the leading party, GG related what he saw and how he saw the situation. These hombres did not look or act like rustlers. The two groups were still intact and no one had broken away to scout ahead. Scobie and Clikka were sent to scout the plain where the herd was grazing and make sure there were no other intruders moving in from a different direction.

"I reckon GG's right, Will, they do look trouble, but is it us they're after? Could be they're working their way into Cheyenne the quiet way. We've about three hour's daylight left, enough time for them to make it into Cheyenne just as night falls. I'll get back and get the ranch prepared for any attack. You look after things out here, keep them observed but don't let them see you. If they do skirt around the ranch, all well and good, we'll let them move on, but if they are intent on raiding us, we will be ready. I'll take Chas with me, you keep Scobie, GG, Clikka and the two range hands with you out here, and if they do attack the ranch, we'll get them from both sides. If we are attacked, I'll send a red rocket up to warn you. If they do skirt around, I'll send Chas and Hogan in to warn the sheriff to expect 'em, but they do look trouble; 'I just hope it ain't us they're looking for. You happy with that?' Will nodded; he knew the siege plan for an attack on the ranch – all the women in the bunkhouse where there was water, food, heat and beds, the windows would be shuttered and the boss would have Sammy, Spud, Roger and other range hands well positioned and ready to give any galoots a very nasty taste of Henry rifle power.

Trigg eyed them through his glass from the hayloft door in the top of the big barn as the four riders came sauntering up to the ranch. They were edgy, mouthing to each other – probably how they were gonna take this ranch over. He let them come on until one rider moved towards his house.

"Nobody at home, hombre; they're all out, house is locked, what's your business?"

The hombre stopped and looked to his boss. The bossman was looking around, trying to locate where the voice was coming from but was obviously not seeing what he needed to see, and his hand slid onto his pistol grip.

"What's your business, stranger?"

"Get out here and I'll tell yer."

"I can hear good and clear from where I am. What's your business here?"

The hombre was getting riled and his three hoppos were sliding their hands onto their pistols, they were expecting the bossman to get real angry real soon.

"What's your business here, stranger; easy enough request, ain't it?"

"Get out here where I can see you and I'll tell you."

"No, you get out of here and fast; this is private property and you are trespassing. I have asked what your business is and you won't say, so turn around and get gone fast. The hombre drew his gun and waved it around, still not sure of where to shoot. A rifle shot took his Stetson clean off his head, spinning it into the dust. The rifle shot had spooked the horses and caused them to jig about.

"Hombre, you have two options: ride out or get carried out, your choice." Whether the hombre intended to, or the horse lunged forward towards the barn of its own doing, who knows, but another rifle shot took his gun shoulder out and the hombre crumpled down into the dust. Trigg wanted this hombre alive, the other three could be corpsed.

"Get off your hosses, throw all your guns away and lie flat on your bellies, arms well spread, or get shot – your choice." They chose to fight. Trigg gave the signal and they were corpsed.

Will Lawton heard the gunfire, as did the other five hombres he was observing, and he saw the smiles on their faces through his telescope as they kicked their horses into a canter.

Then Scobie pointed out the red plumes of the rocket and Will levelled his rifle and took down the leading rider. The other four were not ready to die and surrendered.

GG then led the major back to where these hombres had stashed their saddlebags, but it was getting too dark in that deep gully to see much. They returned at daybreak and recovered all nine saddlebags and these were placed in the wagon along with the four corpses and the five captured hombres and carted into Fort DH Russell. Eight of the saddlebags contained very little of interest, but one contained $9,467, and screwed up in the bottom, a receipt for $30,000 that bore the name of an attorney in Marshalltown, Iowa, and was dated a month earlier.

As usual, nobody was talking, maybe too scared to with the main hombre still alive, and he wouldn't be dying anytime soon. He had a smashed shoulder bone which would be next to useless for the rest of his life but he would not die.

Trigg completed his report of the incident and passed it to his colonel. The colonel read through the report of this incident. It was an awkward situation that had arisen and with the benefit of hindsight, it would have been better if this boss hombre had been corpsed, but he fully understood why Major Hemmyng had only shot to wound him then he'd be able to find out who he was and why he had been trespassing on NY land. This report had to be delivered to Divisional Headquarters, but as there were no real facts as yet, as to why this incident had occurred, the colonel decided not to forward the report.

"Before I report this incident to Omaha, Major, I think it would be wise to write to this attorney in Marshalltown and see if he can shed any light on these galoots. Unless one of these prisoners talks, it appears that is our only potential source of information. Get a letter off to him. In the meantime those galoots can stew in jail until we decide otherwise." A letter was immediately despatched and Trigg returned to his routine duties.

One consequence of this incident that had reawakened a fear that he had was that as an army officer, he could be transferred to another posting at any time should some top-brass officer back in army HQ so decide. Fort DH Russell was seeing more and more of these HQ-based top army officers now that the railroad had made the journey so easy.

Also, the only big problem the army now had with the redskins was with Red Cloud and the Sioux/Cheyenne uniting together and there was an awful lot of them. With Red Cloud having won the Bozeman Trail War and having burnt those vacated army forts to the ground, there was continued speculation and rumour that Congress and the Army, stirred up by the warmongers in the East Coast newspapers, wanted the 'Indian problem' resolved once and for all.

Having got the NY. up and running, the last thing he needed was to be posted up into Montana or Idaho or North Dakota. He wanted to resign from the army when he was ready, but orders were orders and very few orders were changed, and should he be posted, that was his only option. It was not the end of the world, he was well pleased with his personal situation, but another two years in the army would be ideal. Maybe he ought to become a more social hombre and keep his ears tuned to the internal grapevine of rumour and speculation that he had always scorned before, being more reliant on the more truthful information that the colonel made available when it had been agreed and needed to be expedited.

But that was his problem now – fitting in his army work and getting the ranch up and running. With the army, its business was keeping law and order, and that meant that they had to react to whatever came at them. The ranch had to generate its own business, and that meant having to think well ahead, like any other private business had to, whilst at the same time fighting to keep what was legally theirs.

Now, after this latest incident, he had another nine horses in the NY corrals, and these had been notified to the army. Any hombre who could prove that they had legal ownership of these horses could claim them, provided they settled the livery and any vets' bills and expenses incurred. With this bossman hombre still alive, it would be interesting to see if he thought it worthwhile to try and reclaim these horses. To do that he would have to produce either paperwork or witnesses to verify his claim. But he just might have stolen these horses himself and now he knew he was in an even bigger stew. Things were stacking up real good against this hombre; a reply from the Marshalltown attorney could tip this hombre into an even bigger hole. The Marshalltown attorney didn't reply to the letter; instead he boarded the first available train West and came scuttling across to Fort DH Russell like a bear with its arse on fire. This incident took on a whole different aspect when he confirmed that the receipt for the sum of $30,000 was genuinely his. He had brought his countersigned copy of the settlement with him to verify his story.

The $30,000 was the result of the sale of a ranch, its land and the savings of a recently deceased client, and this money had been paid to the sole beneficiary as the signatures on the receipt indicated. The attorney had passed this money over and received the receipt confirming acceptance but within an hour of this transaction being concluded, the beneficiary had been found murdered and the money was gone.

The local lawman had investigated and drawn a total blank. The murderer and the money had simply disappeared, seemingly into thin air, but then this letter from Major Hemmyng had arrived requesting information with regard to this crumpled-up receipt.

The attorney had the murdered man's widow to protect and was determined to give every assistance in resolving this dire situation. He had very little regard for the local lawman who had carried out the investigation of the murder, so little regard that he had not notified the lawman about this enquiry from the army; he had kept his own counsel and headed to Fort DH Russell as rapidly as he could.

With this situation unfolding as it now was, the murder and robbery in Marshalltown the month previous to the incident on the NY, and now these hombres under lock and key in the fort,

Trigg enquired as to whether the attorney might recognise any of the prisoners. The attorney was doubtful, but he was more than ready to cast his eye over these galoots, provided he could retain his own anonymity.

A screen was obtained and these galoots were paraded, or carried, past for the attorney to view them. Four of these he had seen before, but he did not know their names, but they were definitely from the Marshalltown locality. But he knew someone who would know who they were, and was so keen to resolve the situation, he would pay for this fella to travel to the Fort and carry out his own identification parade.

"Buddy Deans is the deputy; he is not the sharpest knife in the cutlery drawer, but he is, in my experience, the only fella I would trust in that sheriff's office. He is a big raw-boned lad who the sheriff uses for his brawn and ability to handle the drunks and the brawlers, but he is indebted to the sheriff who provides him and his kid sister with rent-free lodgings. Buddy's parents took ill and died leaving Buddy to look after his little sister. With your permission, Col. Stratton, I will return to Marshalltown and make the arrangements and then telegraph you the details."

The colonel was in full agreement. This case was well out of their jurisdiction, but if he could transfer these galoots and their identities to Div. HQ in Omaha in a well-packed report, ideal; they had done all they could, it would be up to Div. HQ to pursue the matter. Trigg was equally content – it was out of his hair, they had made the arrests, and now let the Omaha team resolve the case whilst he concentrated on his local situation.

Buddy Deans arrived three days later and was exactly as described, a large but amiable fella who had lost both his parents suddenly and had taken the deputy's job to keep a roof over him and his kid sister. His pa, a blacksmith with a rented smithy, had suffered a seizure and had died leaving debts that had overwhelmed his ma. She then caught some ague and she had passed away as well. Trigg could easily imagine that Buddy's pa was one of those fellas who was quick to do the work but slow to ask for payment, kind-hearted as some folks call these fellas.

When the four who the attorney had said were familiar were paraded past the screen, Buddy was nearly out of his seat and at them, but Trigg restrained him. "It ain't your problem, Buddy, just give us the names and your job is done."

Buddy had seen the boss hombre before but didn't know his name, but he gave them the names of the others and where they lived. Buddy was thanked and sent on his way home.

As Trigg ushered him out of the fort, he offered Buddy Deans some good advice. "Buddy, don't say a word of your visit here to anyone. Keep your eyes and your ears open and your mouth shut tight. If anyone asks where you've been, say Omaha, looking for a blacksmith's job on a ranch out West that you heard was going. Any trouble, see the attorney and get your kid sister and yourself over here; a good blacksmith farrier is a useful man to have around."

Sammy Wheeler was wanting an assistant and Buddy looked just the right guy for the Job: young, fit, strong, good raw material.

The colonel compiled his report and the whole scraggy lot were transported to Divisional HQ in Omaha and the nine horses stayed on the NY Ranch in Sammy's remuda. Somebody talked too loose during the Omaha-led investigation; apparently a smooth-talking, smart-witted lawyer had been recruited to contest this investigation by a hombre in Chicago and was making counterclaims against the army.

Trigg had received this information directly from the attorney, not from Army HQ and he showed the letter to the colonel. Forewarned is forearmed and the colonel made a casual enquiry to Omaha as to how the investigation was progressing, but was not at all happy with the reply he received. Trigg knew the score – when the fighting started for real, those in the front line got hit first and Buddy Dean's name was in the report. He telegraphed the attorney.

"If Buddy wants a job, tell him to get themselves over here pronto."

Since Buddy Deans had come into Trigg's world, the NY had acquired another fourteen rustlers' horses. Sammy was getting desperate for a full-time assistant. The range hands, even old Ragnar, had been helping out, but Sammy Wheeler needed an assistant to work 'iron', as well as all the other livery jobs, and get Jake set up as well. When Buddy Deans and his kid sister arrived, Sammy had him working within an hour. Buddy's six-year- old sister was drafted into Nancy's egg-collecting team; those pesky hens were laying eggs all over the place. Buddy was in his element – no more drunks to manhandle and the chance to restart on the trade his pa had started learning him and both were safely ensconced well away from that bad situation that was beginning to unfold in Marshalltown. There weren't any losers on the NY but there would be in Marshalltown.

It turned out that the hombre who had been the bossman when they had tried to attack the NY was a failed gambler from Chicago. Along with a hoppo, one of the men who had been corpsed on the NY, they had robbed a gambling house where a big pot was being played out, and skedaddled out of Chicago to Marshalltown, where his sister was married to the sheriff. Just how he came to know that the fella was carrying $30,000 was not known, but he did know, and he shot the man and fled into the shanty town where he had some cousins and they had laid low. Again, why the sheriff had decided to take a posse out in the other direction was yet to be satisfactorily explained, but it had afforded his brother-in-law the opportunity to depart Marshalltown and head west with a gang of galoots out of the shanty town. Where they had been in the month before arriving on the NY was again unknown, but they were being connected with other robberies as the dates and timings made it highly likely that it was them. Again, why had they departed the train at Pine Bluffs when Cheyenne was only another forty miles or so up the track? But they had and it was their downfall.

The big argument back in Omaha now was that the slick-talking lawyer in Chicago was alleging that his client had stashed more than $40,000 before being captured, yet only $9,000 had been declared. The inference being that somebody else had pocketed the rest.

Trigg's response was that the army could send a search party to look for the stash anytime they wished, and was it not possible that this money could have been stashed anywhere between Marshalltown and Pine Bluffs. Alleging that the stash was on NY land could be a clever ploy to deter anyone else from looking for it. But this stash could be found anytime in the future, and it would be deposited in the fort's safekeeping and used to recompense any of the victims as the judiciary saw fit. Trigg had consulted with Roland Simons, his attorney, and the response was all he could make, but he had a worrying inkling that this would not be the last he would hear of this matter. Roland Simons had had other dealings with these Chicago law firms before and it seemed a well-used ploy to try and spread as much sewage as they could, and they were very persistent.

Trigg's attention was then taken away from this situation when Jimmy Hanson, his accountant, put a proposition to him concerning shipping beef back into Indiana. Jimmy had been ferreting around looking for business and had contacted some of his old colleagues back East, fellas who he had been at college with and, as accountants seemed very good at, they had kept in touch as they went their separate ways after graduating. Jimmy was a lively fella despite his portly build and thick-lensed spectacles. Behind all that he was as sharp as a tack. He had been corresponding with his old college pal and spotted an opportunity he reckoned the major could well be interested in, if not now, then certainly in the future.

Jimmy met with Trigg and Roger in the upstairs office at the hardware yard and he outlined his proposal. His college pal had joined a food-supplying company which were intending to expand the business to meet growing demand and was actively seeking more suppliers of high-quality beef on the hoof. They were geared up to do the rendering, and it was good-quality material they wanted but they were having trouble getting regular supplies. They had taken on other suppliers but kept getting let down. Jimmy knew well that this was the business the NY was looking for but when were they looking to get started?

"Jimmy, you and Roger do the numbers, talk to your pals and find out how much they will pay and how many cattle they need to make it viable. If the numbers are right, then we will meet with them and see if we can do business, but if I don't like em, I ain't doing business with em. It might not be the best criteria for business, but I ain't dealing with hombres I don't like; it's just the Yorkshire in me, but that's how it is."

Roger and Jimmy did the numbers, and checked and double-checked the numbers, then put the paperwork away for a few days and got their heads into other items of business that needed attending to. Then they re-read their calculations and were convinced that they had got their numbers correct. The bogeymen in all these numbers were the market prices and these were dictated by the big auctions, but those prices could hurt both buyer and seller, it needed an agreed price for a stipulated period so that both buyer and seller knew what they were earning or paying. It was a swings and roundabouts situation – you had to do a deal and stick to it but some would and others wouldn't. Major Trigg Hemmyng had no debt, no mortgage, and a steadily rising inflow of cash from the hardware yard and the horse sales. His army income was not taken into the equation as that might stop if he had to resign his commission. It was make your mind up time – did he want to pursue this deal or wait till he had grown the herd and look at bigger deals? – single deals when the auction prices were in his favour, then sit tight if the prices fell and grow the herd again.

The reality of being a rancher was staring him hard in the face and it was looking at him wide-eyed and naked. A bird in the hand was worth two in the bush; if they could agree a deal with this C. Brandt & Sons, and he liked em, then he was ready for the NY to start trading in earnest. It was a 'walk before they tried to run' situation but you had to take the first step sometime or other; was he ready?

"See if you can agree a deal, then invite them over to see our spread and the herd and I can have a look at em."

The two Brandt sons arrived, with apologies for their father's absence.

"He says as we're running the business now, we can do the travelling. My pa's been made aware that a good colt that he likes may be for sale, so he's gone off trying to buy the horse. That's his real interest now: horse racing and breeding."

They liked the spread, were introduced to Sammy and Will, and Adalia and Helen cooked up a fine dinner for them. Trigg nodded to Roger that he liked em. A deal was agreed on a fixed price for six months with a minimum weight stated for an animal and payment to be made within fourteen days of delivery to Brandt's railyard pens. One hundred animals a month and a deal to be renegotiated unless either side wanted out.

Roger's next letter home was to his old boss, Colonel Barton, as he had promised to keep him informed as to how he was finding things in America and why not, when he had always been told there was always a place for him on the duke's payroll if the venture failed. It was the least he could do to keep his old boss in England informed. He told him of this deal they had agreed and that the NY was really in business now.

Col. Barton was quick to deliver this news to the duke. Unbeknown to Roger, the wily and astute old duke's hunch was coming to fruition. His hunch was that those two young fellas would be successful, and he was in a position to help them should they show that they had what it took to be successful in a tough business. Young Hemmyng had succeeded beyond his expectations, rising like that in the army and showing he had the guts and determination to command men and be very decisive in dire situations. Now young Stead was beginning to show his potential. He was ready to make his move and place a proposition in front of them that would increase their earning potential greatly. Nothing was guaranteed, but this chance would be a big fillip to their business.

Two months later Trigg eyed the very impressively addressed letter, then very carefully sliced open the envelope and gazed at the letter heading:

The Delaware Investment Group (Livestock Division) Washington DC.

For the attention of Major T.R. Hemmyng.

In Strict Confidence. He read the expertly composed letter outlining their involvement in managing livestock investments of American and European investors. Maybe it was too expertly composed. Trigg was well aware that there were plenty of these slippery varmints in the East – the carpetbaggers who had roamed the South in the aftermath promising the world on one hand and robbing you blind with the other. They were that slippery they could get under a snake's belly with a top hat on! Rustlers could steal your cattle but these varmints could steal your land as well and smile doing it. He was minded to burn the letter but hesitated. No harm in having Jimmy and Roland see it; maybe they could make some enquiries. He then let Roger read the letter, voiced his fears to Roger, then suggested he pass it to Roland and see what his thoughts were.

There had been reports in the newspapers on these investment deals and the trouble that had ensued when the rancher had fell out with his client. Nothing was easy in this business but the rewards were reputed to be very good. The NY had the land and Adalia and himself had chosen to create a home and a business on it, so no opportunity would be discarded until they were sure it was not viable for them. If Roland's enquiries proved satisfactory, then Roger and himself would talk with these livestock investment hombres – nothing ventured, nothing gained. It would be dependent on Roland's advice. He had his army business to attend to that needed his immediate attention. Captain Rinker had uncovered a gang of hombres that was marauding north of Cheyenne and Lt. Rossi had another rumpus to sort out in the Laramie Mountains involving some miners who he reckoned were robbing stagecoaches and hauliers – nothing new but every one of these problems could be very nasty.

The Shoshone lads had come across a robbery and followed the tracks back to a trail that led into a mine and nowhere else. The hard part then was getting in close enough without being spotted. These robbers often posted guards above a trail to give the mine owner plenty of warning if uninvited hombres were approaching. Scobie and GG had followed the trail back to a 'one way in, one way out' sort of place. One option was simply to take an uniformed troop straight in and parly with the owner, but that gave the owner plenty of time to make sure his place was spotless. Searching the tunnels was a no-no. It was too dangerous; the tunnel props could be booby trapped and any loot would be well buried under a well-disguised dummy tunnel. The other option was to remove the guard and get in quick, but even then you were likely to be involved in a shoot-out. Every one of these places was different. They had even got into one of these places posing as a tinker man with a cartload of pots and pans to sell, but this one was only suited to removing the guard and then piling in as quick as they could with the intent of catching them napping

Removing the guard went to plan, but they didn't get the surprise they had hoped for and the shoot-out took place. Even though all the troopers were clearly uniformed the miners weren't ready to cooperate or even to parley. After downing four miners, the white flag was waved and the rest of the miners were bound and gagged and loaded into one of their own wagons. The cabins were then searched and loot was found; that was good enough for the major. The main tunnel into the mine was dynamited to seal it – no way was he taking risks sending any of his men in there. The miners' cabins were fired and the items of loot, and the remaining live miners and their corpsed hombres, were loaded into one of their own wagons and carted back to the fort for the colonel and his internal team to carry out the questioning and further investigation, as he saw fit. If he decided to recover more of the loot from within the mine, he could form a troop of infantry soldiers to undertake that work, as was the normal practice in these situations.

Capt. Rinker had set up a tasty-dish ruse to lure in the marauders north of the fort and it worked superbly. In came the marauders expecting some easy pickings, only to get a good blast of shotgun pellets, which was more than enough to rid them of any thoughts of resisting. They now had the perpetrators of this raiding and killing; now the hard bit would be finding out where the loot was stashed and who had done the murdering. The promise of a certain hanging or a long spell of rock-busting down in Leavenworth concentrated the minds, but remission could be earned if they chose to cooperate. These were hard nasty galoots and not too smart, and their brains, what few they had, could be toyed with. It was in for a penny, in for a dollar – all was fair in this business

The scrap timber was still arriving and Ragnar took heed of the stories that Scobie was telling him of the devastation that the winters of the seven year's snows could wreak on the livestock. Even bison caught in a bad place would freeze to death in these winters and although the last seven year's snows had not been that severe, it was more gales and driving rain that had flooded vast areas of low-lying land and caused the North Platte to burst its banks and swamp the land for hundreds of square miles.

Trigg could verify this; his first winter at Fort Laramie had been perishingly cold, so cold that Henri knew he couldn't take this weather and transferred over to a posting in Nevada. Then Trigg had endured the last seven year's snow which had been the colossal rains that had caused widespread floods as the Union Pacific's tracks had been washed away in the North Platte area. With warnings of the likelihood of dire weather in store, Ragnar had put his thinking cap on and had devised a plan to erect, using this scrap timber, some very basic but effective livestock sheds, sheds that would protect the calfers and ewes from the driving rain, intense frosts and blizzards.

"Get me a sawyer and two handy lads and I will supervise them. We will cut all this scrap timber into 1½ inch thick boards – width won't matter, it'll all get used up like this." He showed his grandson his sketches and Trigg saw the simplicity of his detailing and the ease in which these sheds could be erected. Every scrap of wood would be used, even the sawdust could be used for packing the eggs in Nancy's egg boxes, and should they ever need to, a shed could be pulled down and the wood used for winter logs.

Trigg's uncanny knack for making the right move at the right time manifested itself again. He went to see Herbie Brunner and learnt that the Casements' lumber yard was being moved to Green River. With the Union Pacific now laying track into Utah, all the backup works were moving on as well

"I've got two brothers, trained em up myself to be sawyers, but they don't want to move to Green River; they're staying with their ma in Cheyenne. I didn't like the thought that I'd got to lay them off. This job will be spot on for them. They can do the cutting and then with Ragnar keeping his eye on them, they can erect the sheds as easy as pie. I'll call em in."

Two sturdy young fellas appeared and a deal was agreed.

Trigg would supply them with a wagon and team to get them and their tools about and they could use the bunkhouse through the week, then travel back to Cheyenne on Saturday afternoon and be back on the NY early on Monday.

"It'll be a real good start for you lads to do some carpentry work. It'll get you started on that side. Could be the making of you. Tommy Brennan worked for the major first and look how well he's doing now."

Roger ordered in new blades for the vertical saw; it was only a basic machine but it was all they needed.

Trigg and his grandpa decided on some good level sites. The sheds would be sited so the open-fronted side faced south, the winds, rains and blizzards would blow over the roofs and carry on into northern Colorado, and the animals could park their arses in the shed and watch them go whistling by. The calvers and the ewes would be warm and dry.

The more Trigg thought about erecting these sheds, the more he liked it. His grandpa had come up with a really useful use for this 'scrap lumber', the quantity of which was much larger than he had envisaged it to be. Ragnar's other responsibility that Trigg had placed on him to keep him occupied was also paying good dividends. Most of the ewes were 'dropping' two lambs, and the value of these extra lambs would easily pay for these two lads to erect these sheds. If next season's lambing was as good, the value of his sheep holding would be well in excess of the budget they had set, and these sheds would only be more helpful in keeping the ewes in good condition through the hard winter weather

He was in a very happy frame of mind as he entered the ranch office, but he was immediately thrown into a real load of trouble. Tempers were getting frayed and threats were being made. This time all by Nancy of all people and she was ready to carry out a gelding. Her blond pet bitch, Lucy, was in pup, and there was only one miscreant to blame, but The Dodger was admitting nothing. The Dodger had been sat in his usual spot on the corner of the verandah, a spot that allowed him to survey nearly all the ranch and the corrals, but on seeing Nancy advancing with a kitchen knife, he had scarpered. There were plenty of places to hide on this ranch and he knew them all so he made himself scarce.

Trigg and Roger found it hard to suppress a grin, but they didn't want Nancy upset for longer than necessary, and it was Ragnar again who came up with the solution that took the venom out of Nancy's anger.

"Nancy, if The Dodger is the sire, they'll be real good pups and I'll look after all the nursemaiding – done it loads of times with my collies back in England. Nance, don't let it bother that pretty head of yours. I'll look after everything and find good homes for the pups once they're weaned. You just leave it to me, Nance."

"He's telling the truth, Nancy. He was well respected for breeding and training Collies; your Lucy couldn't be in better hands."

Trigg's backing for his grandpa helped to placate Nancy somewhat but she was still not a happy lady when she departed the office, with Lucy traipsing home gingerly behind her mistress.

When they saw Nancy disappear into Sam's forge, all three let rip with a guffaw that they had been straining to suppress. Trigg knew The Dodger was adventurous. He had gone missing on many occasions, but like the trooper he was, he was always back on time and ready to roll. He was a fit, very athletic dog and had earned his right to his pleasures, with his unblemished record of duty. Not one trooper who had served with him, would deny him that right

Trigg caused further hilarity when he declared he would be claiming his stud fee as the owner of the rascal and Ragnar knew exactly what that was – first pick of the litter – but he would be careful to choose the most opportune time to register his claim with Nancy.

This situation settled down, but a month later when it became known that Nancy herself was in the family way, the boot was on the other foot now, and Ragnar was not backward in coming forward.

"Pot calling the kettle black, Nance – you cheeky, little madam. Lucy must have thought it was the proper thing to do." Then he scarpered quickly having got his jibe in and before Nancy could find something to swat him with.

Word had leaked out on the NY about this little shemozzle and the range hands had taken to giving The Dodger a round of applause when he called in to the bunkhouse for his nightly bowl of beer from Spud. The Dodger did not want his bowl of beer in the bunkhouse to get out; even the boss had not been aware of this nightly arrangement. He thought the bowl of beer that Helen gave him in the kitchen was the only one he got, and he wanted it to stay that way. He might be the boss, but he didn't know everything that went on. No, sirree.

Then Roland Simmons and Jimmy Hansom were wanting to arrange a meeting concerning this Delaware Livestock Agency business. Roland had received a written reply from his head office in New York and they were wanting to inform Trigg and Roger of the situation, tout suite if not sooner.

"These people are from a very well-regarded company with extensive contacts in Europe. If they are interested in discussing a business arrangement with you, then my head office suggests you would be very well advised to meet them and investigate their interest in more detail. I would readily agree to be at the meeting with you to assist on any legal issues that could arise, as will Jimmy Hansom on any financial requirements, but my head office is very impressed that this company is interested in doing business with you

Roland Simmons passed him the letter from his New York

head office which Trigg passed immediately to Roger. Trigg would not have been surprised in the least if Roland had advised him to avoid these people like the plague, but this was a totally different message he was hearing from him. Was he jessing him? Had Roland developed a wicked sense of humour? But as he eyed him and Jimmy, they didn't even blink, just sat there with the very contented gaze of men who were on solid ground.

Roger passed him the letter back with the slow nod of an impressed man.

"So we talk to these hombres then and see what is on offer?"

"I think you will be very wise to do so, Major, and as I have said we will be there to listen and advise."

"Write to them, Roger, and agree to meet them here in Cheyenne; let's see if they are prepared to come all the way out here. Apologise for me not writing personally – give them a cock and bull story that I have been called out on patrol. Let's start off with these hombres on the right foot, on our terms."

Roland and Jimmy were thanked for their attendance and would be notified of any further developments and the dates of any meetings. Trigg was still not convinced that these hombres were genuine. Bigger fiddles than this had been worked before – the Union Pacific came readily to mind. The Credit Mobiliere and another French-sounding fiddle had been splashed all over the newspapers and was the talk of the workforce. Nothing it seemed was safe from these smooth-talking shysters where land close to the railroad was involved. The following day, Chas came hurtling back onto the ranch needing Will's advice. GG and he had found a herd of 124 horses quietly grazing and drinking on NY land. GG had stayed out to keep an eye on them; it was a case of leave them be until they had more men to round them up. Will pulled in four range-hands and followed Chas back.

By the time they got back to where GG was waiting, the buzzards were up and circling around. GG had spotted them and was now also scanning the plain through his glass for any more hombres who could have taken these others down, but he had not seen a thing, nothing that looked suspicious. Will espied the herd; they were still quiet and content so leave them be and go and have a look to see if it was some dead bodies that the buzzards were interested in.

They found eight very dead hombres in a swilly in the plain, and then tracks that led down into a gully. GG and Chas followed the tracks but were soon convinced that the riders were moving quick and heading towards the Nebraska border. They went back and reported to Will. This was army business. Will had these horses rounded up and taken back into the NY's corrals. He left Chas to keep the buzzards off the bodies until they had a wagon out there to cart them back in, then he sent a runner into the fort.

Sammy looked a bit bemused – another herd of hosses to look after; he needed more corrals. These horses would have to be rope-tethered.

Trigg sent a detail out to inspect the scene the quick way, on a train to Pine Bluffs, then a ten-mile canter northeast, survey the scene and then back into Pine Bluffs, to make enquiries in the railyard as to whether they had noticed anything suspicious. GG and Chas would be waiting for the detail at the site where the bodies had been found. Trigg left the fort early to give himself plenty of time in the fading light to have a good look at the bodies in the wagon as they were carted back to the fort and then to have a good look at this herd of unbranded horses that was now in the NY corrals. Sgt. Harry Pickering, who was now his regular company, when not with the troop, and himself would do the inspecting and then the report could be completed and presented to the colonel. Two days later, Chas was again galloping in for Will's help. Five riders were heading across the NY land. They didn't look trouble but they had passed a signboard notifying that they were on private land and trespassing, but they carried on riding.

Will took three range hands with him and instructed Chas to keep out of sight but keep them observed.

"You're trespassing, gents. Anything I can help you with? I'm the range boss."

"We lost a herd of hosses here about a week ago; know anything about em?"

"Sure do, they're in the army's possession now. You need to go see the colonel in Fort Russell; he's in charge." Will did not want these hombres anywhere near the NY. They did not look trouble but were well-armed and looked capable of stirring some up.

"Easiest way there for you is back into Pine Bluffs, train ride to Cheyenne, then skirt west around the town and the fort is about three miles; you can't miss it."

"Quicker if we ride straight on, ain't it?"

"No, it ain't an easy ride, and it looks like we're getting a good storm within the hour or so and you fellas ain't got slickers. Pine Bluffs is your best choice."

They looked west, saw the storm clouds gathering and reined their horses around and trotted off east towards Pine Bluffs. Will then sent Chas to get into the hardware yard quick. Jake could telegraph the fort from there and warn the boss. When nobody arrived at the fort, Will was not surprised. When he had informed these hombres that the herd was in the army's control now, a grim look spread over their faces. Also, no enquiry was made about the dead men. Will conferred with the boss. He had told those hombres the truth. Although the herd was on the NY for safekeeping, it was still under the army's jurisdiction. Will gave Trigg a full description of these hombres, and they posted some guards on the approach to the ranch. He then took a stroll around Cheyenne that evening but did not spot any of these hombres. Eight dead men, 124 horses gone, but where were these hombres now? Or had they admitted defeat knowing the army was involved and scarpered while they could?

Jake, in the H&S, as the people were now calling it, had been informed of this incident and being a former sergeant, he understood the situation and was now carefully watching and listening to any well-attired hombre who came into the store as he did all the negotiation for the buying and selling of horses and the boss kept him well abreast of these types of situations. Forewarned was forearmed, and seconds could be vital if a galoot turned nasty.

When a well-attired hombre sidled into the store as Jake was attending to a lady customer, who was collecting an order that her husband had placed, Jake ran his beady eye over the hombre. This hombre was fancying a silver-plated, ivory-handled Colt pistol that Jake had displayed in a locked glass cabinet and he was eyeing it from various angles.

The order for the lady needed another box of shells and Jake had called to his assistant to fetch a box from the storeroom. As he waited, he enquired of the gent whether there was anything he could help him with.

"Yes, could I have a closer look at the ivory-handled Colt please?"

The hombre looked well able to afford the pistol, so Jake unlocked the rear door of the cabinet and passed it to the hombre. Then Jake's young assistant arrived with the box of shells and Jake asked him to wrap up the order for the lady.

The hombre inspected the pistol and then declared that this pistol was his and had been stolen from him and that Jake was a scoundrel for selling stolen goods. The lady customer was taken aback at this accusation and cowered away from the counter. "Sir, we know where this pistol came from, we have not stolen it from anybody and my boss will be very ready to discuss this situation with you. Give me the gun back and we will arrange an appointment to discuss this situation sensibly."

"No, you scoundrel, I will not – this is my pistol and I will not be handing it back." Then he produced a Derringer and pointed it at Jake and squeezed the trigger, but the gun jammed. The lady screamed and Jake slid his hand under the counter onto his Colt. The hombre fumbled with the Derringer and then took aim at Jake again and squeezed on the trigger, but again the Derringer failed to fire.

Jake took aim and shot the hombre, plum centre in his chest, sending the man crumpling into a mess on the shop floor. After two misfires, Jake was not waiting for a third.

"Sorry about that Mrs Tinnion, but I had no option. John Boy, go call the sherriff."

Jake then ushered Mrs Tinnion away from the counter and into his office as Roger came swiftly down the stairs with a shotgun at the ready.

"I saw it all, Mr Stead, Jake had no option. It could be him that were shot; that fella's gun misfired twice!"

Roger threw an old blanket over the corpse, then telegraphed the fort for the attention of Major Hemmyng. The major and his detail arrived before the deputy. Apparently there was a big pot being played for in the jailhouse. Even Doc Townley arrived before the deputy. When the deputy saw the army already there, he tried to back out but Trigg firmly ordered him to stay put and witness this situation.

Statements were taken. Doc Townley inspected the man and pronounced him dead, but who was he? There was nothing on his person to identify him. Where had he come from and when? When no identification could be gained, this hombre was carted off to the fort and booked into the morgue. Attempts would be made to identify the dead man. Will Lawton went up to the fort as he believed he may have been one of the hombres he met on the plain, but he wasn't. The hombres he had met then were younger than him.

The dead man's suit which was of Eastern manufacture, and a copy of the poster displayed to identify him, were stored away, and he was buried. Another mystery man to be added to the long list that lawmen in the West had compiled.

What was known for certain was that the railroad would continue to pour immigrants and settlers, mostly young, single men, into Cheyenne and the other new towns that had been created as the railroad stretched westward.

All these fellas needed to eat and Beattie never missed an opportunity to obtain more business for the NY. Every new shop, store or eatery that opened for business was visited by Beattie. With her existing customers ordering more, as their businesses flourished and these new accounts were added, trade for Nancy's dairy department was very good.

The letter from the Delaware Livestock Agency was back by return of post it seemed and they were asking for an appointment, just as quick, in Cheyenne as well. Roger agreed a date with Trigg and a letter was posted off confirming the date and time. Also a suggestion was made that they wire the expected time of arrival so that they could be met off the train and coached to the venue. Cheyenne could get some heavy downpours that time of the year.

The NY had had a run of petty rustling, just mundane work that Will and his men were very competent at handling, but more and more horses were going into Sammy's remuda.

Ragnar's shed building lads were switched to erecting more corrals for Sammy, smaller than the previous two, where he could keep the horses separated and easy to handle. But nothing was moving on that 120-strong herd, and they were gobbling feed and hay in big quantities. That case had gone totally quiet; the army had not been able to make any progress even though it had notified the nearest towns and forts of the situation, but nothing had been reported elsewhere.

Trigg and Roger imposed the six-month rule. If these horses were still unclaimed by this date, he would claim ownership by right of possession. He knew this might also inform the 'owners' where the herd was being kept. The army's notice only stated that the herd was being held under its control, not where it was being held, but Trigg was prepared to take this risk. If anyone came looking to reclaim the herd by force, then it was a safe bet that there would be reward money posted on these hombres and he was confident that he had the men to deal with the situation.

He could get the reward money and the herd. If nobody claimed, he got the herd anyway. 120 horses was a good deal.

Roger was wary of this plan but Will and Sammy were up for it. The claim was registered and Will and his men became extra vigilant.

The Delaware Livestock fellas soon proved amiable hombres. Not the sharp, slick hombres he expected. They explained that they bought cattle in large quantities, on behalf of the investors, and then these cattle were dispersed on to the ranches of the cattlemen who they had appointed to hold and nurture these cattle. Their business was to buy cheap and then sell when the prices were good. What they needed were honest ranchers, ranchers who when they were instructed to load, say 10,000 head of Shorthorns, onto the railroad, they did just that, not 9,400. That only soured their deals, caused trouble for everybody and was bad business all round.

"How do you know we are honest ranchers, sir? We have only been up and running for a year or so. I set the ranch up with the intention of only dealing in good-quality Shorthorns, and to develop the stock through breeding. We now have a regular supply contract and will be looking for more similar deals as we progress. We are also doing well with horse sales, this being Cheyenne."

"Your military position indicates that you are a man well versed in the law and order of this land, and we have a very important investor who is very confident that the NY ought to be added to our list of appointed ranchers. We have many who apply to be added to our list who we would not touch with a barge pole. You, Major, come highly recommended."

Trigg turned to Roger; it could only be one man.

"Is this investor English and ennobled?"

"Yes, Major, very much so."

What had become an attractive proposition as the discussion progressed, now became a deal that he wanted to be part of. A simple nod between himself and Roger and he was very content to agree, subject to the financial details being viable.

"I am very interested, Mr Drummond, subject to Roger and Jimmy reaching an agreement with you regarding the financial details and also Roland being satisfied that the contract is fair and viable."

He had only one other main consideration that concerned him, that of having thousands of these investors' cattle on his ranges over the winter months. This was a follow-on from Scobie's warnings, and that they were already erecting some stock sheds for his own cattle. But the numbers of cattle these hombres dealt in were far too large to provide the kind of severe weather protection that he was providing for his own livestock. But this could wait until the financial negotiations were underway. He was sure these investment fellas would want to inspect the ranch and the ranges before they got talking money.

Cowhands could be hired in the numbers that would be required. Will Lawton would need some range foremen, Sammy would need more staff, but they only had to be hired after a deal had been agreed and a starting date agreed, and that would not be until next spring. With all these thoughts racing through his head, Trigg suggested that Roger and Roland take over the negotiations; he needed to stretch a leg and grab a lungful of fresh air.

Roger was obviously thinking the same, and he called down to Jake for a big pot of coffee and six mugs and plenty of biscuits. A meeting that they had thought might only take a couple of hours of cut and thrust questions and answers now looked as if it might well last all day and even into tomorrow if these investor fellas wanted to go and have a look over the NY.

Roland was then handed the contract to peruse. When he was told there was no hurry, he could take it away and study it at his leisure, he excused himself from the meeting. Like Trigg, he was thinking it might be a shortish meeting, but now he could attend to his more urgent business first, then study this document later. Again, when Jimmy and Roger began talking money with these two investment fellas, there was no hard haggling. They appeared quite happy with the rates for ranching these cattle; it simply appeared they wanted the NY in their deal, on their side. Even the issue that bothered Trigg the most was quickly agreed. If he wanted the livestock off his range by a certain date, then no problem, that can be done.

Roger and Jimmy's negotiating was being quickly concluded with smiles all round, then yes, they would like to look over the NY but not till tomorrow morning. What they wanted to do now was to take up their hotel booking in Cheyenne and study some paperwork that they had to attend to later in the week.

Trigg agreed a time for his lads to collect these investment fellas from their hotel in the morning and safely escort them to the NY. A shaking of hands, a 'see you tomorrow', and Trigg, Roger and Jimmy were left staring at each other in slight wonderment.

"They must be damn good at buying, and then selling when the prices suit them, Roger."

"I reckon that the honesty factor is the big factor in their deal. If they need 10,000 head on the railroad, ten it has to be because that is what their customer is expecting and paying for. Any less and it would sour the deal. We'd be the same, wouldn't we?" You'd feel you were being cheated, wouldn't you, and that don't make for a good business deal, does it?"

Trigg nodded agreement as did Jimmy Hanson.

"Need me tomorrow, gents?" "I don't think so, Jimmy, but

come back in when we have to fill in the forms and send them back with the contract, thank you for your assistance."

"No wonder the old duke and Col. Barton encouraged me to take up your offer and come to work with you in America. No flies on them, is there?"

"Do I sense a touch of regret in your voice, Roger?"

"No, no, I didn't mean it like that, but it's like we said, there ain't no flies on them, is there? Investing his money in American cattle and now he's got two of his minions out here making sure it pays off. No, I couldn't imagine anywhere better; it is the New World, ain't it, and I'm enjoying every minute."

"Well, he'll get his profit, Roger, and we'll get ours. This investors deal has just made my brain turn a cog or two and now I can see clearly what I couldn't before. I can see where a lot of these rustled cattle 'disappear to'. We'll get this new business up and working, be as honest as the year is long. Then there are hombres who I came across in my military days who I might just look up again, but not wearing a uniform."

Roger saw the glint in his eyes. He realised this investors deal would hasten his leaving the army now. There would be too much involvement in the NY, too much money to be earned, but just exactly what he was thinking he didn't know, and it didn't matter because if Trigg Hemmyng had a plan formulating in his head, that he deemed was achievable, not much would deter him. It might take a week or two to fully decide on the plan but when he was ready, somebody was going to be sorry. As Ragnar would say, the Happening Man was roused up and mean.

Roger had read the situation spot on. Trigg now knew that as soon as this deal was confirmed and a start date agreed for the first 20,000 head of cattle to be driven up from the Pine Bluff cattle pens, he had to be out of the army. With this first delivery up and on the NY ranges, another 10,000 would be following on. 30,000 head would give them a good Income. Adding in their own herd made the income real good, but more cattle meant more rustlers and more trouble. He needed to, wanted, to be here on the NY, not twenty miles away, and he could be a father as well by then. It was time to talk to the colonel and ensure his leaving the army was correctly carried out and he left on completely amicable terms with an unblemished service record. If this new strategy went to plan, having his service record unblemished could be vital. There would be other business opportunities, but he was determined that his army record would be unblemished. Trigg, Adalia, Roger and Ragnar talked long into the night that evening. A deal had been agreed verbally, but nothing was signed or sealed yet. Now was the time to sort out any fears or doubts. Once the contract was signed, the NY and everybody on the NY had to be fully committed. The following morning, Spud Murphy and Scobie took the coach in to collect the Delaware fellas. Chas and GG rode scout but stayed in the H&S, rather than follow them into the town to the hotel. Some folks were still very wary at the sight of a well-armed redskin riding loose, so them keeping out of sight was wise. They would pick the coach up as it came out of town and then ride scout as the coach headed out to the NY. While they were away, Trigg called Will Lawton, his range boss, and Sammy Wheeler, his stockman, into the office and outlined the deal and who these fellas were coming out to look over the NY. As he had done in the army, he liked his main men to know exactly what the plan was, and understand what the objectives were. He didn't like keeping them in the dark; he liked them to be fully aware and have their say, before not after. Again, all were in favour. The Delaware Agency fellas were impressed with the new ranch: good barns, big bunkhouse, plenty of fresh water, more than adequate ranges and very handy for the Pine Bluffs stock pens, on the main Trans Continental railtrack, easy to get cattle to and away from. Adalia and Helen served a tasty lunch during which the deal was agreed verbally, and then Spud and Scobie coached them back into Cheyenne in good time to catch their train. All the handshakes had been made, and now the contract could be posted when Roland had made his perusal of the conditions and the deal was on. Trigg and Roger sat back and took a few good breaths. They had the winter to get properly organised and there were many plans to make with Will and Sammy. Trigg talked with the colonel and the schedule for his leaving the army was agreed. Now he had to keep his nose clean whilst he served out his notice. Having submitted his notice, he had ensured he would not be posted or, worse, sent on some harum scarum campaign up into the Black Hills, or into Montana, as the rumours circulating around the fort were speculating. A campaign had been ordered by somebody in the top brass back in Washington at Army HQ but then had been deferred when the plan had no provision for severe weather conditions. The climate had been ignored when the plan was made. They must have thought it was just like New Mexico or southern Arizona up near the Canadian border. Thousands of infantry soldiers would have been marching about up to their knees in snow by day and suffering hard frost by night, and not a redskin would have been found. Congress was still steadily reducing the army's manpower. With only the troubles of the northern redskins to be resolved, the government had been ordered to slim down the army. This had helped Trigg's situation as regards his resignation, so both sides were happy, but the likes of Captain Rinker and Lt. Rossi were not pleased. Promotions were increasingly difficult to earn and they were likely to be in their present positions for years to come. The only chance of a promotion would be if another war broke out and the only one likely was if the Sioux and the Cheyenne got angry with the Indian Agency and went back on the warpath. Not a long-shot since Red Cloud had lost control to Sitting Bull and Crazy Horse. Scobie was hearing that these two were hankering after a big showdown that would let the white man know that they were far from down and out. Many dollars from the government handouts had been spent acquiring repeating rifles, or stealing them if the chance arose. When Scobie received word that some of the army's Shoshone scouts weren't being retained, Trigg put him to selecting three who he deemed would be suitable to work on the NY. With this investor's herd to guard, three more Shoshones would be ideal. Sgts. Harry Pickering and Joe Kennedy were also getting a touch worried about the situation and Harry, being his regular escort man, had raised the subject with him. Trigg obviously wanted to keep this investor's deal under wraps as long as possible, but Harry and Joe had been with him since Fort Laramie and were well tried and tested soldiers, and they were not daft. Talk was bound to take place on the NY. Will Lawton was a long-standing buddy of theirs, and Harry and Joe were regular visitors, both to the NY and the H&S. Trigg did not want to offer them work until his leaving paperwork was finalised – all part of keeping his nose clean. He didn't want accusations being made that he was taking the pick of his cavalry troop with him, which he intended to do but not until this deal was signed and sealed. Once this deal was signed and sealed, he would be offering them work and if his other plans came to fruition, Capt. Rinker, Lt. Rossi and Sgts. Fred Stockham and Billy Medsen would be offered jobs as well, but that might not be for a year or so. Fred and Billy worked with Capt. Rinker and Lt. Rossi and as such he did not see that much of them. Harry and Joe had always worked with him and Will, Harry even closer now that he was his regular escort man. He knew it would be a problem keeping them happy but that was the conundrum he had to solve: keeping them happy but not giving too many of his intentions away. To keep faith with Harry and Joe and to keep them on his side, he took them aside and swore them to secrecy. "Listen, you two, this is in total confidence between us three. I have resigned from the army, it's all been agreed with the colonel and the paperwork is being finalised as we speak. I have just agreed a big deal that will make the NY's operations a lot bigger. I also have a plan to develop another company which I intend to have up and working in the next year or so, and there will be jobs in this company for both of you, at double your current salary. I ain't telling you any more but stick with the army and I'll keep you informed, and you two will be the first in." Both Harry and Joe were well pleased with that. They shook hands on the deal and promised to keep their eyes and ears open and their mouths shut tight. The rains came early and heavy that winter, slanting down in the wind, and the whole area was soon flooded and waterlogged. These stock sheds looked a lot better investment each day. On one of the more temperate days in this very wet winter, Trigg and Roger were in the new office discussing how to amend Beattie's increasingly busy working day. The point both were concerned with was that Beattie was collecting a lot of cash as she did the rounds of her customers and that some galoot could easily rob her before she had the money safely deposited in the bank. They settled on a routine that Beattie would leave an agreed invoice with her bigger customers and Roger would organise the collection of this money by someone else. The last thing they wanted was for Beattie to be attacked and robbed, and maybe badly injured, so the easy way was to remove the need for her to be carrying the cash. They needed someone to do this job, but who? As they deliberated, Trigg's attention was taken by a voice below, a voice he had not heard for years but he knew exactly who it belonged to. Trigg raised his finger to his lips in a gesture of quiet to Roger as he listened to the voice talking to Jake below. He slipped down the stairs and eased open the connecting door and eyed the scene through the hinge gap. Captain Tom Benson, the first officer he had served under at Fort Laramie, was here in Cheyenne and alive and kicking. Time and involvements, particularly the Civil War, had caused him, like many others, to lose all trace of former colleagues but, no matter, here he was in the H&S after all these years. As Jake parcelled up his customer's goods, Trigg pushed the door open and greeted his former well-liked officer. "Capt. Benson, it's good to see you again." Tom Benson's hand slipped inside his coat as his eyes flashed from Trigg to Jake and then back to Trigg. Trigg raised his hands to show his lack of aggression. "Fort Laramie in '60, when you had to leave to help your folks in Charleston." Tom Benson eyed the epaulettes denoting a serving major and then the hombre behind the counter slid his hand onto a shelf. "Lt. Hemmyng as was, as I remember it; am I correct?" "You are, sir; have you time for some coffee and biscuits?" Tom Benson nodded as he relaxed and reached across the counter to accept the hand extended. Jake lifted his counter-flap and then slipped the package onto a shelf under his counter. Trigg could not miss the difficulty that Tom Benson had as he struggled to climb the staircase. The half-space landing was a welcome relief for him. "This is Roger Stead, all the way from England to look after my private business interests." "So it looks like you've made all the right moves, and I've made all the wrong ones, Major." Tom Benson had not wanted to make this journey to Cheyenne but had found he had no option. His latest attempt to find an occupation that his injuries could manage to allow him to earn a decent income was proving problematic in more ways than one. "So what brings you to Cheyenne, Captain? I'm based here in Fort Russell but will be leaving the army in the New Year. Is there any way I can be of assistance? I am always ready to help a former colleague, legally, of course."

Tom Benson felt the request bring him back his memories of serving with the Lieutenant – short, sharp and straight to the heart of the problem, no shilly-shallying. But he could be the answer to the problem he had here in Cheyenne. "I bought an interest in a private detection agency, Major, run by a former Pinkerton man. I got knocked about bad several times in the war; others got a lot worse but I ain't the fittest old soldier. The position I bought was that of a surveyor, Jack Laidlaw's name for a fella who assessed his potential client's needs, and his setup before he puts his 'detectives' in to progress the case. Also, I am used to try and locate the known varmints who have scarpered. Jack Laidlaw was honest with me; he wanted an ex-army officer, someone who would give added gravitas to his operation, before he let his hounds loose. I am here in Cheyenne to locate two hombres who we believe are here. When I locate them, I wire our new office in Omaha and Jack sends his heavy men to nab them, whichever way they can, and cart them back East. My job, when the heavy men arrive, is to point out the varmints and then retire to a safe location, my job done." Trigg was very interested, it was exactly the sort of business he was interested in. "Tell me to mind my own business if you wish, but has your visit here in Cheyenne been successful? We may be able to help, although we only carry out work within the town limits if requested by the mayor, or the territorial governor if he feels the local police department is outgunned, but we can still find things out." "Half and half – I've located the nephew, but not his uncle, which surprised me as they usually stick close together. The nephew I've seen is busy gambling but I ain't seen hide nor hair of the uncle in two days. The uncle is the brains, gets into all sorts of fiddles and scams and his nephew is the brawn and gunman. Could be that the uncle is out drumming up a fiddle somewhere but I've been here three days and haven't seen anything of him. They usually work quicker than that." "What name do they go by? I'll ask if they are known at the fort." "Clary Rigsby is the uncle; Jack, often called Sonny Rigsby is the young'un, but I'm wiring Omaha tonight. If we only get the young'un, Jack Laidlaw's men will get him to talk, and I want to be home. I'm married now with a daughter." Tom Benson was running short of money. He had nearly spent his expenses money and this parcel of goods he was buying would clear it out. "I'll ask in the fort if they're known. I'll wire Jake later; check with him before you leave. But it's real good to see you again, Captain. I'll tell the lads; still got most of them with me.

They'll be well pleased to know that you're alive and kicking." "I'm alive but I ain't doing much kicking, but a lot got it worse than me. Got to look on the bright side, aint you." "Take a note of our telegraph number, wire me the next time you are coming across and you can stay out at the ranch. Will and the lads will be glad to see you again." "Will Lawton still with you? Who else have you got?" "Scobie and his Shoshone lads, Harry Pickering, Joe Kennedy, Spud Murphy – you left me a good team. Henri transferred to Nevada; couldn't stand the winters." Trigg took him back into Jake's shop. When Tom Benson presented the cash to settle his bill, Trigg waived it away but slipped the receipt into Tom's breast pocket. "This is Jake Smithers, Will Lawton's first sergeant. Jake, meet Capt. Tom Benson, my first operational officer at Fort Laramie." "I reckoned I'd seen him afore; Fort Bridger, was it?" Jake saluted. "Yes, sir." "It's good to see you again, Captain. If you're over here again and needing some help, talk to Jake if I'm not around, he knows who to talk to. Be careful and stay healthy." Clary and Sonny Rigsby were not on the army's list of wanted men. Not surprising as most of these galoots usually adopted a new name in a new town. A week later Tom Benson was back and wanting help. Jack Laidlaw had sent his heavy men in to nab Sonny Rigsby but Sonny had gotten real friendly with his gambling pals and they had given these heavy men a good hiding when they tried to nab Sonny. When these heavy men arrived back in Omaha, battered and bruised, and empty handed, Jack Laidlaw had blown his top, thrown $300 at Tom Benson and told him to sort it out. Then he had gone whoring, not for the first time. Tom knew the business was sailing close to the wind; his buying in investment was in real jeopardy of disappearing, and with it his job and income. If they didn't nab these two Rigsbys, their client would boot them. No client, no payment – it was desperation stakes and Tom knew he had only one option. If his plan worked, he might just get his one grand's worth of buying in dollars back and get out unscathed. If it failed, he was in big trouble. Captain Tom Benson caught the train to Cheyenne and checked that this Sonny Rigsby was still in Cheyenne. He was and seemed to be doing rather well by the wedge of dollars he had on the table. The next morning, Tom visited the H&S and threw himself on the good offices of his former lieutenant. Will, Harry and Joe were more than ready for some 'out of hours' assistance to help a well-liked former officer, now not enjoying the best of fortune. "We need to lure this galoot out and away from his hoppos. Do you know who his buddies were before he came out West, Tom?" "He was thick in with Lew Danner and Wes Tobin; that's who he rode with." "Tom, take Harry and Joe and point him out. We'll have a go at nabbing him tomorrow night. Keep your head down and scarce until tomorrow, Tom. If this don't work, we'll chase him out of town, then he's on our territory, but we'll try this one first, it'll be better for us." Harry Pickering was squiring the lady owner's daughter of Madge's Bar and Rooming House. Madge was not altogether happy with this but the advantage of having an army sergeant around the place regularly, since her husband had poisoned his guts with the cheap rotgut that he had become addicted to, and now gone to meet his Maker, had balanced the books in her opinion. If, as seemed the case, Martina was happy, so was she. Harry was still a randy bastard of an army sergeant but he was their army sergeant, and his ability to 'magic up' some brawny troopers at very short notice also mitigated his position. Madge's Bar never seemed to get trashed – not the case for a lot of others. Marti, as she was known, was being raised to the trade and well-schooled in the female side of this business, in all its facets. Sonny Rigsby was passed a message by a very comely waitress, verbally. Anything written was not trusted, only the spoken word was accepted in the gambling world; they liked to see the face delivering the message. "Sonny, Lew Danner is holed up in Room 8 at the Greenwood. He needs to see you urgent." "Deal me out boys, I won't be long. I've got an old buddy to see urgently." He scooped up his wedge and headed for the Greenwood. Room 8 was Tom Benson's room and they had informed the clerk he was expecting a visitor who would be asking for a Lew Danner. The $5 bill tucked into the clerk's breast pocket bought his undying connivance. Joe Kennedy watched as Rigsby departed the saloon and quietly followed, giving the thumbs up to the window of Room 8 as he crossed the street. "Yes, sir, first floor, fourth room on the right." Rigsby, as expected, didn't bother to knock. This was his buddy, Lew, and he barged straight into and onto Harry Pickering's well aimed-fist that hit him side on and rammed his head into the wall, and he went down like a bag of taters. Joe had skipped up the stairs and joined in as Rigsby was rope-gagged and hooded, then bound and hobbled and marched down the back stairs and out to the waiting wagon. Scobie soon had the wagon moving nice and slowly out of town. Marti had found out where Rigsby was rooming and his room was emptied and thoroughly searched. When they met up the following morning, Tom Benson totted up the loot that had been 'collected'. There was more than enough to placate the client. Rigsby was then bundled onto a freight wagon of a train that had halted at a water stop halfway up the Sherman Rise. Well tanked up it would not stop for a long time after it crested the Rise and rolled west, maybe as far as Green River. Tom Benson was coached out to the NY to have a good drink and a meeting with his former army colleagues. When Tom Benson arrived back in Omaha, Jack Laidlaw was full of admiration for Tom's efforts. Their client had his losses made good and the Jack Laidlaw Detective Agency had another satisfied client who had paid his fee promptly. Unknown to Jack Laidlaw, only Tom knew he was the winner. He had deducted a grand, at source, and the client was still totally recompensed. Everyone had won – only the whorehouse was out of pocket, or its takings were not as high as they might have been. Tom Benson had been reminded of his former lieutenant's ability to get the job done. Little wonder he had made major, was it? Tom and his wife, Sally, raised a toast to him each night for a month, and to all his former troopers who had helped out and then refused any payment. When the rumour reached Tom Benson's ears, and was then confirmed, that Sonny Rigsby had been found alive and well, but battered and bruised in Rawlins Springs, questions were being asked about the whereabouts of his Uncle Clary. Tom confided in Jack Laidlaw that he had not seen the uncle at all in Cheyenne and that was why they only went looking for Sonny Rigsby. Tom had only organised the detention of Sonny and relieved him of the cash he was carrying, and that had been returned to the client from whom it was originally stolen. How Sonny came to be in Rawlins Springs he did not know and the whereabouts of his uncle were equally unknown to him. Maybe some of Sonny's new hoppos might know, but where were they now? Cheyenne was full of transients looking for any opportunity to get rich quick, any way they could, and everything was a mystery when you got involved with these galoots. The NY had its now routine involvement with some petty rustlers, the H&S continued to flourish and Ragnar's shed-builders were now in full flow having become very competent in the erecting of these sheds quickly. Adalia's pregnancy was progressing very satisfactorily as Doctor Mae Townley's visits, often accompanied by her ma and pa, became more regular as the two women became firmer friends and both women were moving towards big occasions: Adalia's first child and Mae's apple blossom springtime wedding. There was a lot to discuss and plan for both of them. This spring wedding was turning out not to be ideal, with the investors' deal now certain but with Will as range boss, who would then be away on his honeymoon, won't he? It was a good job that Trigg had tendered his resignation, as he would obviously have to take over the full running of the NY. He had to make sure he was out of the army by then completely. He also had to ensure that they had lined up some range hands for when this cattle arrived and a couple of range foremen. Cheyenne was becoming more and more hectic as fellas that may be up in the hills during the year were now crowding in to Cheyenne before the winter really set in. In the past, many of these men had chosen to stay up in the hills but had frozen to death as the frosts and the blizzards took their toll on them. A week before he was due to move across to Green River, Herbie Brunner was attacked and robbed and left for dead. Herbie had been carried into Doc Townley's barely alive and the doc had him settled him into the little three-bed hospital he had built in his yard. Knowing that Jake and Herbie had become buddies, the doc had sent the bad news to Jake, and Jake was now raging mad. Roger was now struggling to stop him heading out to look for the attackers, but nobody knew who they were as Herbie had been found unconscious in an alleyway, but Jake was having trouble understanding that, such was the ferocity of his anger. Trigg and Will were sent for; they would be able to calm him down before he had a seizure. Beattie was out on the NY talking with Nancy, probably very fortunate as she was just as fond of Herbie. They had spent many evenings each week in their cottage, carding and talking, keeping each other company and now this happens. Trigg and Will galloped in, leaving Scobie to coach Beattie in nice and steady, giving them time to assure Jake that these galoots, who had attacked and robbed Herbie, were walking dead men. "Jake, we'll get them. Doc Townley reckons he'll survive – it might take a long time but he'll mend. You ain't fit enough to go after them, and if you get hurt what does Beattie do then? I have two good, well-led troops who will find them quicker than you can." Jake knew that was true and began to settle down. When Will looked him square in the eye, placed his hands on his shoulders and promised him that he would do all he could to catch these galoots and bring them to justice,

Jake's anger and frustration burst out and the tears began rolling down his craggy, weatherbeaten face. Will patted him on the shoulder. "Let it all out, Jake; it takes a good man to show how much he cares." It was the Shoshone lads who came across some galoots who had made a camp in one of the more remote gullys on the NY. They had found a steep bank and camped right under it. So steep was the bank that a campfire was even hard to see in there, and the horses were tethered right behind some shrubbery growth, but they had spotted them and reported back to Will. They were on NY land, they were trespassing, and Will called them to come out peaceable, hands raised, guns laid on the floor, and they would be carted into the army's jurisdiction at Fort Russell. But, as was thought likely, they refused. They were given the chance to reconsider but, again, they refused. "Fellas, we can sit here and watch you starve to death, we ain't coming in, but you ain't going anywhere and anything we see move, we'll rattle some bullets into it. If you don't believe me, try us out – your choice." They stuck it out for the night, then hunger must have begun to take effect, as two came out firing, but were taken down. Not killed – they wanted them alive. Then the other four tried to make a break for it but were quickly taken down. Will was in no rush – wounded, moaning men were not new to him. They had had the choice, now they could stew in their own juices. He was not risking any of his men on galoots like these. When the army detail he had sent for arrived, he explained the situation and handed over the operation to the lieutenant with a warning to be careful as one or more of those galoots could be feigning injury; it was always a possibility. The lieutenant repeated the warning to his men and as they edged their way closer, two of the galoots began to move as if to open fire and were shot. A wagon was made available to the lieutenant, as Will and the Shoshone lads mounted up and moved away to let the Lieutenant do his job. Herbie's leather wallet with his name inscribed on the front was found containing $62, just $10 a man and a bad beating for Herbie, but that's how it was on the high plains. Satisfied that the situation was under control, Will took his leave of the scene and took his men back to the ranch, to report to his boss. "$62 in Herbie's inscribed leather wallet. They hadn't the sense to ditch the wallet. Maybe they can't read and it didn't mean anything to them." "We saw worse on the railroad, Will, $2 could get your throat cut in those 'hell on wheels' winter stoppages. Desperate men do desperate deeds." Trigg informed Jake that Will had Herbie's attackers in the army's control. "The Shoshone lads found some squatters in a remote gully and notified Will. He called for them to come out peaceable, as trespassers, but they refused twice and chose to shoot their way out. Will shot to wound and all six were injured. They penned them in overnight, then when the army detail they had sent for arrived, he handed over to them. When the army moved in and searched their dugout, they found Herbie's wallet with $62 in it. Will gave them the use of a wagon and left them to complete their work. I expect to see these hombres arrive in the fort later. I'll keep you fully informed, Jake." Jake's response was the same. "Sixty two lousy dollars, two dead, four looking at years of hard labour, and Herbie even more injured. At least they won't be hurting anyone else." It was another reminder if anyone needed one at how tough life could be. If you were kind to hombres like these, they would treat you as weak. Will could have let them walk away and they would either shoot the cattle or return to rustle some more. Galoots like these were trouble. They liked to use force, enjoyed using force, it was their stock-in-trade and Herbie Brunner had just had a severe dose of it. His new injuries would likely plague him longer than their memories of inflicting it. Beattie had learnt, during their evenings socialising, that Herbie had a younger brother, a carpenter like Herbie had been, who was well out West with the Casements Construction Team and this brother had been christened Gordon but was usually known as Gordi.

Trigg sent a telegram out to Railhead with the sad news of his brother's misfortune. Maybe it would reach him, if he was still around. Nancy was in the ranch office chasing Roger as to where the mixing bowls he had ordered for her were. "I'm going into the H&S tomorrow. I'll make enquiries in the UP freight office to see if they know." "Just arrived, Mr Stead, according to our records." "Good. I'll send one of Jake's lads in to collect them after dinner." As Roger made his way back from the station buildings, he spotted an elderly couple looking very perplexed and asked if he could help them. "I think we've missed our train – there wasn't anyone to ask." "Where were you going to, ma'am?" "Ogallala, to see my sister, but it's the first time we have used the train and it's so confusing." Roger saw the train disappearing east, they certainly had missed the train. "Let's go and enquire at the ticket office, see what the time is of the next train." Just as they were about to start walking, shooting rang out behind the troop train that had just halted. Steam was still spurting out of the engine, and soldiers were jumping down off the steps of the carriages. More shots were heard, orders were being shouted and bullets and shotgun pellets were flying. Roger ushered the couple behind some packing cases as three galoots came rushing out of the clouds of steam. One man ran away but the other two came heading straight to where Roger had the couple hiding behind the crates. One galoot was bellowing in triumph at having blasted a soldier, the other was berating him for being stupid saying he had dropped them in the shit now. Roger drew his Colt out of his shoulder holster and cocked it, just as these two who were busy reloading saw him. "Hold it there, you two; drop the guns quick." One did, but the other started to swing the shotgun towards him laughing and started to mouth something at him, but Roger squeezed on the trigger and down he went. The other one backed away in fear as he saw his buddy crumple to the ground. "You allright, Mr Stead? We'll sort this out, you get that old couple away and safe." Sgt. Fred Stockham had his gun trained on the cowering galoot and some more soldiers were coming to help them.

"Go on, Mr Stead, and get those old folks sorted out. It looks like this ambushing is all over now."

Roger did as he was told. He ushered the couple into the station, bought them a pot of coffee and found out when the next train to Ogallala was, in what seemed to him like thirty seconds. His heart was racing, he needed to walk. He took the long route to the H&S and he had just about composed himself when he got there.

"Was that some shooting we heard in the railyard, Roger?"

"It was, Jake. Some galoots were taking on the army; I don't know why."

"Fred Stockham's just ridden in. Maybe he knows what it's all about."

Roger was still not feeling too good, he felt a bit sick in his belly, but he made sure he got to Fred first and led him away from Jake.

"What happens now, Sergeant? Do I have to make out a report?"

"What about, Mr Stead? Like I said, we'll take care of it. It ain't nice but you had no option, none at all as I saw it. The major will wrap it all up as an army incident, which it was. You try and put it out of your head. It's all done and finished. The elderly couple will be on the next train to Ogallala. I'm only here passing on their gratitude to you for your help."

Roger had just had his first taste of how quick a bad situation could erupt out here. There he was minding his own business and then he was killing a man to keep himself alive.

Three hours later when Major Trigg Hemmyng rode into the H&S it was an eyeball to eyeball stare.

"Fred told me all about it, Roger; are you all right?"

"I will be if that's the only time I have to do that. It ain't good in any way, is it?"

"No, but if it's necessary, what were your options? I don't want you shooting people, you have better things to do, but some of these galoots don't see it that way."

A week later, as if that incident was just Roger's introduction to his involvement with the lawless side of life, Roger was in the firing line again.

A nice peaceful morning on the NY and Roger is in the office attending to the paperwork that had to be kept up to date and in order. Will Lawton was out on the range. Trigg was in the fort supporting the colonel in a meeting with some visiting army officials, when Sam Little comes hurtling into his office. "The Dodger warned Spud; there're ten riders heading straight in here and looking real trouble. Grab a rifle, Roger."

The Dodger had smelt them on the breeze as they came towards the ranch and gone to Will, from his days out on patrol with Spud Murphy.

"Spud and Buddy are watching them ride in, Ragnar's in the house, keeping the women inside, and a range hand has gone to alert Will, then I told him to get to the H&S for Jake to wire the boss up at the fort, but that's going to be two hours at best before he can get here and these hombres are going to be on us in ten minutes, could be sooner."

Roger checked his Colt and slipped it back into his shoulder holster. Then he took a Henry from the rack, threw a box of shells to Sam, picked up another box for himself, then headed out after Sam to where Spud and Buddy were watching these riders from up in the big barn hayloft.

"They split into two fives, gaffer. Looks like one is heading straight in, the others are circling around getting behind us."

Then they heard Ragnar calling to tell them he was getting the women into the bunkhouse, so one less place to worry about.

"They're coming up the crease in the plain. You'll see em soon, gaffer. Can't see the others yet but they'll be up to your left, about two hundred yards away, I reckon."

Roger and Sam eyed them through their telescopes as they came up onto the crest and halted, looking the ranch over through their telescopes.

"They ain't saddle-tramps, Roger, and they're well armed with good horses."

"Want me to put a big '50' through em gaffer, just to let em know we know they're there?"

Roger's first thoughts were to refuse. But why not – they were about four hundred yards away, be as easy as downing a bison, and it could spook em, discourage them.

Roger nodded up to Spud and the Sharps rifle barked. The hoss went down like a bag of taters and the rider rolled clear and took cover behind his very still former mount. Roger was playing the waiting game, for Will to get back in with GG and Chas, and the other Shoshone lads were down on the grass bluffs helping Hamish with a spot of sheep-stealing problems, and Scobie was with Trigg at the fort. There were about four hours' daylight left and the clouds were looking heavy and the wind was rising. The other five galoots had not shown as Spud predicted.

"I ain't seen the other five yet, Spud, can you see em?"

"No, and them other four are dropping back down, maybe scared of another big '50' into em."

Roger and Sam ran into the barn and up into the hayloft. Those two doors gave them the best view and they also needed to get Spud's soldiering advice, the tactics that he had learnt from Trigg and Will in their army days. By the time they had scrambled up the ladders into the hayloft, Spud was wanting to be back down on the ground, leaving Buddy up in the hayloft to observe and notify him of these raiders' direction and progress.

"There're six riders coming at us hard, riding low in the saddle and weaving around. I'ts hard to get a bead on em; these hombres know how to attack. Buddy can stay up here, but we need to get well hidden down here to stop them getting into any of the buildings and setting them afire. We've got real trouble here. Take good cover, don't give them anything to shoot at, but don't take your eyes off them." Six riders coming in hard. Buddy up above would pour plenty down on them as they came in. If they got into the yard and among the buildings, it was one-on-one fighting. Six of them, four of us – not the time to waste shots and give your position away, but you had to keep them out.

The range hand had alerted Will and then, as ordered, had hightailed it to find Jake. Trigg had received the wire from Jake but had become mired in this meeting with the delegation from Army HQ hombres and next on the agenda was cavalry matters, Trigg's department. The colonel needed him there for the practical problems that this territory caused them. He sent Sgt. Joe Kennedy and six troopers to see what was afoot and provide a military presence if it was needed. Also, Joe Kennedy was to inform Adalia that he would be staying in the fort overnight. This delegation was led by an infantry colonel who needed every aspect of the cavalry requirements explained in detail.

Capt. Rinker, Lt. Rossi and his troop were out on patrol and busy. Scobie, as his chief scout, was in the fort with him. With Will out there with the other Shoshone lads, and Sgt. Kennedy with a detail heading out there, he was confident that this incident would be taken care of but there was always that niggling doubt that wormed its way into his thinking, that this time might be real bad. But as his thoughts were taking him elsewhere, this visiting colonel seemed to be generating more need for each of his questions to be answered in great detail. Trigg countered this colonel's questioning by throwing his long-held feelings back at him.

"Why does the army keep the cavalry manpower so low in an area like this? It is so vast with thousands of redskins to be placated which infantry soldiers cannot do. They spend most of their time digging new latrines, then filling in the old ones, then drilling themselves to the point of boredom. Then they're either bored silly or get paralytic drunk and are put on sick leave as unfit for duty. Then when they get supposedly better they desert. If the numbers were balanced up and we had more cavalry, we could manage this big, wild country more efficiently

Colonel Stratton sensed the anger rising in the major's tenor, and was quick to realise that maybe something else was bothering him. Was Major Hemmyng venting his anger on this HQ colonel while he could? His resignation papers were already signed and sealed. There was very little the army could do now, as long as he didn't thump him or personally abuse him.

The visiting colonel had started to show some signs of sweat on his brow; he was not liking this counter questioning, and not one of his aides seemed ready or willing to reply. They had been keen to throw queries in to bolster his questioning, but now nothing was being said to assist him.

A sharp kick to his ankle was enough to settle Trigg into a more calm demeanour, but there was still this 'feeling' across the table.

"Sort the Indian agents out, locate more cavalry up here, honour the treaties and you will diffuse the situation. Just give it time. Also, ignore the Eastern press's ranting and ravings, they only want to sell newsprint, most of which is invented anyway. The railroad is in and working and the redskins can't damage it – it is too well protected. Those redskins who want to integrate, will, like the Cherokee did, and as Red Cloud is now advising the Lakota nations to do, but they are a very proud people – push them hard and they will fight back. Give them more time to understand the white man's world and my guess is that most of them will adjust and adapt. They will have to now that the bison are being slaughtered to extinction. What is left for them?" Trigg eyed the visiting colonel. "My apologies for the lecture, colonel. Maybe it is time for me to move on and let the army carry out the government's policies."

"Time is not a commodity that we have to work with, Major.

Congress wants action, the newspapers are demanding action, and we have the onerous task of giving Congress what it is asking for. I can't argue with your convictions, Major, and I thank you for being so honest in your beliefs. It is not usual for us to be given honest answers."

The atmosphere across the table had become more amenable now that the visiting colonel was content he was going to be given truthful responses to his questions.

Out on the NY it was stark reality. The raiders came galloping in and were met with gunfire coming at them from all angles, particularly from above as Buddy sprayed bullets at them relentlessly.

The raiders, having scanned the ranch buildings with their telescopes and seeing no one moving, with only one '50' shell being aimed at them, had made the assumption that maybe only one or two people were at home. So it was a matter of getting in and taking the place over pronto, and being in position to waylay the residents. The reality was that more than a few of them were at home and ready for the attack. But as Spud had judged, these hombres were not new to this work, and could handle some of this resistance. Two had been taken down but the other four had leapt off their horses at the first chance and sought refuge in one of Sam's corrals, and were using the railing boards and fence posts for protection as they crept closer to the main buildings. Now it was a cat and mouse fight as gunfire ripped out in both directions, as both sides took any opportunity to get in a telling shot that might tip the advantage their way.

Suddenly Roger,who was raging mad, took a gamble. He broke out of the cover he was hiding behind and legged it across to another vantage point nearer the bunkhouse where he could better defend the women. As he ran, two of the hombres raised up and took aim at him, giving Buddy his chance to get a better shot at them. Buddy managed to slam a bullet into one of the raiders who crumpled over one of the corral's rails and hung there, writhing in agony. Another of the raiders tried to reach up and pull his hoppo down, but Spud's shot shattered his helping arm and more screaming and agonised moaning was heard. Two left, and Spud called for them to surrender.

"Stand up, throw your guns away and come out with your hands in the air. We won't gun you down."

As the other two were heard talking about this offer, Chas came hurtling in on his 'paint' from the direction that the raiders had approached, saw the two raiders huddled behind the horse trough and emptied his pistol into them.

"Which way did you come in, Chas? There're four more out there somewhere, and where's Will?"

"Coming in steady: his horse has gone lame. Which way to these others?"

Spud pointed out the way and cautioned him. "About half a mile, but only locate them and keep them observed, don't take them on; the boss will want them alive, savvy?"

Chas nodded acceptance. He knew the boss would have his guts for garters if these hombres were not able to talk.

"Good man, we'll send some men out to help you once we have these galoots trussed up and gagged, just be careful. Away you go."

No sooner had Chas urged his pony away and back on to the plain, than Sergeant Kennedy and his six-trooper detail came galloping onto the NY from the opposite direction.

"Will Lawton is that way somewhere, his horse has gone lame, and young Chas has just gone out to locate four more of these galoots, that way. We've got these six galoots sorted, Sergeant."

Joe Kennedy eyed the scene, then congratulated Spud on a

good job well done, then spotted one of the captured men had decided to resist and leapt from his horse and gave the galoot a good kicking to subdue him.

"You three go and find ex-Sgt. Major Lawton pronto, afore somebody else does, and keep alert, there could be more of these galoots marauding around. You three fellers keep your eyes peeled."

Both tasks were carried out without incident. As they returned to the ranch, the place was regaining its normal way of working. Sgt. Kennedy had the four hombres added to the others, the corpses were then bound and hooded, and the galoots were then humped into the wagon, ready for delivery to the fort. He had about one and a half hours of daylight left, just right for a steady roll back to the fort, after they had sampled a few beers in the bunkhouse. Chas was then tasked with taking up the observing duty from the hayloft.

The focal point creating all the hilarity in the bunkhouse was gaffer Mr Stead's sudden skedaddling run across the yard as he sought to take up a different defensive position nearer the bunkhouse.

"It was stalemate, Sergeant, and then he lit out like a scalded cat to the bunkhouse. One of them galoots raised up to plug him, took too long to get a bead on him, and Buddy had got him afore he had lined up on the gaffer. This galoot was then draped over the middle rail rorping like a babby when an arm reached up to pull him down, but I plugged it first shot."

Roger met Joe Kennedy's look of mild scorn.

"I know it was rash, Sergeant, I shouldn't have done it, but all I was thinking about was getting closer to the bunkhouse to protect the women – must have been a rush of blood to my head or something similar."

"A noble thought, Mr Stead, but you ain't any good dead, but as the major will say, 'all's well that ends well.'"

They all had a drink to that.

"Oh by the way, Mr. Stead, the major will be staying in the fort tonight – these HQ fellas are being real finnicky. I'll inform him that all is well out here, but stay alert."

When the wagon arrived back in the fort, Trigg ran his eye over the prisoners and the corpsed men, and then inspected the saddlebags. Nothing of any real substance was found. All the horses were in Sam's corrals and they could be inspected tomorrow. Trigg then went to talk to the colonel.

Early the next morning, Scobie was released from attending any further talks with the visiting delegation, and allowed to return to the NY. Trigg needed the plain scouring for any indications as to where these hombres had been prior to the raid on the NY. Had these hombres left the train at Pine Bluffs? If not, where? These hombres were not local, their clothing, saddles and tack confirmed that. Also, there was very little money in the saddlebags. Had it been stashed for recovery later?

Scobie knew the routine, and he was despatched to go looking for anything of interest before the tracks were obliterated by any bad weather.

As usual, none of the prisoners were talking and they were left to stew in the mire of their own making. Time, and their increasing desperation as they realised they were in a bad situation, usually loosened a tongue or two.

Trigg had no reason to question Roger's involvement in the shootout, rather he was quietly pleased. After a relatively easy introduction to the West, Roger was getting a more realistic experience of the brutal side, and in Trigg's mind that was all to the good. You could talk about these situations until the cows came home, but being in the thick of it was where you learnt. With the investors' deal now signed and sealed, having more livestock on the NY was very likely to attract this type of trouble. This was the trade-off they were in. More livestock, more money but more trouble. You just had to learn to deal with it, and those two experiences would be invaluable to Roger. Two days later

Trigg was back in the fort. He had gone out himself with Scobie onto the plains. Tracks had been found but not much else, no old camp sites or likely stash areas. The prison duty sergeant had not heard any of them talking, and this situation was drifting into a stalemate situation. They were not learning anything. Then a message was delivered to him from the gatehouse. A Mr Gordon Brunner was asking to see him – said he had been wired about his brother. Trigg told the corporal to bring him up to his office. He was pleased that the telegraph had got through to him. Trigg described Herbie's injuries, which, added to the other injuries he had received, meant that Herbie might not regain much mobility, if any, when his general health recovered. "Herbie is still in Doc Townley's little hospital, but Jake and Beattie Smithers are going to take him into their cottage shortly. I'll take you down and introduce you to Jake." "I was reckoning on taking him back with me. I've left the Casements, and have got me a place and a good job in Green River." "I don't think so, not yet awhile, but I suggest you go and see Doc Townley and he'll explain." Trigg introduced him to Jake at the H&S. Jake knew full well Trigg's regard for Herbie and likewise Trigg knew that Jake would not let his brother take over until Herbie was well enough to travel. As Trigg took his leave of their company, Buddy Deans appeared with four more horses for Jake's sales stable. "Buddy, these hombres that we have just captured on the NY – did you get a good look at them? " "No, boss, I was up in the hayloft keeping a lookout in case there were any more galoots marauding around. By the time I was down, Sgt. Kennedy had em roped and hooded and they were being humped into the wagon." "Buddy, before you return to the NY come up to the fort and ask for me at the gate." He had not been there but this raid appeared similar to the one those hombres from Marshalltown had attempted. Buddy had identified those galoots; maybe he just might know these hombres. Why not let him have a look, nothing ventured – nothing gained. The off-chance worked; Buddy did know one of these galoots, not personally but from the time he had given him a thumping in his time as a deputy, back in Marshalltown. This galoot had refused to go into his cell after being arrested for brawling. Buddy had had to drop him, then drag him into the cell and lock him up. "He's called Lou Viarra. He's one of the Iti's from the railway shanties. I ain't seen him for two years or so. Heard he'd moved to Chicago. He thinks he's a hard man; probably is with a gun in his hand." Trigg thanked him and let him go on his way. Then he went to see the colonel. "Buddy Deans has just identified one of those hombres. He knew him as Lou Viarra from Marshalltown but he also thought he was now living in Chicago. It looks to me, colonel, that this latest raid is connected to the first raid. How is that case progressing? Can you get an update from Omaha?" "I will, Major. Point the prisoner out to me, and I will ensure he is kept in solitary confinement. We will get him separated from the others and leave him to wonder why." Trigg was content with that, but his thoughts were still on who this guy was and why they were still coming to raid the NY. They alleged that a great deal of money had been taken from the saddlebags, by others, i.e. they were trying to cast slurs on him and his men. He was certain though that no money had been stolen. If these hombres from Chicago were still convinced that this money had been taken, was it stashed somewhere on the NY? They had looked twice now but had found nothing. With these hombres now either dead or locked up in the fort, and out of contact with any top dog back in Chicago, would any more now come looking? He needed the colonel to get an up-to-date assessment of how Omaha were progressing with those first hombres. Trigg then considered Spud's concerns. Spud had been worried when he had seen these latest raiders galloping in, well-experienced and determined. If The Dodger had not caught the scent, or the breeze had been coming from a different direction, the outcome might have been too nasty to contemplate What were his options now? Keep Will on the ranch full time and a permanent lookout up in the hayloft, or leave Will to carry on doing his normal work and still be close by, and have either Joe Kennedy or Harry Pickering work a rota so that they were on the NY full time leaving himself to be around as well?

He talked with the colonel again, and obtained his agreement to allow him to have Harry and Joe work a rota so that one of them was on the NY every day. "This is an ongoing case, Major, there is a perceived threat, and I agree that there is, so take the actions you deem necessary to enforce law and order." He called Harry and Joe together and let them agree a rota that suited them, then he headed into Cheyenne to purchase the tripod and the 50x telescope that had just been placed on display. The hayloft had a wicket door in both gables, one faced east, the other west. Two more hatches were cut into the north and south-facing roof surfaces. Now one man could view anything approaching from all four points of the compass, from a vantage point that was out of the wind and the rain. He retained responsibility for this rota, with his grandpa acting as his deputy when he was off the NY. The Dodger had saved their bacon the first time but from now on, until this situation was resolved, there would be a constant observer up there during the daylight hours. The night times were The Dodger's domain. He could hear sounds and sense trouble way before even the Shoshone lads could. Trigg, Roger and Will agreed the number of range hands they would need based on the initial 30,000 head that the investors' men would arrange delivery of. Also, two range foremen, working directly for Will, would also be a first requirement. Get those two in place and then they could fit the range hands around them. Will and Roger went down to visit George Dobbs, manager of the UP Livestock pens at Pine Bluffs. George had been notified previously, in confidence, and fully appreciating the need of as much hush hush as was possible, he had kept his eye out for suitable men that he knew were reliable and well-experienced, and were looking for new work.

"There's one of them in the bar. I only talked to him earlier and he said he was going to ride over and look you up. I'll send down for him; he's still there – that's his hoss yonder, the black. Charlie has a hoppo, they have worked together now for years, real good pair they are, rode every trail from Texas up to Ogallala."

Charlie Parker looked every inch a trail foreman and his hoppo looked every inch the hard man, fall out with either and you were in trouble.

"I've heard of this NY. How long have you owned it?"

"I don't own it, I'm the range boss, and Roger here is the ranch manager."

"Where's the boss then?"

"He's minding his own business, Charlie. You'll work for me, I work for Roger here."

"Sounds like it's a lot military. You bin in the army?"

"Yep, Union, but that's all over now ain't it? We had some galvanised Yankees with us; they were good lads, did as they were told, no problems, or do you still see it different, Charlie?"

"Not now. I did for a time, but there're a lot that still don't."

"What are you looking for, Charlie? A Missourian, ain't you?"

"Somewhere to settle, but it won't be down there, it's got too many bad memories.

"Wyoming ain't a state yet, but Cheyenne is growing real fast; you could do worse."

"We was going to ride over and have a look at yer, that be allright?"

"No, you had better ride over with us or you might get shot otherwise."

"You getting rustlers already? Giving you plenty of trouble, are they?"

"Worse, but it ain't anything we can't handle, and your hoppo looks useful – quiet type ain't he?"

"You serve good grub I've heard, and pay top dollar, is that right?"

"Yep, with roly poly treacle, sticky toffee or baked rice pudding for afters – sound OK?"

"Sounds like we'd better get riding. I ain't had any sticky toffee for years."

As they moved onto NY land, GG and Chas came riding up. Charlie eyed his hoppo and both looked a bit pensive at the sight of these well-armed redskins.

"Rest easy, Charlie, they're our scouts. This is deeded land, not open range, and like I said, we can handle any trouble that comes our way."

"Twenty a week and all found I've heard."

Roger looked over at Will and then took over the talking.

"Twenty for your hoppo, twenty-five for you and a cut of the reward notices, and that can easy double your money. Wyoming is running wild, and we seem to attract plenty. And beer is sold at cost in the bunkhouse, but whisky or rotgut are banned. "

"How far have we got left, and how many long drives do we do?"

"Another six miles and that's it. It's either down to the pens or we collect from them."

"We ain't got shot and gone to heaven, have we, Larry? It sounds better every yard we go." Larry nodded in agreement; seemed like he nearly broke into a smile!

"Charlie, this hoppo of yours is a mite too noisy for me; does he ever say much?"

"Good sign that, Mr Stead, if he didn't like what he was seeing or hearing, we wouldn't be here now."

"So, what's his name? We'll need it for payroll purposes."

"Hadwick, with an H. Larry lets his fist do the talking and he's good with a gun as well."

One night in the bunkhouse, and a day on the NY was good enough for Charlie, but now he felt he had to spill the beans on his domestic situation.

"I've got six kids, Mr. Stead, and maybe there'll be one more when I get 'ome. There has been for the last six years. We like the spread and everything about it. We could easy settle here, well away from down there. Would that be on? I see you have some cottages built."

As Charlie was talking, Trigg, Harry and Scobie came cantering in after having spent another night in the fort. The sight of three Union uniforms was not too welcoming for Charlie but he had already been informed that the ranch owner was still a serving cavalry officer. Roger introduced them.

"This is Charlie Parker, boss. He comes well recommended by George Dobbs, and this is his hoppo, Rowdy Hadwick. Will wants him as a range foreman, but Charlie has just raised a domestic situation."

"Pleased to meet you, Charlie, Rowdy. If George recommends you, and Will wants you both on his staff, we'll hire you. It ain't nothing we can't handle, is it, this domestic situation? You ain't got twelve kids, have you, and need your own bunkhouse, do you?"

"No, only six, but maybe there'll be another one at home waiting for me."

"Where do you call home, Charlie?"

"Near by Springfield, Missouri."

"You got enough money to train your family all that way, Charlie?"

"No, we'll use a wagon. We'll get here."

"If you want the job, Charlie, it's yours. I'll advance you $200. If you don't turn up on time, Scobie here and his lads will come looking for you. Get your missus and the kids on the train. They'll like it a real lot and it'll save you a real load of time. That a deal, Charlie?"

Charlie shook on the deal.

"Roger will tell you when he needs you here. I reckon we'll get on well, Charlie."

When he gave Adalia the news, she added the numbers up and made the comment that they ought to be thinking of building a schoolroom. Trigg knew well that the range hands, like ordinary soldiers, were seldom capable of reading or writing or doing the numbers. It was a big factor that caused a lot of trouble. Fighting, and worse, often broke out with fellas who lacked a basic education and sensed they were being cheated. Then they got angry when they were made to look thick and stupid and started to lash out.

The NY was too far from Cheyenne for a daily coach in and coach out, and come the spring when the investors' stock arrived, there would be many range hands who would be in the situation of not being able to read or write; it wasn't just the kids that needed schooling.

"We've plenty of that 'scrap' timber left, I'll get something sorted out, but who is going to do the teaching?" Trigg knew that Adalia would readily do the job, but he didn't want that. She would have their baby to look after, and he had all winter to resolve this poser. Gordi Brunner realised his brother was in far better care than he could provide for him and also Herbie had told him just that. He wasn't leaving Cheyenne now or any time in the future, he had too many good friends here. So it was, good to see you, brother. We'll keep in touch more regular in the future, but here I am and here I'm staying"

When Will found the other range foreman he was looking for, this schooling issue only increased. Monty Delucca, an Arizonian, was wanting to wed a lady who already had two young daughters. Deserted by her husband she was living in the back of the shop where she worked in Denver. There was just one cottage left and the deal was done. Monty would marry his lady, if possible, but if not, they would move into the cottage and get married when this desertion business was legally resolved. Will had the two range foremen he needed and now he was ready to start hiring the range hands they needed. No gangs or known trouble-causers would be contemplated and these two experienced range foremen would have a big say in who they hired. The boss was keen to keep any potential trouble-causers out; there were already plenty out there trying to get in and with 30,000 head of investors' stock plus the 4,000 head of his own livestock, the last thing he needed was someone on the NY being in cohorts with a gang outside. After a discussion with Roger, Trigg Hemmyng placed an advertisement in the local printers and newsheets' window. 'Bookkeeper/teacher required. All applications in their own handwriting to Doctor Mae Townley, 5 East Street, Cheyenne, or in person at 10.00 am this Saturday.' Not a soul replied or turned up at the appointed hour. Not daunted, Trigg assumed that with the winter about to break, maybe folks were more interested in battoning down the hatches, than looking for work. Instead, he asked Herbie, to give him something to occupy his mind, to prepare a sketch for a schoolroom with a two-bed cottage on one gable and a small bell tower above the front door on the other gable. Also, he asked him to do a cutting list of all the timbers required so that a prompt start could be made in the spring. A nice newly built schoolroom and cottage – they might just be the main attraction when he next placed an advertisement The colonel received bad news concerning these galoots from Chicago. Omaha was being stymied by a slick-talking attorney who was somehow managing to baulk the army's attempts to put these galoots up for trial. Also the colonel had mentioned this latest raid and the fact that one galoot had been identified as coming from the same Marshalltown shanties as the other galoots on the first raid. Then, as if to add salt to the wounds, an order had been made that all these latest prisoners were also to be transferred under armed guard to Omaha as well. Orders were orders, and they were delivered, but Trigg Hemmyng vowed secretly to himself that if any more of these galoots raided the NY, from the direction that these had, that they would not walk out of anywhere. The coyotes and buzzards would dine out on them. His anger and frustration were coming to the boil, unlike he had ever felt before. But a message came for him from Lt. Rossi that diverted his thoughts. There had been further altercations in the railyard since Roger had shot those two hombres, not as violent as that incident but, after a tipoff from the railyard's manager, Lt. Rossi had donned the workwear of the yard's workforce, gone to work in the yards and kept his eyes and ears open. Due to the turnover in labour, and the volume of work that needed to be done, Max Rossi easily assimilated himself to the routines of the yard, basically handling crates – they may be a two-man lift or however many were needed. He soon latched on to the manager's complaint. A gang who had arrived to collect deliveries was very loud and demanding that its crates had to be ready quick or the men would get threatening. Max got a good look at these hombres, then ducked out of working in the yard and took to trailing these galoots and the crates they had collected. The trail they took was unexpected but of much interest to the army. That was when Lt. Rossi sent a message to his major – he needed assistance and advice. Trigg read the message, plotted the routes on his map, then called in Scobie. Satisfied that Scobie knew enough of this terrain, he met with the colonel and gained his consent to pursue these hombres. He needed his consent as it looked very likely that they might be moving out of their area of jurisdiction and impinging on areas officially delegated to other forts. The old problem of 'affiliations' was discussed – who did these hombres know in which forts, because a slip of the tongue, or a wrong word at the wrong time, could scuttle an operation. With Colonel Stratton being prepared to shoulder this operation, it removed this problem – the less people involved, the better. With this aspect covered, Trigg organised a troop for a week-long patrol to meet up with Lt. Rossi and pursue this operation. Scobie's prediction was that the heavy weather would be on them in two weeks, give or take a day or so, therefore they had to be gone quick, and move quick. They looked to be heading to the foothills of the Rockies, maybe into the Snowies. Three supply wagons would follow on; they would take packhorses with spare saddle horses, giving them the best of both options. Roger was left in charge on the NY and also to notify Adalia that they were on the move. Two days later after some hard riding, and relaying on the spare horses, they caught up with the lieutenant. Now the pace would slacken, as the hombres' wagons that they were following took a twisting route to rise up into the foothills. Then a packhorse team was observed moving down out of the Rockies to rendezvous with these hombres that they were trailing. They watched as the crates were transferred onto the packhorses, the larger crates being placed on a travois, and the whole caboodle carried on upwards into the mountains. No regard was given to the tracks left by the poles of the travois – the expected rains would wash away any signs, like they always did This operation was purely to observe, and that was all they did. The packhorse teams went into the mine adits, were unloaded and then led away to rest and recover, and be ready for the next delivery. Scobie's lads also found well-worn tracks that led more to Laramie City than Cheyenne. Major Hemmyng carefully withdrew his troops and returned to Fort Russell to report back to his colonel. "We only observed, but it is safe to assume that there is a well-established cache of stolen goods secreted in those mine tunnels. Tracks were also found that led towards Laramie City, and some that headed south, possibly to Denver. This place needs raiding, sir, but it will be nigh on impossible to do that until the winter snows have thawed and a troop can get in there and be fully effective. Anything less will incur unnecessary army casualties." "Trying to fight going up those slopes is giving the defenders too much of an advantage.

Well-aimed dynamite would cause carnage, and maybe they had a cannon. Surprise is the crucial element and without that it would be very difficult." "Not being experienced in infantry tactics, I still cannot imagine being able to position cannon close enough on those slopes to be able to have the necessary elevation to shoot upwards. Maybe the officer who leads this operation may think differently. I will complete my report and leave it in your safe custody, sir." "Is there no access from the rear, Major?" "No, it's in the Rockies, sir. There may be packhorse tracks following the contours of the mountains but not even the redskins venture up there as it is too difficult even for their ponies." "Well, you've uncovered it, major. It will lie on the operations log to be undertaken as soon as possible in the future." It was an interesting discovery to Trigg, but with only six weeks left to serve, it was not for him. It went into his own log as well, along with the many others that he had experienced, many of which, like the trouble with these galoots in Chicago, had not been fully resolved to his satisfaction. The raids that had obviously bothered him the most were those on his home. The order to transport these latest prisoners over to Omaha had riled him even more as he foresaw that these galoots would simply be added to the others, and added to the stalemated situation. Annoyed at this, he had written to Tom Benson in Omaha on a personal basis. He had helped the Laidlaw Detective Agency and maybe it could help him. For the cost of a mail stamp, nothing ventured, nothing gained. Scobie's weather prediction had been accurate. The rains came sleeting down, and the ever-present breeze turned into a gale; winter was here and wasn't likely to go away for months. The stock sheds would be fully tested. As was usual, the lawbreakers were more restricted by the weather than the army. Cheyenne had its troubles, but outside the city limits, the winter had them in its grip. Nancy's bitch produced a litter of four dogs and two bitches. Trigg claimed his first pick of the litter as owner of the sire.

Ragnar made his choice based on his invaluable method, handed down through the family, and Trigg became the owner of another dog. Ragnar had a list of would-be owners eager to acquire one of The Dodger's offspring. Nancy's bitch was in fine condition and proved to be a very attentive mother. A month later Adalia gave birth to an 8½ lb boy, mother and baby were fine, and Ragnar was like a dog with two tails – he was a great grandfather now. Trigg, even with six months' notice, found it hard to believe he was a father, but that little bundle of arms, legs and fair hair soon convinced him he was. Doc Townley whispered to him, "Now you'll really know you're married. Good luck"

It started to snow real heavy a day later but Trigg took no notice. Adalia's confinement went as Mae predicted, and the NY was a happy place. There was a baby in the house and the baby proved he had a good pair of lungs. "Just like his father was, soon to let you know he wanted a feed," was Ragnar's comment. Even The Dodger eyed his man of a job well done. A month later the ceremony at Promontory Point confirmed that the Manifest Destiny of the United States had been achieved. The nation's East and West Coasts had been connected by the Transcontinental Railroad. Trigg quickly realised the world was moving on, and he needed to move just as quick, maybe even quicker. Now he was out of the army, he no longer had the direct protection of the army and no colonel to consult with on a daily basis. Trigg Hemmyng spent a very enjoyable and peaceful winter at home with his wife and their new baby son With only the NY and the H&S to concern them, he and Roger were able to sit and talk, thinking about how the future might develop using the income from the investors' deal to finance, through its payments, for wet nursing their livestock. They had agreed to an initial 30,000 head of investors' cattle on the NY but the NY could hold double that, maybe treble, and the figures, on paper, made attractive reading. They would be in good profit this year when they added in the

NY's own herd, the horse sales, and, most profitable of all, the sheep sales. They agreed on the steady plan for May '69 to May '70, to consolidate, just see how this deal worked out in practice and then look again in November '69 as to what they might do from May '70. A letter arrived from Tom Benson saying they had not been able to gather any real information on the matter of interest, but they would persevere

Charlie Parker arrived with his family and was greatly surprised when he saw that the cottage he and his family would be occupying now had four bedrooms, the two upstairs and two more that had been added on the back, and all were accessible from inside. It was a good job as Charlie had found another baby waiting for him when he arrived home. His wife, Jessy, was ecstatic – a proper home for them, and Charlie would be home most nights. Roger met Charlie's quizzical gaze, but nothing was said. Rowdy Hadwick would be bedding down in the bunkhouse in silence – what else? Monty Delucca arrived early the next day and was introduced to Charlie. Both had heard of each other but had never met. Monty and his new family settled into their cottage and his lady was also extremely pleased to be in a nice new cottage with her two daughters, after having lived in the back of a shop for so long. This cottage had previously been used by Will but he was moving into the ranch house prior to his late April wedding, after which he would have some riding to do. Mae Townley was staying in town, to do the doctoring she had come out West to do. Not for the men, her pa could do that, but for the womenfolk. Medical science in the West was largely digging bullets out of feuding men and stitching up the wounds, whether caused by bullets, knife wounds or arrows. Womens' needs were often tended to by using old wives' remedies, often effective, but Mae was fully intent on using her experience gained at the medical college she had attended prior to becoming a practising doctor. Herbie's plans for a schoolroom had been approved by Adalia, and work would begin when

Tommy Brennan could fit it in. Word had spread around the ranch about this new schoolroom and a lot of interest had been generated. Helen and Nancy were reserving Tuesday and Thursday nights for Women's Night when the women could meet, away from the fellas and the kids and have a natter, do some dressmaking or whatever took their fancy. The room had a good hearth and a chimney so they could use it all year round. That was fine by Trigg. It made it all the more worthwhile building it and if it pleased the women, so be it. When Tommy Brennan and his carpenters arrived to start work, Trigg placed another advertisement in the printers' window for a teacher/ bookkeeper with the instructions as previously stated. Percy and Anne Toulson stepped off the train and a 'hansom' dropped them off at a small elegant rooming house on Main Street. They booked in, then sallied forth up Main Street to view this new territorial capital of Wyoming before the sun dropped behind the Rockies and the unruly behaviour was known to begin. It was Friday. They read the advert and Percy noted the details. Percy and Anne Toulson were looking for a new start in life. Their twin sons had been killed in the Civil War, but they had stayed on in New York hoping that time would soften their loss, but the opposite had occurred. As the other lads who had marched off to war with their sons and then returned, without hardly a scratch to show, were now marrying and raising children, every year was making it harder for them to bear. There were too many memories. Their sons had been guarding an armoury that had taken a direct hit. 'Vaporised' was the army's description of how they had perished. They did not even have a bag of bones to bury. With the railroad now complete, they had decided to seek a new life in the West. Cheyenne would be the first place they would look and see if this new territorial capital was the place they were looking to settle in. If it was not suitable, then they intended to board the train and carry on to Sacramento

At five to ten on the following morning, Percy rapped the big knocker on the door of No.5 East Street. Mae Townley answered the door and Percy stated the reason for his visit. Adalia was inside talking with Margaret Townley, and Doc Townley was in his surgery dealing with the queue of Friday-night brawlers. Mae explained that it was her friend they needed to see and took them into the parlour and had them seated comfortably. Mae liked the well-cut, long frock coat of this gent and his wife was also attired in New York fashions. It was a quick, friendly warning to Adalia as to who was waiting to see her. Mae and Adalia had talked previously thinking they would have to be content with a nice young lady schoolteacher but now Adalia was about to meet two very suave-looking folks, not that that would be a worry in any way but forewarned was always useful. "Thank you for responding to our advertisement. My name is Mrs Adalia Hemmyng. My husband has recently retired from the US Cavalry, and we are establishing a horse and cattle ranch just east of Cheyenne. We are now seeking a schoolteacher cum bookkeeper as both the ranch and our staff are growing very quickly. I need to mention this at this point, because the position is based out on the ranch, not here in Cheyenne. Excuse my cheek, but you do not look like typical Wyoming ranch-dwellers. Would that be suitable for you both?" "Pleased to meet you, Mrs Hemmyng and thank you for being honest. We have left New York seeking to find a new life which being on a ranch would certainly be but we are more interested in the folk we are working for. Anywhere out here, even in Sacramento, if we do not find a position here in Cheyenne, would not be like New York, and that could be good for us." Touche.

Percy Toulson offered her his qualifications, both as a bookkeeper and a school- master and his wife's in bookkeeping. Adalia liked this couple a lot, but were they too good for what they needed? Would they get bored and move on? She passed the papers across to Mae as she gazed at this couple. "I apologise for not introducing Mae. Mae is a fully qualified doctor, has practised in Philadelphia where I grew up, but is here in Cheyenne supporting her father. This position, Mr Toulson, will involve teaching full-grown cowboys, as well as children, probably more of them than the children for a year or two, so would that be acceptable to you?" "If they want to learn, I will gladly teach them, but it certainly will be different." Margaret Townley appeared with a pot of coffee and some biscuits, and then Mae intervened as she passed the papers back to Adalia. "Excuse me butting in, Mr Toulson, but this place is totally different to the East, although it is not as bad as the papers describe it, but it can get dangerous. You could easily see fellas being gunned down. How would that affect you?" "It would not be nice but Abe Lincoln got shot just sitting in the theatre back East so it seems that getting shot can occur anywhere these days." Adalia had read through the qualification certificates and was even more impressed with this couple, but still had the doubt that these two were maybe too good and would get bored, and leave. "Mr and Mrs Toulson, you are clearly well trained, very experienced and very suitable for this job but I think it would be wise if you came out to the ranch and saw the spread for yourselves. I am sure we can agree a salary but I would like you to see where you would be working. We have a small coach that can collect you from your hotel and bring you out. Tomorrow would be ideal. Would that be acceptable to you?" "Yes, certainly. What time would you be collecting us?"

"Would eleven be suitable and if you give me the name of the hotel, and our men will ensure that you have a safe journey both there and back? Before you leave Mrs Toulson, you have been very patient but have you anything that you would like to ask?" "No, Mrs Hemmyng, where Percy goes, I go. I know he would not put us in a position of danger, but thank you for asking. I look forward to seeing you again tomorrow." As Mae returned from escorting them out, she met Adalia's gaze. "They would be ideal for you, and I think he has more backbone than his clothes indicate, and she is no wallflower. Best of luck tomorrow, girl. I'll be keeping my fingers crossed for you." Over dinner that evening, Adalia related the meeting to Trigg and how much she was hoping that they would be taking the job. "Who will you be sending to collect them, Soldier boy?" "Scobie and GG. They usually go in early and have some banter with Jake and Herbie, probably a game or two of cards – Sunday morning, ain't it?" "I'll go in with them then. Ain't seen Herbie for a few days. I'll see how he's getting on." This was Ragnar's way of getting in on the conversation. "Struth, Soldier boy, make sure Scobie meets them out of the rooming house, we're trying to give them a good impression. If GG goes in or that rascal there, they might not bother coming!" "Eh, just because you're a mother, I'll just pretend I didn't hear that." "This is the West, liebling, they got to get used to it. We have to start as we mean to go on and all that banter. They'll be all right, you'll see." They were all right, after GG had pushed his battered face into the carriage to have a look see at the passengers, and had made some comment to Ragnar, and then with a flourish and a redskin squeal, had leapt onto his pony and rode off to carry out his scouting duties.

Ragnar had then carried on a running commentary on all the dangers that were close by, coyotes, wolves, rattlesnakes, vultures and grizzly bears that weren't that far away, but they arrived safe and sound at the NY and were quick to clamber out of the coach and into the ranch house. Adalia introduced them to Roger as he was the ranch manager and it was him who they would be working directly for. Roger showed them around the ranch and into the office where they would be working and discussed with them the bookkeeping records that he needed keeping up to date and he then explained that the boss was busy with his range boss with an issue concerning the horses. With the work on the schoolroom and its cottage nearly complete, he was able to show them this new building and the cottage they would have should they wish to take up this position. Roger then took them on a conducted tour of the ranch, explaining that they had two herds of cattle, then all about the horses and how they acquired them, the sheep herd out on the Bluffs and the dairy work. He also explained that the H&S in Cheyenne was a hardware store and horse sales yard and that would also be included in the bookkeeping and, of course it would involve the pay ledgers being kept fully up to date. Questions were asked and answers were given, and then Roger escorted them back into the house and into Adalia's company. He went back out to see Nancy as Adalia took Anne upstairs to show her the bedroom they could use until the schoolroom and cottage were finished, that is of course if they wished to take up the position.

Percy was invited to take a seat while the two women went upstairs to inspect the bedroom. He settled into an armchair that had a view right down the plain, but no sooner had he settled into the chair, than the back door burst open and a hound came hurtling in and straight at him; its fangs were showing and it was looking like it intended to eat him alive. Percy grabbed the armrests as he cowered away from the growling hound. Then a voice called out from the kitchen, "Dodger, where are you? Get back in here." Then Percy saw a tough, grinning face poking round the door as the hound growled at him one last time, then it did as it was told.

"Mr Toulson, I presume. Take no notice of the dog, he's all growl, just doing his job. Would you like a beer?" Percy nodded, maybe something a bit more medicinal but a beer would do. "Major Trigg Hemmyng, pleased to meet yer, everything all right? Forget the dog, he'll be snoring in a minute. Hope you've liked what you've seen. We are just getting going and we've secured a good deal that will really boost the business. We have a lot more range hands starting soon, most of them can't read or write, and the two new range foremen have got nine kids between em. We've just been blessed with a son. Nancy who runs the dairy is due any time soon and the blacksmith brought his kid sister with him, bright little lass, so we've put the schoolroom up and now we need someone to make it work." The back door opened and mutterings were heard in the kitchen. "Wat's bothering you, Pop?" "I can't get these new boots off. They fit allright but theyre damn hard to gerrem off." "Excuse me, Mr Toulson, drink up and I'll fetch you another beer." "Sit down, put your foot up and quieten down." The Dodger had been roused from trying to have a snooze and had smelt the beer . Percy watched as the major returned with a tray with three beers and a metal bowl on it. As he set the bowl on the floor the dog was straight in. "Steady on, you mucky pup, you're slurping it all over, you won't get another!" The dog looked doleful, and then began to drink his beer more slowly. "If we have a beer, Mr Toulson, he has to have one. He started that when we were at Fort Laramie in '60."

"Toulson, did you say? I had some distant cousins called Toulson, lived over in Cumberland somewhere, best place for them as I remember, but they didn't look like him – he looks a bit edifacated." Percy had taken his time drinking his first beer, he liked it and was savouring every swallow. The dog had slurped his up and was eyeing the glass that was sat there, apparently not wanted. The Dodger looked at his man, then at the beer, then back at his man. "Don't you dare. Go and sit over there and behave yourself. He's after your beer, Mr Toulson, thinks if you don't want it, he'll have it. Ragnar intervened. "Come on, Dodger, get your bowl. I'll get you another, it's Sunday ain't it?" Percy watched as the dog scooped up the tin bowl in his teeth and followed into the kitchen. "Smartest dog west of the Missouri, he is, Mr Toulson. He has met and shaken paws with territorial governers, generals, colonels, rail road building tycoons, river boat captains, and politicians aplenty, bit hesitant with them he was, and was revered by the troopers on those patrols we met when were camping out on the plains. Incredible hearing and sense of smell and never a scrap of trouble. I'll introduce yer properly an' he'll show yer his party piece." The Dodger sat down and raised his paw. Percy Toulson took hold of it. The Dodger gave him a wink. Percy had been entertained by the earlier antics, and this undoubted wink was the final straw – he couldn't hold back his mirth. As Percy was still holding The Dodger's paw, Adalia and Anne entered the parlour. Trigg introduced himself, then when she assured him that everything had gone smoothly, he sent his pop to tell Scobie to fetch the coach. "It'll be dark soon; best if you get back in Cheyenne in good time. Have a good think about the position and tell Dr Mae what you've decided tomorrow. It's been a pleasure meeting yer. Enjoy your stay in Cheyenne and good luck for the future." He had them out of the house and into the coach real quick, and away they went. "That was a rush, Soldier boy, why?"

"They look a devoted couple, she will decide, so let them cuddle up tonight and make a decision. I ain't railroading them into deciding. They are, as you said, ideal but if they want this type of life, let them tell us. He seemed happy, but is she? I hope they do, I liked him, but I reckon he will do what she wants to do."

Then Roger appeared. "What impression did you get, Roger? Do you think they will take the position?" "Yes, his eyes were twinkling, he liked what he saw. They want a new life – the Happening Man has struck gold again, two in one throw of the dice, Adalia. My money is firmly on them joining the NY, and I will be very pleased to have them here." Roger was proved correct; the message came back via the H&S, and Adalia had the coach readied again to go in and collect them. Whilst that was organised, Percy had returned to a furniture shop where he had seen an upright piano for sale. A little bit of haggling and he bought it, and agreed a delivery date. When they arrived back on the NY later that day, Percy checked with Trigg as to whether he had any objections to them having the piano. "None at all, Percy. The army has a band in nearly every fort. I ain't very musical but I can admire a good voice when I hear one. Which one of you is the piano player or do you both tinkle the ivories?" "It's Anne; she can't read music very well, but she can pick a tune quick. She only has to hear it once or twice and she has it. If it wasn't for the music, I don't think we would have survived the dark days." "Tell me to mind my own business, Percy, but what were the dark days?" Percy's head dropped as the memories came flooding back. "We had twin boys, be twenty eight-years old now, and they marched off to the war about six months before it finished. The army letter said they had been 'vapourised' when the armoury they were guarding took a direct hit. We struggled on hoping time would lessen the anguish, but it only got worse as their school pals married and began to raise families, so here we are, hoping a fresh place and a new start will soften the torment." "Percy, I'm deeply sorry for stirring up your sorrows. Forgive me please. Must be this army life has dulled me from thinking too deeply about folks' losses. I'm sorry for asking." "Well, they say a trouble shared is a trouble halved. Let's hope it turns out that way."

Trigg was quick to have a word with Roger, Will, Ragnar and Adalia. He wanted them to hear it from him, so that they knew and didn't ask similar questions of either of them. Raking up those sort of memories up was not good for anybody and these two folks did not need to be reminded too often of sorrows like that. Other people had suffered worse than that, but that would not lessen their grief. It was a tough unforgiving world. There no point in making it worse. Over dinner, Trigg raised the news that Percy had purchased a piano. "They could expect to hear the kids learning the songs. That will liven the nights up. When Tommy gets finished and Anne has the ivories tinkling, be real good for the NY. Nothing like a good sing song on a rainy old night in Wyoming." As the investors' cattle rolled in and more range hands joined the NY, they all soon learnt that this feller in the long coat might not be a bronc-bustin' cowboy, but he knew the meaning of every word and how to use it in the letter they sent home to their folks, and he could total money as fast as a storekeeper's till. He shared a few beers with them every day in the bunkhouse, looked them square in the eye and let them know they could knock on his door any time if they needed to know anything. He had the patience to sit one-to-one with them and help them learn, no mocking or derision, just steady progress to suit them. As the investors' cattle rolled into the Pine Bluffs' livestock pens, Will, Charlie and Rowdy were there to meet them. Cattle didn't only get rustled off ranches, animals could be be stolen at any stage, sometimes only a few, but whole truckloads out of a train were known to go missing somewhere between loading and arrival. Will was there to ensure the delivery dockets tallied with the cattle count. As the herd built up, Percy became involved in visiting Pine Bluffs; he was a whizz at adding the numbers up and it left Charlie and Monty to spend more time on the range. Also Will's wedding to Mae was fast approaching and he would be away for a few weeks, honeymooning in California, care of Henri Watson de Silva. Henry and his lady were coming over for the wedding, and he had arranged a mystery honeymoon for them, somewhere in California, details to be arranged when they met. Trigg, having lost the full time services of Harry and Joe, had taken to using Charlie's hoppo, Rowdy Hadwick. Charlie had been right, Rowdy was good with both the rifle and a Colt, as a short practice session had proved. Charlie did not mind losing his hoppo for the odd day or two now he was in his own cot every night.

Whether he was as useful with his fists was soon likely to be tested; the more time he spent in the Pine Bluffs yard, the quicker he was gonner bump into some galoot who reckoned he could give him a belting. No need to go looking for it, it would find him – a new man in the yard to be challenged, it was guaranteed. Whilst Percy was involved in these inspections, Anne busied herself getting the schoolkids organised and setting up the schoolroom. Also helping Nancy as her 'time' was getting nearer and nearer, and getting acquainted with Beattie and how the H&S routine worked so Nancy would have no need to fret. She soon became friendly with Helen, both being of a similar age and with similar attitudes. With one baby already on the NY and another due very shortly, there was plenty to occupy a caring lady. What she had thought might be a mite quiet time, even lonely, was suddenly seeming that there weren't enough hours in the day, but she was not complaining, she was well content: a new cosy cottage, furnished to her taste; it could be a whole lot worse. The investors wanted to place another 8,000 head on the NY, on top of the 30,000 they already had. Would they take them? It was urgent – they needed them moved onto a safer ranch, too much trouble where they were. Trigg had a quick word with Will – they were managing easy enough, he was happy, send them here. Roger wired confirmation that the NY would take them. When they arrived, there were only 7,460 fit to trail. 540 were done in, too lame to move, looked underfed and over trailed. Where had they been? Will moved the fit cattle out, not enough daylight left to hang about talking, leaving George Dobbs to wire the investors' men direct from his office. Next morning Roger was in the H&S early expecting a wire regarding these unfit cattle, but nothing arrived. Was this an example of the troubles the investors' men kept getting with some of the ranchers? A wire did arrive, but not one they were expecting. Tom Benson was on the train and heading for Cheyenne and needing to see his old lieutenant urgently. Roger advised Jake to have Tom Benson escorted straight out to the NY, no need for him to book a room, he could stay on the NY.

Nothing more was heard of the cattle Trigg had refused to trail. With only enough light left, they had trailed the bulk of the herd onto the NY. Maybe these others could be collected when they were rested up and fit to trail. Tom Benson arrived with a tale of woe, business for the Jack Laidlaw Detection Agency had been picking up steadily, then as the result of carrying out a very tidy and efficient job of detection for a new client based in St Louis, this new client had recommended them to a good friend, a top man in the Garcia Brothers business, no less. The Garcias was an old business of general dealers, trading in high-quality merchandise throughout the South, the Caribbean and also into the South American countries. "Me and Jack had been to meet this Ricardo Diaz, son-in-law of the Garcia brother who lives in Havana, and it went well. The trouble he wanted clearing up was right up our street and we're just preparing our offer. Then Jack takes his wife and daughter to see his in-laws, not a frequent occurrence, when two hick galoots derail the train they're riding on, just to see it plunge into the river. They weren't even trying to rob it, just sat there laughing after it had plunged into the river. Word is they were brain-addled on rotgut, and this passenger who got out brained em with a spanner they had used to undo the bolts in the fish plates. Now I'm in a big tangle. I ain't got the money to run this deal. Are you interested in buying the company and keeping this deal going with the Garcia's?" "Steady on, Tom, how much time is there, when do these Garcias want your team in and working, and how much is the company worth, how do you work your men?" "I reckon this Ricardo Diaz will be all right. He said it was trouble that they'd had for a while, and some others had tried and failed to resolve things." "Have you brought any of the company's books with you, and any details of this deal with the Garcias?" "Yep, got them here in my bag; knew you'd need to see them." "Who is looking after the office while you are over here?" "Feller called Enoch Pound. It was him who sorted the job out that led to this recommendation. Only been with us a few months – just walked in and asked for a job one day. We gave him a try and he did well. You'd never take him for a detective, but he gets the results and that's all that matters, ain't it?" "So what are your movements now, Tom?" "Got to be back in Omaha by Thursday night; its Jack's funeral on Friday." Roger scribbled on some paper and passed it across to him.

"Consolidate, remember." "So if you're on the night train tomorrow and back in Omaha early Thursday?" "Yep, that will suit me fine." "We might as well give this full consideration, Roger. Tom's travelled a long way, it's obviously very important to him, but I ain't making any promises, Tom." Trigg sent for Will. He wanted a rider to take a message to Jimmy Hanson. "Make sure yer see Mr Hanson and he gives you a reply. Be careful." Trigg was arranging to meet Jimmy in the H&S office at 10.00 hours. "Right, Tom, tell us all about these Garcia brothers. I reckon I've heard of them but only in passing sort of thing. What is it that they actually do?" "Where do I start? They're like general dealers, have been for a hundred years I believe, and they buy and sell all sorts of expensive furnishings, carpets, fabrics, house- wares, everything the rich folk want. The boss man lives in Havana. It was his son-in- law we met in St Louis, nice gent, very refined, and they trade all over. St Louis is only one of the main centres. Materials and goods come in from Europe and Asia, all over the place." "Seems to me they would be a good company to get acquainted with, Tom, I'll bet they get a lot of robbers and thieves prowling around, with all that amount of expensive stock on their hands." Roger felt the anticipation in Trigg's voice; the consolidation looked like being on the next train East, if Jimmy Hanson's figures made sense. The Happening Man had the look of a hunter about him – sit tight and enjoy the ride. Jimmy Hanson asked all the questions he wanted answers to, then perused the books that Tom had brought with him. Lastly it was how do you finance your detectives, hourly paid or on a price plus a slice of the reward monies, agents in other words? "The company isn't worth a carrot. It only owns three horses and a surrey, everything is rented, including his house, and there was only $80 in the bank plus whatever there was in the petty cash or under his bed. No safe was mentioned. Fortunately all the agents had been paid up to date, and the work in progress was not substantial. It was like many other detective agencies – very easy come, easy go. The only real item of value was the potential in this Garcia Brothers deal, but to value that was like wetting your finger to measure which way the wind was blowing. Would this Mr Diaz run a mile if you wanted to carry out this work for him with a different owner?" '

Mr Laidlaw was an ex-Pinkerton man, and Abe Lincoln had used the Pinkerton Agency to gather information on Confederate Army operations, and maybe the government was still using them. It was a crucial point that Jimmy had raised, a point that had to be cleared before anything else was discussed. "You had better go see this Mr Diaz and make him aware of the whole sorry situation. Jimmy thinks your rates need to be another 10% higher to cover for a bigger contingency, but that might not be of any relevance if Diaz loses interest. Take my private card and if Diaz is prepared to continue to negotiate, show him my card and tell him I am interested if his deal is on. Make sure he knows that the same team is doing the work, but with a new owner. Best of luck, Tom. Let me know how you get on." Trigg waved him off on the train, then went back into the H&S office. "It could be a good business if that Garcia deal is on, Major, but the stories I have heard about Garcia could make yer hair curl; well, not yours – it's curly already, but the brother who lives in Havana has a fearsome reputation. Maybe the both of them are getting a bit long in tooth, and the sons-in-law are not out of the same get out and get them mould. Probably too well educated for the cut and thrust of getting your goods or money back without involving too much law. Be interesting to see how it all turns out." A few days later, as they were trailing the last of these extra investors' stock up onto the NY, a rustling mob came out of a gully that led up from NY land. This last delivery was in addition to the other extra stock, but had arrived in the railyard pens and the only option was to get it onto the NY and Roger and Percy could sort out the mix-up in the numbers. Rowdy Hadwick had his horse shot out from under him, managed to roll clear and got real mad with these thieving hombres. He leapt at one of em, dragged him off his hoss and hammered him senseless, then pulled another hoss and man down and piled into him. He nearly got shot, but this other galoot turned and rode off looking shit scared. We've got em all, boss, no need to worry about that Rowdy, he can scrap, takes the hosses as well." "Tell him to be careful, Will, losing yer temper ain't good, too risky – the next one might not get scared." "Already have, an' he took it right. Here's the only saddlebag they had. We'll cart them up to the fort and book em in. The horses are in Sam's remuda and I've stripped the dead one and left it out there. Be gone in a day or two. Anything else?"

"Go see Percy, he might like a visit to the fort and it'll be useful if he knows the booking procedure, that's if he ain't got any teaching duties." Percy accepted the opportunity but was not too keen when he saw the two dead men and heard the other moans and groaning from the rope burns from the hobbling and the handcuffing. The hoods weren't that tight, just tight enough to stop em falling off. The saddlebags had a 'bravado' reward notice. Some of these galoots liked to carry a reward poster showing they were wanted. Seemed to be a bragging honour when they were carousing with their buddies, and it made naming and claiming easier as well. The eight horses went into the corrals, and the $87 into the petty cash box. Six more saddles and tack and some ropey old pistols to sell. There was some other paperwork that had no relevance to him, but it would be attached to the claim form that Roger, or maybe

Percy now, would submit for payment. Some body might make sense of it, no point in throwing it away until the Army had a chance to read it. Another rustling raid was made four days later, and they came in at sun-up, in two waves, straight from the west; the galoots had set out from Cheyenne, or congregated in Cheyenne, maybe directly off the train. The three extra Shoshone boys that Scobie had recruited as they had been released by the army saw them first, from the hayloft where Scobie had berthed them. They didn't want be in the bunkhouse, and some of the range hands didn't want them; there still was plenty of dislike, on both sides, between the whites and the redskins. Comments had been made, followed by snidey looks, when they had arrived, and Scobie had wisely moved them up into the hayloft. It was a 'give them some time to get used to each other' type of thinking. Unlike before, Trigg, Will, Spud and Sammy knew these Shoshone lads well and trusted them, but Charlie, Monty, Rowdy and the new range hands didn't and were still not sure. Then another three had arrived to cause some more uncertainty. Trigg and Will had schooled these new men in the 'stay well hidden, give em nothing to shoot at, and pick your shots' – too many shots gave your position away too easy – make them look hard to find yer. GG was straight up into the hayloft; he would keep those lads up there well hidden and not spraying bullets all over. Now it would be clear if Charlie and Monty had taken full heed of the advice. These hombres coming cantering in looked determined.

With no time to get the women into the bunkhouse, Trigg sent Will into the bottom of the Barn, and Buddie into the schoolhouse, while he stayed in the house with Roger. Ragnar took his shotgun, with Adalia and the baby and Helen upstairs. With Buddie and Will in position, and himself where he was, they were in like a triangle, not shooting from either side and liable to shoot each other. He would shoot first. The tactic was keep well covered up, let them come in and see what they had to say, if anything, then he would let rip if he was not happy, and after that it was take no prisoners. Trigg could see Scobie up in the hayloft; it had been built that way purposely so signs could be given, pointing out where any attackers were. It was like holding the high ground and viewing the battleground. Three riders held back, the other three came in and started making their demands. As the hombre started to call out his demands, Charlie Parker stood up and started calling him out, with real venom in his speech. "You ain't getting hoss shit here, Rat Face Ford. Git your arse out here before" … A pistol shot from one of the other riders smacked into the timber very close to Charlie's head, but then Trigg took the gunman clean off his horse with a rifle shot that hit the man just in front of his ear and shattered his skull. "Get yer head down, Charlie, and keep quiet." Trigg signalled up to Scobie and another rifle shot hit the hombre making the demands, in his shoulder and he crumpled off his hoss and onto the ground. The other rider jigged about as his hoss shied then hightailed it out to where the other three had hung back. Will appeared at the hayloft door. "Big 50 into em, boss?" Trigg gave him the big thumbs up, then enquired as to where the others were. With the new hatches that had been cut into the barn roof, an observer had a clear view in every direction. Scobie reappeared at the hayloft door. "They're still back about 300 yds, boss; don't appear to be too keen." The Sharps big 50 barked and a hoss went down like a bag of taters, trapping its rider's leg underneath it. Will was reloading the Sharps and ready to fire again. He looked down at Trigg and got the big thumbs again. The Sharps barked again and another hoss went down. The two other riders scarpered, closely followed by a hobbling rider. Scobie came across to the house. "They've scarpered back to the others, boss. We can get saddled up and out and around behind em. GG can keep watch."

"Do that, but don't take them on, just stand off and look real menacing." Trigg called Buddie to look after the house, then ordered Charlie to get his range hands out and up onto the range to relieve the night shift. He kept Rowdy back; that gave himself, Will, Rowdy, Sam and Buddie time to wait for Scobie and his lads to get to the other side of these hombres and see what they did then. If they came back he was confident they would quickly even the numbers up. With Scobie and his lads behind them and five of them in front, and all good shots, it was down to these galoots what took place next. Charlie seemed to know the mouthpiece – that would be sorted out later. There wasn't anybody bothering the herd or one of the Shoshone lads would have been in, so what were these galoots after, and thinking they needed to come onto the NY at daybreak to get it? "They're still milling about, boss, Scobie is behind em now, but they might not be aware of him yet." Trigg had them saddle up. The situation needed resolving and it was better sorted out there, well away from the house. GG had ordered Chas and Clickka to tidy up the mess of those who had been downed, with the usual caution to be alert as they could still be dangerous. Trigg and Rowdy rode out wide to the right, Will, Buddie and Sam to the left, and they stood off and hailed them. Seeing only five men facing them, the galoots began to look more brazen, until a rifle shot took their attention from their rear. Seeing six more riders well spaced out and higher up the plain, they looked for an escape route, and four took flight down the plain eastwards. They had a long way to go thataway, and Scobie had three of his lads tail them – the usual, keep them observed, unless attacked, "We'll follow on when these galoots are sorted." The mouth knew the game was up, and they surrendered. He tried to make out that they had got the wrong place, but there wasn't another place for miles, and they had passed the NY nameboard only a mile back. Disarmed and handcuffed, they were marched back into the barn: not what cowboy boots were intended for; those big heels were intended to keep the boot in the stirrup, not for tramping over high plains.

"So, Rat Face Ford, just what were you here for?" The galoot stuck to his story, and the others clammed up, as usual. Will and Scobie had taken three more Shoshone lads and caught up with the other three who were sat watching four very lost and weary galoots arguing between each other as to which direction was the right way to go. A couple of rifle shots close to their feet had them wondering where the hell they had come from. Will called for their surrender and they laid flat down, arms spread wide, and were disarmed. They also were made to walk back to the NY. Will and Scobie cantered back to the NY, leaving Chas and Clickka and co. to trail these galoots back. Charlie had been sent for. Would he be able to shed some light on why this galoot had arrived making, or trying to make, the demands he had? Whilst they were waiting for Charlie to get back in, Trigg and Will had a look in the saddlebags of Rat Face Ford. $8,000 in used, old, $10 bills, and a receipt made out in the name of an Archibald Woodman, from an attorney in Laramie City. There were scrawled signatures, but not readable. The other saddlebag had another $630 in a cloth bag. Charlie Parker was taken into the office and given some coffee and biscuits to settle him after the canter back in. "We've got em in the barn, Charlie, but the boss galoot, the one you didn't seem to have much regard for, ain't saying anything except that they attacked the wrong spread, just made a stupid mistake. You called him Rat Face Ford; is that his real name, or does he use several names?" "That's my name for him. He's lower than a snake's belly, snidiest bastard you'll ever come across. His name is Archie Ford, but we were always feuding after we stashed some loot. When we went back, it had gone and he had too. I did the graft for that loot and he did the dirty on us. Never capped eyes on him since, then he shows up again this morning an' I got mad. That was his brother-in-law you shot – nearly did for me, didn't he?" "Well, he missed, that's all that matters, but the next one might not. Keep yer head down and be more cagey; jumping up like that ain't very clever. Charlie, where do yer know him from?"

"Missouri, we was running wild as the war ended. We acquired some loot, Yankee dollars, from a battlesite that had been hidden in some old buildings. He told us it was there. I snook in while he kept a lookout, then we stashed it again and scarpered. There was three of usin' it, but when we went back it had gone; could only have been him where we had stashed it. Jimmy, the other lad in it, never left my side until he was killed. I promised him that his mother would get his share, but it had gone. I've done some wrong things in my time but I'd never cheat on a pal like that." "Any idea what he was doing up here then, Charlie, long ways from Missouri?" "I ain't ever seen him since we made that stash, but I've heard talk about him, all bad and about similar cheatin' and thieving on folks who helped him and thought he was all right, but he seems to have a talent for cheating and robbing, sly and nasty." As Trigg was about to ask whether he knew anyone in Laramie City, Will came bustling into the office. "That mouthpiece has had a seizure, dead as he'll ever be. I had just released one of his arms, Spud had brought a bowl of stew and some spoons for em, trying the 'be kind' routine to get em talking, but he reared up moaning, then collapsed. His face had gone all lopsided and his tonque shot out. We doused him in water but he's a gonner." "Get em loaded up, Will. I'll cart em into the fort and book em in. Charlie can come with me and tell the colonel what he knows. You stay alert out here, and make sure GG stays up in the hayloft and scans the plains." When they arrived in the fort, the colonel was occupied by visiting army staff and Capt. Rinker was deputed to take the statements and prepare the report. Charlie confirmed the identity of the two he knew, but had no idea who the rest were – likely they were some galoots he had assembled to form another gang. Trigg talked to John Rinker privately about the money in the saddlebags and the receipt for the $8,000 that was nicely parcelled up and separate from the other money. "Could be these galoots had just been in Laramie, collected this money, then had for whatever reason decided to raid the NY. The attorney in Laramie might be forthcoming." He submitted the NY's claim on all the money in the saddlebags and then registered that the nine horses were in the NY corrals and would be included in the six- month rule. All as previous claims. Also he reserved the right to claim any reward monies on the galoots now in the army jail. He carefully pocketed the receipt for the saddlebag monies, then accepted the assurance from Capt. Rinker that he would be notified, in writing, of further developments as they arose. He shook hands with his former colleague and bid him farewell. He called into the H&S to notify Jake of the day's events, had some of the usual banter on the latest goings-on in Cheyenne, then they mosied on back to the NY. "That Clay Patrick hombre, Charlie, Rat Face's brother-in-law. You told the captain he was a Virginian. Where'd yer meet up with him – in the war?" "Yup. There were four brothers, all good soldiers, but he was real mean that Clay, real mean and cruel, but it was war and there were plenty like him on both sides. We rode with em for about two weeks, then we separated. Ordered to different locations as the battles raged, but the older one, Clancy, I reckon they called him, was the leader – good soldier him." When they arrived back on the NY, Roger had been into town and collected the mail, and waiting for the boss was a letter addressed to Major T Hemmyng, postmarked Omaha. Tom Benson had been to see Mr Diaz, and yes, they were still very keen to progress this deal, but the urgency had been removed due to Senor Emilio Garcia's illness. He was expected to recover quite quickly, but until he was back and fully fit, nothing would be finalised. That was good news; they could think it out more fully before a decision needed to be made. Then another decision needed to be made. "I reckon we ought to keep two o' them pups. The one we chose is a real determined cuss, but so is one of his brothers, they're like twins, always together and rough and tumbling each other; be real fine dogs them. Don't like letting him go." "Pop, if you want to keep the pair, so be it, I ain't ever gonner doubt your judgement when it comes to pups." "Good, glad you've seen sense. Now what yer gonner call em? We need to start training em to a name. Jake's taking one for H&S, Will's having a bitch for the Doc, the other bitch is going to Herbie, and two customers of the H&S, can't remember the names but Jake says they're good fellers, are having the dogs. Now I need two names from you." "Pop, sort the names out with Adalia. Let her see the pups, then you two decide."

A week after delivering Rat Face Ford and his cohorts into the fort, Capt. Rinker was wanting a private word with his old boss. "We can't find hide nor hair of an attorney who signs his name anything like the one on that receipt. None of the officers in Fort Sandars recognise it, and those galoots that you brought in with Ford don't know anything. That's understandable as the two might have met one evening in a private place to do their business. Could be there's a rogue attorney on the loose over there; wouldn't be the first, would it?"

"No, you're right there. Thanks for letting me know. Keep me in touch." He decided to let sleeping dogs lie, and use the Trespass Law to claim the money now lodged with the army as evidence, as the army had tried but had been unable to locate or identify this attorney. He had done things correctly, leave it at that. The only other item that had taken his notice was that every horse these latest raiders had used had a different brand on them: twelve horses, twelve different brands. "Have you seen any of those brands before, Sam – twelve, all different. We see plenty that have been altered, some have grown over, and some without a brand, but twelve all different – what do you reckon?" "I'll make a sketch of each one, and pin it up near the forge, be interesting." "Put a star near the ones that the two main hoppos were riding, the light grey and the strawberry roan, tell Buddie about it as well." Gordi Brunner was in the H&S, deep in conversation with his brother, when Trigg rolled in two days later. It was a quick acknowledgement from Herbie, then the pair were back into their seemingly serious conversation. Herbie was obviously recovering his health good and fast. Jimmy Hanson then appeared and he went straight upstairs to join Trigg. "I want to go over that deal for the Laidlaw business, Jimmy. We've got some extra time to make sure our figures are correct; the Garcia brother in charge at St Louis ain't too well at the moment, and the deal won't be agreed until he's back." The deal was talked over, taken apart, bits added in, but it still added up to a viable proposition, and like all those kinds of deals, the beauty was in the eye of the beholder

Most businessmen wouldn't touch it with a barge pole, but the potential was too good to be ignored if the man doing the deal was confident, and Major Trigg Hemmyng was confident. This deal was stirring his juices. He had intended to get into a detective type of business and his initial thoughts were as a livestock detective type of business. His army experience had shown him that, like other already established cattle detectives, there was a business to be made, and with these investors moving in as well, it could only get better. Now here was a viable business with a feller in the top spot who he knew and liked, and a deal ready to be had with an impressive client. He had two men waiting in the wings, Sgts Harry Pickering and Joe Kennedy, who could slide in alongside Capt. Tom Benson to strengthen and support him, and when they had the opportunity to get into the livestock side, the Shoshone lads could be used for tracking and observing where the rustled cattle or horses were being kept. He had the men lined up, now this deal could produce the opportunity, and he was ready to give it a go; this could be the second string to his bow that he wanted. Cattle could be an unreliable business, and it was hard work holding onto your stock. Horses were better, but there were thousands of horse dealers and, like cattle, they could easily be trotted over the hill and away, but lawlessness was a fast growing business, if you were suited to dealing with these hombres. The investors were good, but for how long? If the prices dropped, they would look elsewhere to invest. Another good line of business was well worth the trouble, and trouble was there in abundance, whichever way you chose to do business, remember Abe Lincoln. In Trigg Hemmyng's thinking, you had to make your choice and go for it. The train ride over to Omaha had given Trigg plenty of time to sit, take in the scenery, and think. Tom Benson introduced him to Enoch Pound, the detective who had unravelled the case that had led to this introduction to the Garcia potential deal. Trigg eyed the scrawny looking middle-aged feller. Tom had been exact in his description, the last type of hombre that you imagined a detective to look like, but he was proving very successful to the Laidlaw Agency. The old saying was proving true: it didn't matter what he looked like, could he do the job, and Enoch Pound was proving he could. As Trigg was being introduced to Mr Ricardo Diaz in the old but very comfortable entrance foyer of the Garcias' St Louis office, another coach came trotting in, and outbustled a well-worn faced feller of Hispanic appearance, elegantly dressed, but with the air of a man who knew exactly what he was about, and who caused Mr Ricardo Diaz to suddenly divert all his attention away from his visitors.

"Susannah, quickly, go tell Mr Emilio his brother is just arriving, quick." Trigg nodded to Tom Benson to take a step backwards and give this hombre all the space he needed. "Ola, Ricardo, how is my brother? I came straight to the office. Is he here or still at the hacienda?" "He is here, he has recovered and we were about to meet with these two gents on a small business matter, Senor Silvio." "Who are these gringos, Ricardo, what is the business matter?" Before Ricardo could answer Senor Emilio appeared and the two elderly brothers embraced, then a short splattering of Spanish took place that ended when they turned to face Trigg and Tom. "This is Major Hemmyng, and this is Capt. Benson, representing the Laidlaw Detective Agency, here to discuss the El Paso department problem." 'El Paso' – the words caused Trigg to look urgently at Tom, who shrugged his shoulders in disbelief. "You two gringos were not Jonny Rebs, were you?" "No Sir, I served in the army of the West where I met Capt. Benson who later did become involved in the Civil War. We were both in the 2nd Cavalry Regiment." Senor Silvio eyed them both sternly, then asked where the Laidlaw gringo was. "He and his family were killed recently, in a railroad derailment. The purpose of our meeting today was to discuss whether you would agree to me acquiring this business and allow the Laidlaw Agency to undertake work for the Garcia company." Senor Silvio flashed glances across to his brother, more Spanish babbling took place, then he turned his steely, black-eyed gaze back onto Trigg. "You said you served in the cavalry. What you do now Major?" "I ranch cattle mainly but also horses and sheep, sir." "How many cattle on your range, Major, do you know?" "As of Tuesday, 41,000 short horns, 600 saddle horses and 4,600 sheep up on the grass bluffs, sir. The ranch is located just east of Cheyenne, in the territory of Wyoming."

The black-eyed stare seemed to intensify, but then a hand was extended as if a truce was being offered. Trigg wrapped his big farmer's lad fist over the knobbly, hard-skinned mitt. "You do not have the hands of a vaquero, Major." "No, sir, my hands are more attuned to handling a Henry repeating rifle. I trust you are aware of the rustling problem that is prevalent in the business. I employ cowboys to manage the cattle, I shoot the rustlers." There was more Spaniardo banter, then Senor Silvio backed away and raised his hand. "Adios, Major, very interesting to meet you. Emilio will conduct his meeting with you now. Good luck Gentlemen." Trigg knew he had been 'interviewed' Silvio Garcia-style, but felt he had given as good as he had got, that the gringo had stood his ground and not been intimidated, but that was his guess. What would Emilio have to say, and what did the El Paso Engineering Co. have to do with the Garcias?

Then there was the Topeka and the others who were involved with those stolen Winchesters; what had they stumbled into all these years later? Even if the Garcias didn't want to use Laidlaws, there was plenty to poke a nose into and see what came bubbling out. Trigg had got the impression that Tom had not remembered about the El Paso name stamped on those crates, and why should he. He had more important thoughts occupying his mind at that time. A situation that had caused him to leave Fort Laramie at very short notice to rescue his folks from Charleston, before the Secession was created. Any later and it might have been near on impossible for a Union officer to get into Charleston; that was the real hotbed for the Confederates. No, Senor Emilio proved to be a much more agreeable gent than his brother; maybe that was the difference between living and working in Havana and being in St Louis. Also they wanted this problem resolved and the Laidlaw Agency had managed to get itself in front of Senor Emilio Garcia and into the box seat as the next detective agency to be employed to rid them of this problem.

Tom Benson presented the paperwork stating the rates that they were prepared to work for, plus the contingency items. All were readily accepted and a starting date was requested. Again, it was accepted, and the information regarding the most recent thefts of the Garcias' goods was immediately available. It was get started, the sooner the better. The handshakes were exchanged, the chase was on. Tom carefully inserted Garcias' information into his document case, then they headed for the Omaha train, and a long discussion as they headed north. Tom was appreciative of the incoming pair of army sergeants, as his personal assistants, to be used as he required. The added 'weight' could be very useful for when any of his detectives wanted some protection, men that were well-versed in that work. The original lead that Major Dan Arnessen had received was from a manager in the Ben Holliday Denver depot, and that sent them down to the Crow Creek area where they recovered the Henry and Sharps rifles. Who was the manager? Where was Major Dan Arnessen now? After leaving Omaha on the Union Pacific Construction train, Trigg's only contact with the major was the message that he was to meet with Col. Stratton at Fort Sandars and then serve under the colonel in Cheyenne. He would make enquiries at Div HQ when they got back to Omaha. The initial planning was how and who would work with Enoch as they began to read through this information from the Garcias and then organise themselves. Trigg wired Roger at the H&S to arrange for Harry and Joe to be in the H&S on Thursday at 16.00 hrs. The gatehouse sergeant at Div. HQ remembered him. "He's now Lt. Col. Arnessen and he's due here next Tuesday, Major. I'll make sure he gets your note, sir." "I've left a note asking him to contact you here in Omaha, Tom. What is the position with the rented office and Jack Laidlaw's house? How have you progressed in tidying up all the current business? Is there much debt outstanding?" "The rents are being paid, and there're only two outstanding debts that Enoch was confident he could collect this money while we were away. That money will cover another month's rent, then it gets tight."

"Tom, Jimmy Hanson says that the company ain't worth a carrot, just the horses and a surrey are assets, and this Garcia deal could be good, but how do yer value it?" " I will take over the company. I will rename it the Benson Laidlaw Agency. Me as the chairman, you as the operations director and Roger as the financial director. The bank will be my current bankers, they have a branch here in Omaha, two signatures on every cheque. If I am funding it, I need to know where every dollar is going. That is my deal; are you happy with that? Before we go any further we need to be in full agreement." "It's more than I was hoping for." "Good. Now, are you buying your own home?" "No, renting." "Would you prefer Jack Laidlaw's old house?" "Yes please." "Right, vacate your house and move in; the BLA will pay the rent. You take over the surrey and if you need any more horses and tack, we will send yer some from the H&S. These offices – are there any others with a better frontage? There's no rush but keep an eye out for one near the rail line where the telegraph could be easily connected. It's much more private when an operator ain't involved." "Good, that's the basics sorted out, now we have to get earning some money, for all our benefit. Roger will confirm the banking arrangements and deposit some working capital. If it's money, always deal with Roger, or leave a message with Jake, no one else." Tom Benson was well pleased: from fearing for his job and income, he would now have his name in the company's title, and no rent to pay. He knew he would have to earn every dime, but he was ready for what promised to be one hell of a journey. Trigg had left Tom Benson to deal with Lt. Col. Dan Arnessen. They were good buddies at Fort Laramie. It could be a good move for them to get re-acquainted. He wanted to talk to Lt. Rossi about the operation that they undertook well north of Fort Collins, when they had trailed a wagon train into the foothills of the Rockies. That was to observe only. A report had been submitted, but that was his last operation before he had left the Army.

The place where they had found the El Paso rifles was only a half mile or so away. These wagons had been trailed from the Cheyenne rail yard across into the foothills of the Rockies, could be these galoots had shifted their storage facilities a bit further West to fit in with the new settlements, and the railroad? Max Rossi confirmed what he thought might be the situation: not enough troopers and other more important issues to be attended to. The report was still on the list of issues to be investigated, but was steadily slipping further still away from the likelihood of being attended to. Harry and Joe were jubilant at the news at joining the BLA. Both were at a loose end in the army, and were continually being doubled up with either Capt. Rinker or Lt. Rossi, each of whom have their regular Sergeant, Two sergeants in a troop was not good as both had their ways of doing things, and good buddies as they were, friction was inevitable. With the continuing reduction in manpower, and the fact that they had a new job to go to, Capt. Rinker allowed them to leave immediately. No favours had been sought, and maybe not the full story had been told, but the army was happy, Joe and Harry were happy, and the happiest chappies of all were Trigg and Tom Benson. Tom Benson had had a good reunion with Lt. Col. Arnessen, who had expressed much interest in this new detective agency and would be digging out the information that they had requested. The Lieutenant colonel had noticed that his much esteemed former greenhorn lieutenant was not now on the Div. HQ list of serving officers. Now he knew where he was and what he was up to, and he was not displeased. Trigg now complied with Roger's suggestion, and he printed out four large signs and nailed one to each of the offices' four walls. CONSOLIDATION. Roger viewed the signs, and added the date to each one. "Let's see how long this intention lasts." But Roger inwardly recognised that the potential in this new business was colossal, and it had cost peanuts to get into it. "Ragnar, the Happening Man is at it again." And Ragnar sat transfixed as Roger explained,in graphic detail just what his grandson was getting himself into. "He's left the army, now he's creating his own army. Capt. Benson, Sgts. Harry Pickering and Joe Kennedy have enlisted, and that's only after the first week. Add to that Ex-Sgt. Major Will Lawton ruling the range, very ably assisted by ex-Cpl. Scobie Hill and his Shoshone lads, ex-Cpl. Spud Murphy as bunkhouse gaffer, and ex-Sgt. Jake Smithers keeping the H&S in order, and not forgetting Private Dodger and, I suspect, more to enlist in the future, we have a tidy troop all ready." Trigg eyed his grandpop across the dinner table and winked. "Stick around, Pop, I might need a good quartermaster." Ragnar had plenty of news for his next letter home. He and Adalia had taken over the letter writing, with Trigg adding his own lines, and there always seemed to be good news. Annie Hemmyng still saw the good and, for her, the sad bits. A daughter-in-law she would never meet and now a grandson. The christening was now fixed for the day before Will and Mae were to be wed. Stiener Ragnar Hemmyng, named after his grandfather and his Great-grandfather and from the photograph of him in his mother's arms, a robust little feller the spittin' image of his pa at the same age. Her consolation was that they were all healthy and flourishing and she could keep dreaming and hoping. It was only her husband's conviction that kept her hopes alive: he was sure. "He'll be back. I don't know when, but he said he would come home, and who could doubt him?" Names had been chosen for the two young dogs. As Adalia had watched as Ragnar threw sticks and other wooden pegs into the long grass and then set the pups to retrieve them, her German lineage had brought up that they were snufehund. Ragnar, who wanted a different, uncommon name, then split that name, one to be called Snufe, the other Hundy, two names that were highly unlikely to be encountered again, different for each dog. Snufe and Hundy, no mistaking those names. "Snufe and Hundy, that's fine by me, very uncommon, probably unique. Which is which, Pop?" "The Snufe has only two white socks, Hundy has four, but that's about it. We'll have to see how they grow." The Dodger who had trotted along to all these runouts, was looking a touch mystified as these two pups scampered about finding these sticks. He had never been a tracker or a fighter, but nobody had ever taken him on; no, he was guarder, could sniff or hear anything windborne and see for miles. Just what them young'uns was up to he was not too sure. He trotted along beside his man and watched em scurrying about in the long grass.

Trigg had seen enough, his Pop was right, they were determinded little critters, and they were still only halfgrown. Both had come on a bundle since he had last seen them. An idea came into his mind – it was worth a try. Nothing ventured, nothing gained. He pulled some of the old saddlebags out of the barn and took them into the H&S for Jake to get them made into coin pouches. "Get these made into coin pouches, Jake, but don't have the leather cleaned, make sure they're still musty and earthy smelling." Roger handed him a letter, postmarked Washington. Trigg recognised the hand-writing, and carefully opened the envelope. "It's from Lt. Col. Dan Arnessen, following his meeting with Tom Benson He was a major when I served under him, and Tom, at Fort Laramie, learnt me an awful lot in the short time, took me under his wing, yer might say, a real good soldier. Obviously still is." He passed the letter to Roger, and sat quietly whilst Roger read the letter. "He's wanting to meet you again, see where you've settled." "Can't beat having friends in high places, can yer? Its got to be better than having enemies, especially if they're in Washington. The Ben Holliday Manager being in Laramie City now is very convenient as well. I'll get across and make his acquaintance. Both pieces of information he supplied were very accurate." "I got out of Denver by the skin on my teeth, got chased out an' I went East after the army made those two raids back then. I knew who was bossing the thieving back then but it could be different now, might not be; he had three ropey sons. His name was Cally Porteous; plenty knew that but finding him in those mountains was near on impossible. He had men who never missed anything that moved and he knew every hidey hole there was up there, and there were hundreds of old mine workings. Can't tell yer any more, and I'll thank yer to give me a wide berth in future. I took a big risk coming back here but my wife needs to be near her folks. The last thing I need is for them Porteous varmints to know I'm here. I've changed me name and grown all this hair, and stopped drinking. I've a family to feed now." Trigg nodded agreement and thanked him for the name who used to be, and still could be, thieving and robbing the kinds of goods that were of interest to him. The thought crossed his mind as to how Dan Arnessen knew where he was, but, let that alone for now – he had a name to get looking for and see where that took them. He had this information in a letter and mailed off to Tom Benson that evening.

He studied the map; it was a long way from Denver to St Louis, and even further to where those rifles had originally been manufactured. The crates had been stencilled as the El Paso Engineering Co, so that now meant they had been in the Garcias' possession, stencilled up, then moved out, and then stolen, but where? This area was unknown to him, but who did know it? Charlie and Monty had trailed cattle across it. Tom was going to notify him when Enoch had departed for Denver to nosey around and see what he could learn, particularly about those Porteous hombres. 'Charlie, if you had fifty crates weighing two 200lbs each and you had to transport them from Kansas to Denver quickly, no railroad in yet, how would yer do it, and why?" 'No railroad, only quick way is wagons and maybe mule trains. Seems like these crates are needing to be snook in.' 'Could be – no chance of boats or rafts, too many shallows?' 'If yer needed to keep moving and hiding wagons, you could split up and scatter, any time.' That was good enough for Trigg. Ten minutes talking to someone who knew the terrain could save yer weeks roamin' around on a hoss. In his mind, that cut the area down to between Kansas City and St Louis. If there was an inside man, and the crates had been loaded onto a barge going up the Missouri, instead of onto a boat heading for the Gulf of Mexico, a well organised three or four-man gang could carry that out easily, but how could yer tie all that together if Garcias' own staff hadn't been able to, or the other people they had used before hadn't been able to? Sit on it for a few days, and let Enoch go have a look and listen in Denver. Jake handed him the coin pouches; they were just right. 'Here, Pop, stick some dollar coins in them and tie them tight. Then we'll find some rough land to hide them away for a day or two. We'll keep a couple back for Snufe and Hundy to bite on, mess around with, then we'll let them loose and see if they can find the pouches we've hidden. There's no rush, let them have plenty of time to find out what this new game is about, but if they get good at finding these pouches, they could earn me a fortune.'

Trigg explained how these robbers often stashed the loot, then scarpered just in case they were being chased, and then came back days, even weeks, later to recover the loot. Also being robbers, where could they store the loot safely? All this honour among thieves was hogwash – if a couple were skint and needed money, it was not unknown for them to rob the stash and scarper. Gang leaders were also known to stash the loot, then kill the other gang members, keeping all the loot for themselves. They were also known to have forgotten exactly where they had stashed it, might have been a lot pie-eyed at the time, then clean forgot where it was, so they had to do some more robbing, and on it went. 'If these two young dogs can learn to find this hidden loot, we could earn a real fortune. Might have to give some of it up and claim any reward money, but I don't need to tell you how to school em, Pop, if that's what they learn and no other distractions, we just might be on to a good little sideline.' Ragnar was in his element – two good robust pups to school and an interesting new sort of work for him to learn as well. This grandson of his was full of ideas, and this one seemed to be the daddy of them all. He put all of his lifelong experience and nous to work. They used the Shoshone lads to take the pouches out and hide them away, then Ragnar would bring the dogs in from a different direction, so the dogs had no scent to follow, then when he was near, he would set the dogs loose and urge them on, and they soon began to learn this new game. A tasty reward when they located a pouch and everyone was happy. Trigg had left his pop to get the schooling underway, and he could get more involved later; it was better if the dogs had only one man schooling them. Enoch Pound did far better than Trigg had expected him to. The Porteous family was still very active, the sons more so than the father. Cally Porteous had stopped a bullet with his shoulder and then after getting over that, his hoss had gone down in some rough land and pitched him head on into a tree stump. His eldest boy, Solly, was now running the show, with Cally doing the planning from a buggy. But that was not the main information that was causing Trigg to laud Enoch's investigating; it was that Enoch had learnt that Cally's wife's maiden name was Hendricks. Tom had contacted Ricardo Diaz for a look at the wage books for the 59 and 60 years and there it was. Two Hendricks were registered, they were still there, and Enoch had gone back to St Louis and mosied around.

Tom had not said anything to Ricardo Diaz, apart from that it was a normal routine that they did to see if there were any well-known rogues lurking about where they didn't ought to be. Enoch was still noseying around in St Louis, gathering more information as they spoke, regarding these Hendricks and the life they led. Trigg had met with Tom on North Platte station, then ambled into the town for a quiet discussion, mainly on this case but also on another job that a previous client was wanting sorted out. The Garcia job looked to be progressing very well, due mainly to the lieutenant colonel's information and Enoch's clever ploy to find out the maiden name of the wife, but Trigg was wanting to ensure that all this information stayed discreet, that Tom kept it quiet. 'Don't let Diaz know anything at all; we don't want him thinking we're up there with Pinkertons, Tom, we ain't and we probably won't ever be. Let's work this one through and take it as it comes. We know, but they don't need to; no point in making things too hard for ourselves. We will probably earn more staying smaller and leaner, and letting Pinkertons have all the fame, be in all the newspapers. I'm more than happy to liaise with them, help each other, cos that's what they do, as you know well. Share the information, tit for tat, but you do that, and only you, nobody else, not even me or Roger, just you, make it part of your job. If this Garcia job runs as well as it's looking to do, you make contact with them, you make the running and see how they react, and use your rank, Capt. Tom Benson – put it on them. You know how they learn us at the army college – you can be nice and friendly but still be firm, the 'start as you mean to go on' routine. I know you had a hard war, got knocked about a lot, and your confidence got dented, but we could have a good business here, Tom. We all need to be positive, and discreet.' The discreet bit was in regard to the Henry rifles they had recovered on that patrol, and then had gone into the quartermaster's store at Fort Laramie. Major Arnessen, as he was then, had been very lenient with the truth when he had filed his report. He had paid more regard to his men's safety, as a good officer should always do, than to the actual details of exactly what rifles they had recovered; there could even be some still in the stores. It had all been done for the right reasons, and no monetary gain had been made, but some smart troublemaker could raise some hullabaloo if it got into the army's knowledge. There was always someone looking to gain some advantage.

Enoch's detecting raised enough questions that left no doubt in Trigg and Tom's minds that they were organising the thefts. They lived well, had that swagger about them that oozed the smugness that they were too clever, could get materials out of the place and then their share of the loot, but they still had not been nabbed in the act. Ricardo Diaz was not bothered about waiting; he was convinced by the evidence laid before him. He was for getting rid before any more stock was stolen, clear them all out and stop the thieving. Trigg could not disagree, but why not feed some more crates in that were apparently crates of rifles, to be stencilled up as 'El Paso Engineering Co.' and tempt them, see how they actually work the theft, maybe see who else was involved, and which way these crates of rifles made their way to Kansas and Denver, and nab the whole shooting match in one go. Emilio Garcia was in favour of that, clear the lot out in one go.

'We will order the rifles to be delivered into our warehouse, then we will notify yourselves and you can be ready to observe and have them arrested.' That was exactly what Trigg was hoping for. He wanted these new crates of rifles out on the loose and being carted, hopefully from a barge tied up at a jetty on the Missouri somewhere near Kansas, then across country to Denver. Garcias own men could make the arrests in their own store yards. Trigg was more concerned about where the stolen goods ended up. He had no authority now to arrest people. He could detain them simply by shooting em when they were in possession of the loot, but that was risky and too messy. He didn't have enough men to cover the possibility that these hombres might split up and cart the loot to different locations, and also this action was likely to take place in the Denver region, and he didn't know anybody he could trust over there, not even army personnel; the old problem of affiliations could be involved. Who knew who down there? One loose word could sink the operation. Did Dan Arnessen know the area and the personnel down there well enough to trust them implicitly? Men's lives would be on the line, these hombres would not hesitate to protect their interests, and dead men don't tell tales.

To keep this operation quiet, manageable, with the men he had, he realised that he had another observe only job on his hands. Trail them to where the loot was hidden, and then go back in later, hopefully to only one stash site. Being able to use local army units was far preferable, but there were too many loose ends; if he still deemed it necessary to use local army units, raiding one stash site and knowing what was in there could work.

He could prepare a schedule of what they were looking for, then let some hombre try and talk their way out of that if they tried to reroute any loot. He needed to talk with Lt. Col. Arnessen, he was the only feller he could trust, and hopefully, he might know someone – could be in Leavenworth even, that was near enough. But Dan Arnessen was just as wary as his former greenhorn lieutenant was. It was him who had made the lieutenant aware of this possible problem in their Fort Laramie days, learnt from personal experience earlier in his career. His only solution was to use a troop from Fort DA Russell. Lt. Col. Arnessen was now Col. Arnessen. He would liaise with Col. Stratton to assess whether a troop could be spared from DA Russell, as other operations were being planned. Congress was still wanting troop reductions. Whichever way you turned you were meeting obstructions. Trigg complimented him on his promotion. He was told to keep his mouth very tightly shut, it was not official yet, and there was many a slip between cup and lip. A troop out of DA Russell was obviously ideal to Trigg – get down there, nicely secreted in the war-wagons that had proved to be very effective. Nothing was to be used that gave any indication that the army was involved. When he arrived back at the H&S, a message from Col. Stratton was waiting for him. He and Martha would be coming over for Sunday dinner. The telegraph had obviously been busy. 'You can have Lt. Rossi and his troop, Capt. Rinker I need for other, already scheduled duties. Now tell me exactly just what this operation is all about. I need to know everything in case there are problems that need answers – the whole kit and caboodle please.' Trigg explained how this initial meeting with the Garcia Co. had taken a sudden twist with the knowledge that the El Paso Engineering Co. was owned by the Garcias. Those rifles had been recovered but nobody had been arrested, not even after the second operation, because like always, they had not the time to sit and wait for these hombres to turn up.

It was get the rifles – the main priority was stopping the rifles getting into the redskins' hands – and get them back to Fort Laramie. Then he had been transferred onto the UP Railroad Operation and into the establishment of Cheyenne. Then they had come across the Opteka raid where Lt. Clabelle had been killed and Sgt. Lawton severely injured, but they had not gotten the main organisers, but now they were close to doing so.

If these rifles that were due to be shortly used as a lure were stolen and then trailed across to the Denver area and stashed among other earlier El Paso material, that could mean that they had nailed the organisers of this whole thieving operation. But, as the BLA, he hadn't the men, or the authority now, to arrest these hombres. It would be a shootout, unless the army was involved. It could still be, but that meant federal law was being challenged. He talked with Dan Arnessen first because he knew the early history and how long this outfit could have been operating. 'Good, so this will also resolve this recent operation as well, two birds with one stone; that makes it even better.' 'Not necessarily Colonel, if these rifles are not stashed up in those mines, but it may be a good move to get in there was well, while we're in the area with a good team.' 'All right, I'm happy that this operation is viable and needs carrying out. Both myself and Dan Arnessen will have to call in some favours – good job he's got himself well ensconced with Army HQ. But, don't forget, Lt. Rossi is running the operation, it's an army operation, and he will have to negotiate with the local units, as they will come looking when word gets out about what is going on.' 'That suits me, Colonel. I'll be right behind him, protecting his rear but keeping quiet.' 'We'll give it an operational name that can be used by the local units to verify it is a genuine army operation – Leavenworth will insist.' Leavenworth – it was not what Trigg wanted to hear, but he realised that they had to be aware of the operation, but would they be content just to know about it, would someone's ego be rattled, or worse? Dan Arnessen came up trumps on that problem. He would arrange to be there two days before. He had business to discuss with the GOC, that there was an ongoing issue, and he would make the general aware, at short notice.

He would apologise profusely and explain that it had

developed virtually overnight, such was the nature of the operation. This would be largely true, as it all depended on when and where these rifles were stolen, if indeed they were stolen at all. As usual, the whole operation was based on the greed and determination of the robbers. Dan Arnessen would have to be closely involved. As soon as the robbers struck, he would have to get himself across to Leavenworth rapidly, but that was not a problem for the Colonel just let him know, he would get there. Col. Stratton would be wired and Lt Rossi would have to get his troop, including the wagons, on the move south.

Trigg, Harry, Joe and Scobie, with four of his lads, would be keeping watch and trailing the crates whereever they went. The tricky bit would be making contact with Lt. Rossi, but once the theft had been made, they could arrange a relay that would leap-frog the route being followed – no other way to do it, unless yer kept passing a telegraph station. The robbery took place as he thought it would, and the crates went up the Missouri and into a boatyard. Then the robbers gave him a helping hand and left them in there for two days. Two whole days to get everyone in place, rested up and ready to go. And they were too smug coming in to collect the crates – must have been the same old routine, just move them on and collect their wages. But Trigg's biggest surprise came when Dan Arnessen, accompanied by three more useful-looking hombres, appeared, attired as well-to-do fellers, and fell into line behind Lt .Rossi. Trigg assured the Lieutenant that these latecomers were genuine and known, and he could continue to control the Operation Santa Anna, as he saw fit. When the crates went into the mine workings, Arnessen and his three buddies were quickly in there behind the troopers and inspecting everything they could find; they weren't in a hurry. They prodded and probed every nook and cranny and went about their work in an orderly manner and only departed the site when they were satisfied that they had seen all there was to see. As they departed, it was just a short discussion. He congratulated Lt. Rossi on a well-run operation, mentioned he would be in touch again shortly, and they were gone. 'What was he looking for, boss?' was Scobie's terse comment. Trigg explained to Lt. Max Rossi who he was and where they had served together before, but the other three hombres were not known to him, but better to keep it all under wraps as they obviously didn't want to be known. Col. Stratton would know, but the less they knew, the better. That distraction out of the way, they found a whole array of merchandise hidden away in the mineshafts, and it looked like it was from various sources. The robbers were bound, gagged and hooded by the lieutenant and his troopers, whilst Trigg and his men captured the few workmen in the mines, especially anyone who looked like a clerk. These fellers were not fighting men; they looked after the books and the wages. He was confident that these Porteous boys were organising these robberies, and having some of their ledgers and payroll books had to be very useful.

Enoch had found out where they lived, so they could stew in their homes until he was ready to pounce, let them think the stash had been found but they were still on the loose, like they had been for years. Leave them be for a while, then have them followed as there could be other stash sites. The mountains were littered with mine works, most of which had proved barren, not worth a carrot, but useful as storage places. The amount of merchandise in these two shafts was colossal, it would need full-time guarding to allow a knowledgeable surveyor to catalogue the material, and that was the army's job – they led the operation and they would reap the rewards, if and when all this loot was auctioned off. Trigg had Roger and Roland investigate the possibility of claiming a reward for information leading to the recovery of this merchandise. The Garcias were happy to settle their account for the identification and arrest of the robbers, and were cooperating with the surveyor appointed to identify any previous owners of this loot as the catalogue was being created.

It was a complicated bag of who was the loot stolen from and when, and had any reward notices been issued at the time? Even insurers were involved. What a mish mash. But it went down in the army's records as another successful operation. The Porteous family had their homes and business addresses raided by the army, but not before more stashes had been located in other areas not too far from this first location. It had been a good operation, but Trigg knew not to venture into the Denver area again. He had got lucky once, get well away and stay well away – in future. Put plenty of distance between the BLA and any galoot looking for revenge, cos there was bound to be other losers who were associated with the Porteous gang, who had not been identified. The Garcias were offering the BLA more work. That would keep Capt. Tom Benson and his team busy. He could stay on the NY now, and let Will and Mae have a good wedding, and his son be christened. Henri and his lady were coming over, there would be a lot of catching up to do, and the weather looked set to behave, according to Scobie.

The weather did behave – so did his son, he slept through most of the short blessing. Meeting Will's folks pleased him greatly, a meeting he had been looking forward to for a long time, and so had Thomas and Edna Lawton, and together with meeting and thanking all his other army buddies, it sure was a happy time for all concerned. As Ragnar was quick to comment, 'You've seen Will, you've seen his pa, like two peas in a pod.' It was their first real holiday since they had wed, and the first time they had been west of Indiana, and now they were seeing what had kept their eldest son from returning home after leaving the army. Like a lot of other lads after the war or military service, not many had returned home when they had had the chance. The war had changed a lot of things. Now Edna saw for herself why Will would be settling down in Cheyenne. Again, it was the sweet, and the not so sweet, emotions for a mother, seeing her eldest child marry and knowing he would be a long way from his home. C'est la vie' Henri had arranged a honeymoon on the Monterey peninsula, in a hostelry owned by his future father-in-law. That caused some speculation from his Army buddies from Fort Laramie when it had became common knowledge – Monterey, how about that? Just what was this handsome son of a gun, Dixie boy marrying into? Trigg knew the story, but not the full details, and he was just as interested to hear the details. Henri's future father-in-law was a first generation American – the only son of a Dutch trader who had established a hardware store up in the Sierra Madre, and then his son Arnie, had rode the 49 gold rush and the mining boom to increase that single store to a total of forty-four. Now the big companies were buying up the claims and Arnie was adding food sections to every store, sometimes tripling the size of the old store. There were a lot of old miners and new immigrants in California and Arnie was organising himself to feed them all he could. With forty-four food shops to fill, Arnie was intending to get into the food supplying and processing business as well, and he liked the thought of having a Capt. Henri Watson de Silva on his Board of Directors, and even more as his son-in-law. 'Well done, Dixie boy, you sound like you've got yerself well set, and a pretty lady into the bargain. I always knew you were a smart coyote, just never figured out what it was you were smart at, apart from charming the ladies.' 'Listen, you marauding Viking Dog Wolf, you might think I'm a whole lot smarter when I start buying beef from you, an' I ain't joking. I reckon if you can ship cattle into Michigan and Ohio, you can ship it into Sacramento, where Arnie's siting his food processing factory. He's all ready to buy the land in the railyard, right alongside the main railtrack." 'You sure are full of surprises today, Dixie boy, real good surprises as well. Any more in yer back pocket.?' 'Only one: we're getting wed in September, and you're the best man." 'I ain't missing that, best man or not. Are you serious about this cattle into Sacramento? It ain't the beer and the thin air up here in Wyoming that's got to you, is it?" 'It ain't, but that freezing weather up at Fort Laramie did me a favour in the long run. Transferring over to that side of the Rockies has turned up trumps for me, and meeting Rosanna is the best bit. Forget about her father, I would have wed her anyway, we are well-suited and she's a very capable lady. This deal with her father is just the icing on the cake, and I reckon we can do each other a favour. I've been learning about this food business since me and Arnie have been acquainted, and this food processing business he is intent on establishing will sell to every food store, not just his own food shops, and he wants good beef as well as the not so good. If folks want prime steak, he will supply it, but at an extra cost. Like he supplied the best shovels and tools, but they cost more because folks knew they were better quality. We knew in the army that Texas Longhorns only gave yer poor beef – if you are after good steak, don't buy Longhorn gristle. Will told me that the NY only had Shorthorns, so we need to get our heads together and see if we can do business.' 'Arnie is real interested in all this cowboy talk, rustlers and outlaws and such, he's always got his head in a newspaper reading the latest reports. He was a bit peeved when he learnt we were coming up here for Will and Mae's wedding, wasn't too happy he was staying at home, but he perked up some when I said we would have a talk. I remember you saying in one of your letters that you only wanted to raise Shorthorns, so that's why I quizzed Will first.' 'I had the notion that you were more interested in horses up here, seeing that this side of the Rockies is so vast and not many hombres can manage without one. Staging is more developed over in California, always has been since the Mexicans had it.' 'I learnt about beef when I was on the UP Construction train. Jack Casement trailed Shorthorns all the way across from Omaha as his beef on the hoof. Fresh rendered beef every day for the tracklayers as they humped those iron rails day in day out. You know as well as me, the army buys Longhorns purely on price, like it only bought carbines, not the best rifles for its soldiers, and we know why. Most of those Shorthorns on the NY ranges aren't mine. They are owned by an investors group. We just wet nurse them and get a tidy price for doing it. The trouble we handle, that's ranching, but we were well practised in that side through our army experience, but I have close on 4,000 head, and one private contract, and looking for some more, depending on the size of the deal.'

With the investors' deal, we need to dove-tail the work carefully, but a deal with yourself and Mr Arnie Asmusson would be real good. Let's get Will and Mae on the train, then we can add up the numbers.' A wide-awake and busy little bundle of arms and legs was placed in his arms, a podgy little fist bashed his nose, it was business over and hoedown time and take yer partners for a whirl around the dance floor. The following day, after the effects of the celebrating had worn off and Trigg and Roger were discussing the deal with Henri, the Colonel and Martha reappeared on the NY. Having had a very enjoyable day with plenty of socialising and dancing, the Colonel had refrained from mixing business with pleasure, but now he needed to broach a topic with Trigg and Roger that the territorial governor was pressing him for an opinion on. "The territorial governer reckons that the formation of a Livestock Growers Association ought to be formed. This association could represent the livestock growers and make it easier for all concerned to create some guidelines that the ranchers would be able to agree on, and maybe standardise the problems that are being encountered. It could make it easier for the territory to liase with the army and the livestock growers and a more agreed policy would show that the territory is showing itself to be more responsible and more worthy of being a full-blown state and taking its place alongside the existing states of the Union. Livestock growing is becoming a big factor in the territory, and the governor is keen on presenting this image. At present there is no set procedure, and the army and the territory officials have to deal with every Tom, Dick and Harry individually, with a lot of wasted time and duplication involved. An association would show responsibility, be like a local Congress where issues in contention could be resolved by local debate in Cheyenne" The theory sounded fine, but the devil was in the detail, and Trigg, in his Army years, had met most of these prospective livestock growers, only in passing, but close enough to know that they were all ornery hombres who liked to do things their way, and when it suited them. Getting them round a table and agreeing issues would need someone with the wisdom of Solomon and the patience of Jobe, unless everything was set up to suit themselves, and then they'd still find something to feud over. Most of em were reckoned to have 'trimmed' a few herds to get started, but they weren't the first, and wouldn't be the last; on open ranges it was every man for himself. He voiced his opinion to the colonel but if Roger would represent the NY, with Will Lawton to assist him, if he felt he needed support at a meeting, then he would back up the colonel and make sure he got to read the minutes of any meetings, if there ever were any, but he would be too busy, and his former military career would not endear him to those hombres. One or two might even fancy a bit of revenge, better if he was elsewhere. Out of sight, out of mind kind of thinking. Roger was amenable, so the colonel could mark the NY down as supportive. Roger was of the opinion that if this association came into being, then being in and hearing what was being said had to be better than not knowing anything. When the colonel had departed, Trigg cautioned his buddy on the tactics he needed to adopt if and when the association became a reality. "Don't volunteer for any official position. Play it crafty and keep out of trouble, and vote with the majority. They'll be scheming and plotting, and trying to fix any regulations to favour themselves but no matter, support them or suffer the consequences. It won't be boring with those galoots, I can guarantee that; you're in for some lively meetings." Will and Mae were on a train heading up the Evans Pass to California and he had his ranch to look after, and that had to be his main focus of attention. Too much could change too quickly if he let his mind wander and become lazy. All those other things could wait, be stored away for some other time, and then be brought out and looked at afresh. There was still an edge to the evening breeze when the sun dipped behind the Rockies, but that just seemed to sharpen his appetite for his supper. The Dodger was stretched out in his favourite spot on the corner of the verandah, ears twitching, picking up sounds that only he could hear. Even the bunkhouse seemed to have settled down for the evening and the only sounds were Ragnar coralling Snufe and Hundy after another game of find the pouches. The world around here seemed to be at peace with itself, long may it stay that way, but he knew that it wouldn't. It did not have a snowball's chance in hell.

Just enjoy it while yer could, cos like winter, something hard and nasty would be visited on you, it would be back to the survival of the toughest, the most determined. Trigg's thoughts scanned around to the big pay day that the BLA looked like earning from this operation that had begun in the unusual circumstances that unfolded after Jack Laidlaw and his family had perished. Then that fortunate meeting when he had heard those words, 'The El Paso Dept'. mentioned, a name etched in his memory, but a name he thought would just remain a memory, and fade away in time. But then, hocus pocus, it had reared up and set that operation into life. He had other names written in his yearly logs, that were similar, operations where they had nabbed the workmen, but not the main men, and as far as he knew, Omaha Div. HQ had not followed up and collared them either. He had accepted that Fort Laramie was out in the wilds, and that these organisers would be more likely to be in the more established towns, so it made sense that everything should be centred back East, but what about these other operations that had been transferred? The only one that he knew anything about was the Chicago Italians and that was far from being resolved. His other attraction in acquiring the BLA was as a livestock detecting agency, which was where he reckoned he had more going for him, and being based in Omaha, four hundred miles away, was well away from Cheyenne and the NY, again out of sight and out of mind. Pinkertons like to publicise; he was looking to operate on the quiet, get in and nab the miscreants and get out and gone, and get paid. The BLA could continue to work as a routine detective agency, but the livestock side would not be vaunted; it could operate by word of mouth, be recommended by satisfied clients. It could even lie dormant for a time, then burst back into life when a juicy contract came in. Harry, Joe and Scobie's lads could melt back into the BLA or onto the NY. The income from the investors' deal allowed for that. Now if Roger and himself could extract a sizeable pay day out of the army's monetary gain on this Denver raid, they would have to pay an auctioneer to sell off all that merchandise, but there had to be a big surplus even after that fee was paid. Without the BLA alerting them to this stash of stolen loot, it would still be there. Roland Simmons was very much of the opinion that an agreement could be made with the army. He knew from his experience back East that the army had contracts with private agencies for payment when information that led to arrests and the upholding of law and order were made. Roland suggested that Roger, as the financial director of this correctly registered enterprise, should initiate the negotiation and he would provide his advice, as he usually would, but as this was a very involved case, those arrested had to be checked and verified, and the auctioneer had to complete the cataloguing, provisional valuation, and then the actual auction sale. It was a case of don't count yer chickens yet, fellers, this job could take months to complete. Trigg and Roger had foreseen that being the case, but it was a case of getting the claim registered toute suit and taking it there, and that was done. The

BLA had received its fees from the Garcias so the BLA's bank balance was in order. Then Col. Arnessen had wired the H&S. He wanted to meet, on the NY, in private, and had stipulated a date and time, in the immediate future. Roger had replied, confirming receipt of the wire, nothing else needed saying. Jake was notified that a Col Arnessen might be calling in, but if he didn't, don't raise any alarms, just be on yer guard in case he did. It was Scobie, fortunately, who espied them as they came up the trail that the NY used to get to the livestock pens in Pine Bluffs. "Morning, Cpl. Hill, do I have your permission to cross NY land?" Scobie nodded acceptance. He had not been warned of the colonel's possible appearance, but he knew not to argue. The Colonel was only being polite. If he wanted to cross, not even the boss would object, and the same three hombres that he had seen down near Denver were here again and all of them were well-armed and prepared for any eventuality. "Yes, Sir; Do you need me to escort you? Some of our new boys might give yer a hard time, if I ain't around – we've had some serious run-ins afore." "Certainly, corporal but we are on a friendly visit." "That's what the others said, Colonel, until the shooting started, an' as you fellers ain't in uniform, our lads would be in order." "Quite correct, Corporal Hill, good thinking, you better had. I can do without one of them Henry bullets being buried in me. Lead on." Scobie had been out with GG and Laky, one of his new boys, to investigate why some buzzards had been circling. Could be a pointer to some small-scale rustlers who chose to slaughter the cattle out on the plain and load the best bits onto a packhorse for delivery into a butchery, but the buzzards had found a old dead coyote, but for Laky's training, it was always necessary to investigate. Then, spotting four riders coming up the trail, Scobie and GG had observed through their telescopes until both were sure it was Arnessen leading these hombres. GG had stayed well back until Scobie had made contact and signalled it was OK. GG then sent Laky haring into the ranch to alert them, and he would keep himself out there and well hidden until Laky returned. The system had been well refined and it worked well, like it was doing again. Trigg and Roger were relaxed in the office as Scobie led the guests into the ranch, saluted his former commanding officer and returned to his morning's work.

"It's the same three who were with him down in Denver, Roger, we might get to know who they are and why he chose to come in the back way, but then again we might not. I think we ought to take them up to the house and leave Percy in peace to get on with his bookkeeping. Can you go up and make Adalia aware she might have visitors." Roger obliged. "Hitch the hosses there, gents. Sam will feed and water them. Follow me up to the house, some refreshments will be waiting for yer." "You've got yerself set up nicely here, Major; hell of a herd you've got here." Trigg noticed their necks swivelling around as they ambled up beside him. "An' hundreds of hosses as well, ain't there? And brand new buildings to boot." "90% of the cattle ain't mine Colonel, we just wetnurse 'em for the investment people." He then turned to the galoot who had joined in making the comments. "Everything is brand new out here, even the town, there wasn't anything out here three years ago, not even DA Russell and Camp Carling when I first arrived, and most of the hosses belonged to rustlers that the coyotes and the buzzards had dined on. You're welcome to inspect Col. Stratton's log; everything has been registered." Trigg introduced the Colonel to Adalia, then was introduced to his travelling buddies. "Capt. John Spriggs, Capt. Peter Jones, from army H.Q. and Inspector Ed Toyne RS." Trigg had just eyeballed and talked down a tax inspector. Roger entered the room and Trigg introduced him. Then Colonel Arnessen took him to one side and made his excuses as he guided Trigg back out onto the verandah.

"I received your claim letter for that Denver raid. It will be acknowledged and the BLA will be added to our list of approved agencies. All the documentation and payment schedules will be forwarded to you, so that the Denver raid will be covered under the scheme. We are over here looking at one or two individuals and their properties, etc. etc. I need you to give my apologies to John Stratton for not visiting him, but we need to be on a train West as soon as we can. That's it, Major, simple as that. Thank you for the hospitality." When they returned to the room, Adalia raised her eyebrows and nodded towards the table; it looked like the taxman was about to devour his lunch – steak pie, peas and beef gravy, with mint sauce. Trigg knew it was a waste of time making small talk, none of these hombres would say anything, they would too busy stuffing themselves. Then he saw Ragnar heading across for his feed. He too would have to wait. Get these four fed and on their way. If that was all the taxman collected today, he would be pleased, very pleased. Trigg quickly arranged for the colonel and his three cohorts to be escorted into Cheyenne – he didn't want em to get lost, they might come back, and there were two places where they could be waylaid. It was a make sure they got into the station and onto a train, and don't leave until the train is outa sight heading west or east situation – either would do. "They were over here looking at one or two individuals and their properties, etc. etc. that's what Dan Arnessen told me, Roger. He also said that the BLA would be added to the list of approved agencies and that all the regulations and payment schedules would be arriving in the mail – some more goodies for us to read and commit to memory, where will it all end I ask myself." "Point taken but the BLA is on the list. Be interesting to see what exactly that involves, but we're on the list. I reckon that if the others can work to the schedules, we will be able to as well." "Could be we have to work around, or under, or slightly to one side, but, like yer said, we'll find a way to make it work." Roger was, by now, well used to realising that Major Trigg Hemmyng was not slow in finding ways or means to negotiate his own route through life, and this new episode was looking to be heading that way as well. The Happening Man had that determined look in his eyes; sit tight and enjoy the ride.

"Yer ought to be spending more time now with these two pups. They're coming on real good – let em get to know you better, get used to your voice more, you won't be sorry, they're real happy souls and busy dogs. To Trigg that was as good as an order. He knew that his grandpa had these dogs ready. As long as he could remember, his grandpa had bred collies and trained them up, then handed them onto the owner at just the right time, when the larking about was ending and the dog was ready to work. Two days spent with his grandpa and the dogs confirmed this. They were eager, wanting to work, and were well versed in the work that they had been prepared for. Trigg explained to Scobie how and what he intended to use the dogs for, causing a smile as wide as the North Platte in flood to spread across his face. It would be on a casual basis but a serious enterprise, with a share of the income finding its way into their bank books that Roger regularly updated and were lodged in the office for them to inspect any time they wanted. Trigg also had a signboard professionally painted that would hang on the side of the wagon when they were working. It stated, 'The Carlisle Minerals Exploration Co' in clear, easy to read letters. Trigg had been refreshing his not too shabby knowledge of the rocks and strata that they had been instructed about on the topographical segment of his cavalry course, and had kept a steady interest since then, his time on the railroad operation being particularly useful. So he could chew the fat with most hombres when it came to matters involving ground conditions. Just as important was his personal situation. Now out of the army and able to determine his own daily routine, he had the flexibilty to choose where and when he went anywhere. Will and Mae were honeymooning, so stay on the ranch, support the two range foremen and fit the other things in to suit. The incident that had annoyed him the most was when those Chicago Italians had come marauding up from Pine Bluffs and got their comeuppance, but then had tried to imply that the NY had sequestered most of the cash they alleged they had been carrying. Subsequent findings had proven that these galoots had marauded all the way across from Marshalltown, where they robbed and killed a feller, then other robberies had been added to their rampage, but when the eight thousand odd dollars had been registered as found on NY land, these other allegations had been made. No credibility seemed to have been given to Trigg's assertion that all this missing money could be stashed, if it hadn't been spent gambling, anywhere they came across, but this smooth-talking lawyer seemed to be able to stymy the army with his counter-claims. Roger had registered a claim on the money now lodged with the Army, so if no other genuine claim was made, the NY was first in line to get this cash, as it had been found on N.Y. land. Now, what better place to let Snufe and Hundy have a sniff around. The Shoshone lads had searched, to no avail, but even they were first to admit that The Dodger had senses far keener than they had. If they found anything, that could scupper this smooth-tongued lawyer's counter-claims that implied his Shoshone lads had side-tracked this money. He loaded up one of the new, smaller wagons that they used as a chuck wagon cum mobile shelter for the range hands when they were out on the range, lighter than the war wagons and more manoeuvreable to cross rougher land easier and quicker. The rock-sampling tools were in the tool box, and the wrecking bar, clay grafts and the pointed shovels, probing bars, extra ammo, and hessian bags and old blankets for the dogs to rest on were in, and off they went. Two saddle horses tethered to the rear, just in case, with Scobie and GG riding scout, again to make sure there were no nasty surprises, and forty-five minutes later they were alongside the gully where the other stash was found. Snufe and Hundy, watched by the Dodger, were given a sniff of Ragnar's musty old saddlebag, and Trigg, guided by Scobie, led them down into the gully and let them loose among the rock-strewn bankings and down into the bushes where the hosses had been hitched, but nothing, and it wasn't for the want of trying, interested them. Trigg let GG show him where they had watched these galoots from. Maybe the boss galoot had slipped around the bend as the gully turned away from a more severe rock face. From where they had been observing, it would not have been possible to see if one man had snook round this bend. GG agreed but they had searched down there, but still found nothing. They took the dogs back in and urged them to root about in this much rougher area. Obviously the melt waters in spring would be like a torrent through there. Snufe and Hundy worked slowly over these larger rocks, then Hundy stood up on his back legs and straining to get higher but couldn't, and was whining and getting angry. Snufe soon joined him and became agitated as well. Trigg called them off and fussed them for having done a good job, and Ragnar came with a biscuit for each of them, the little tit bit they were given for finding a pouch

Trigg tried to scramble up, but then stopped. Scrambling up rocks was easy, it was the descent that was tricky. With yer weight coming down it was easy to fall, and on rock like this, not worth it – go get a ladder and make it easier. Standing atop the gully, you could see a joint in the rock that looked to get wider. Scobie and GG stayed to keep watch whilst Trigg trotted the wagon back to collect a couple of 10ft ladders, the ones they had made for getting up onto the stock shed roofs. Back at the gully, these ladders were just right,. You could see a saddlebag stuffed deep into this crack as you stood near the top of the ladder and leaned over and twisted a bit, but there it was, in the afternoon setting sunlight, clearly visible. But to get it out he needed a steel bar about 6ft long with a hook to slip over the leather straps that tied the flap down. If they hadn't got one, Buddy could make one – it was the only way to get into that crack. The galoot who had stuffed it in there must have had a stick or maybe used his rifle, but yer had to compliment him for getting it up there and then getting it in there. Scobie was on the opposite side of the gully and he couldn't see it. He could see the crack easy enough, but the crack twisted as it went back. But he knew where it was now, no rush, it had been in there for a year or more now, have a steady trundle out in the morning with the hooked bar, and recover it. The ladder went into the wagon and they returned to Sam's forge where Buddy made a hooked bar to his boss's specification. That evening, Trigg had more thoughts on this situation. If this galoot was of the opinion that he had stashed this saddlebag in a place that was very unlikely to be found, why not leave the saddle bag in there? Pull it out, empty it, then push it back in stuffed with old rags to make it look like it had never been found. Then keep quiet, not a word to anyone, not even the army, then wait and watch, be patient, or, recover the saddlebag and let the the army have it, and then see how that affects the current stand-off between the Army and the slick lawyer. The NY was smack in the middle whichever of whatever developed. If this galoot believed that the saddlebag was still safely stashed, he might sell it off to one of his buddies. That might have already been done if there was enough money in the bag to do such a deal, or he could kid some other galoot into thinking there was.

But the first move was to recover the saddlebag and see what it contained. The following morning everything went to plan. He emptied the contents into an hessian bag, tied it up tight, inspected the saddlebag for a maker's name, then stuffed it full of old hessian bags until it resembled how he had found it, then stuffed it into the crack, and made ready to leave. Scobie and GG had been keeping watch to ensure nobody was keeping tabs on them. Before he left he let the dogs, all three of em, have a run, to do what dogs do. Snufe began scratching at the ground, Hundy went looking at him but just stared at his brother. Trigg went for a look-see, and saw the glint in the loose sandy soil. He picked up what looked like coloured glass, but it sparkled when he held it up to the sun; it looked to him like a precious stone, but he had no idea what it was. When he looked down he spotted another, then another, but no more. He called his grandpa across and asked his opinion but he was just as ignorant as he was on precious stones. He slipped them in his breast pocket, marked the spot by leaving a rough lump of rock there and departed. Back on the NY he gave them to Adalia and explained how he had come across them and suggested she let that new jeweller have a look at them. He then took the hessian bag across to the office. He found what he was sure was counterfeit $5 and $10 bills, all in nicely ribboned packs, never been used. $30,000 worth. Was this the money they were claiming had been side-tracked? Did they know it was counterfeit, or did the galoot think it was genuine? Had he bought it for four or five grand thinking that the seller had to be rid of it quick, stolen cash, make me offer? There was another $3,100 in used bills that looked genuine. Also there was a envelope full of letters, with many different addresses, some in Chicago. He had a rethink about the situation – stuff all this dodgy money and the envelope full of letters into an old battered saddlebag, and let the army have that. The genuine money could go into the cash claimed from a different rustling raid and Roger could share that out in the usual manner. The army would get some more evidence to use against the galoots and give them another line of questions to throw at this slick lawyer, and the NY benefits some. Why not? They were due for another bout of rustling, and it could be easily arranged that there were no galoots around to dispute the money found – not nice but neither was having to protect your livestock

He left all this stuff on his desk in Percy's reliable care when Sam called into discuss the extension he wanted doing to enlarge his stables, providing more room for keeping the expectant mares more comfortable, with some small paddocks, until the foals were more sturdy. He went for a look at how Sam wanted them built, but with three grand lying doing nothing on his desk, it was soon agreed. Beattie was in talking with Anne. He always had a bit o' banter with Beattie, mostly about the goings-on in Cheyenne, and nobody knew as many of the details as Beattie picked up on her rounds. Then as he chewed the fat with Spud, Clickka came haring in. 'Rustlers boss. Only four of em but we've downed em. Laky's bringing em in the wagon. Be in soon.' Four young fellers, but what could yer do? Young fellers either skedaddled real fast or tried to shoot it out; these tried the latter and lost. The one saddlebag had a whole fist full of reward posters. These boys had started young but not lasted long. The reward posters being claimed against went in one bag, the dodgy money and the envelope together with a letter of explanation, went into another bag and both were delivered into the fort on the same wagon that carried the four corpses. C'est la vie. Within two weeks of Will and Mae arriving back after an idyllic honeymoon on the Monterey coast, Will received a letter from his ma that told of a desperate situation back home. Ed, his youngest brother, had fallen in with bad company and had incurred some heavy gambling debts. Martin, his other married brother, and his pa had berated him for being stupid and a fight had broken out. Ed had scarpered and then returned with his new friends, the same galoots he owed the money to. Another more violent fight had erupted when Thomas refused to cough up the money to settle the debt. Martin's wife had been 'promised a seeing-to', more brawling had ensued, Thomas's back had been damaged, and he had then agreed to pay off the debt, but Ed was thrown out, banished. Sally, having been scared by the threat, had gone back to her folks near Indianapolis. Martin had gone to plead with her to return, but while he was away, Ed and his hoppos had returned and he was demanding his share of the farm, in cash and quick, or the house and barns would get fired. When Martin came back, alone, Thomas had sent him back to his wife, away from the trouble. His ma was pleading, at her wits' end, with Thomas bedridden, the law calling it a domestic upset that would most likely simmer down, but she was scared witless.

Will let Trigg read the letter. "I ain't got an option, have I? I need some more time off to go and sort things out. I felt Ed was moody when I went home afore the railroad job started. Martin said he was jealous, with ma and pa keeping saying how good I was doing in the army, but pa said they would sort things out. But it's all boiled over. I've gotta go." "All right, I'll go with yer. It needs more than one if Martin ain't there and Thomas's back as gone. The rank might be useful as well; let's use it. Let's get packed, take a spare hoss and the sooner we're moving, the sooner we're back. We'll get the night train." Roger was shown the letter. Charlie and Monty were put in charge on the range, with Rowdy to support Roger, as required. They padded into the stables, catching Arthur the farmhand by surprise, but very pleased to see Will. 'Ed's just gone in. He's real angry, Will.' Then they heard Edna's screams, and Thomas telling his son to get out in a pain-ridden voice. "I'll follow you. Let's get in there quick."

In the few seconds it took them to get into the house, through the kitchen and into the parlour, Ed had his injured father on the floor and was pounding him remorselessly. Trigg pulled Will back. "You look after yer folks, I ain't family." The panic-stricken look on Ed's face didn't save him any as he was hurled against the wall and his face hammered by a big hard fist as he slithered slowly to the floor. "You oughta have more respect for caring hardworking folk, feller." Then the boot went into his crotch, and Ed retched in agony. "Sorry about that, Thomas, but I can't take that kind of disrespect." Arthur then appeared with an old worn shotgun ready to let blast. "Whoa, Arthur, put it down, someone might get hurt." Arthur did as he was bid. "We got here just in time, Will. Better get Thomas cleaned up and into bed and Edna settled down and rested. If he stirs, Arthur, tell me." Arthur stood glaring at Ed. With Thomas in bed and Edna settled, sobbing her heart out but it was better out than in, they turned their attention back to the moaning and groaning Ed.

"We'd better get the Doc, boss, he don't look very healthy to me." "We ought to let the Doc see all three, him last. Arthur, can you go fetch the Doc. And keep your mouth shut – if yer see anyone else, this is family business." Arthur had heard Will refer to this stranger as boss; he would keep his mouth very tightly shut. Trigg and Will cleaned Ed up some and humped him into a bedroom and onto a bare bedframe. Then Arthur came scurrying back into the house. "That Hogwash Porter and Pumpy Ansell are just coming over the crest; it's them that Ed owes the money to." "Well spotted, Arthur, good work that. Get our hosses outa sight, quick." Will led Trigg into the hallway and towards the front door that gave them a clear view of the track to the farm. "Hogwash Porter, that bastard's still causing trouble round here." "Sounds like it, Will, I take it you know him?" "At school, always was a bully. Used to give him a thumping now and again. His grandpa had a hog farm, never saw his pa, and that's how he got his name – came to school stinking of that lotion they use to kill off the hog shit pong." "'You could be getting another chance; they look to be heading in here." When they did turn in, Trigg opened the front door slightly, then told Will to go stay with his ma in the parlour. He would slip into that bedroom and get behind them. Trigg listened as they hitched the horses. "That tosser had better have me some money or he'll get a kicking as well, if he ain't done the mortgaging, we'll fire the stables today, just so he knows for sure we ain't letting em off. Lookee here, the front door's open." Trigg left the bedroom door ajar as he hid behind it and let them slobber past towards the parlour. As they pushed the parlour door open Will was stood beside his ma and facing them. "Well, Hogwash Porter, never heard yer knock, but you always was an ignorant bastard, weren't yer? How long is it since I last gid yer a good thumping, Hogwash, ten year?" "Yer won't gid me another, army bastard; there's two of us." "There's two of us as well, Hogwash." The voice from behind had spooked him and as he turned, he saw Pumpy being dragged back off-balance and his legs kicked from under him.

Then as he turned back a fist smashed into his face, and another strong hand grabbed his neck and pinioned his head into the corner of the room, as the fist kept pounding his face into the wall. Only the blood and the snot oozing down his ma's wallpaper eased Will's fury, and he relaxed his arm and let Hogwash slump to a crumpled mess on the floor, then the boot went in. Arthur appeared wielding an iron bar just as Will piled the boot in. He looked appealingly at Will. "Help yourself, Arthur." Arthur did, with grear vigour, but was advised to be careful as this boss man appeared dragging Pumpy Ansell behind him all trussed up. "Whoa, Arthur, steady on, you'll hurt yer foot; you ain't been for the Doc yet." Arthur scowled at the feller, but then let rip with his other boot. "Good thinking that, Arthur – whack him in the ribs with yer bar, that won't damage." Arthur beamed in gratitude and laced Hogwash a time or two, but then started to blow some – he was getting outa breath, but he was a happy chappy. "How's the law round here, Will?" "Don't know, state police I think; used to have a sheriff when I was a kid. Arthur, who are the lawmen round here now, and are they any good?" Arthur nodded to both questions. "Arthur, call in and ask the lawmen to get here, as well as the Doc." Trigg wanted these two locked up, but was trying to keep Ed out of trouble. Porter and Ansell had trespassed fully armed, and had criminal intentions and arson on their mind. Both of them had heard that and that was why they had been subdued and restrained – enough of a reason in Wyoming but this was not Wyoming. There was also the fact that Martin and his wife had, in effect, been driven out. This was the statement that he and Will agreed that they would give to the law. Gambling debts would be kept out of it, that would only implicate Ed; but had any money been paid? They didn't want to trouble Thomas but it could be useful to know. Will had a quiet word with his pa, and came back nodding – ten grand, half of what was owed, but all the cash he had in the bank, bar the $300 that was hidden in the house. Maybe they should mention this ten grand payment, Thomas's account would verify the withdrawal, and let Ed stew – he had caused all this family trouble in the first place.

The Doc was the first to arrive and busied himself attending to Thomas first and then Edna's more mental injury. When he was satisfied with his treatment of Edna, he was told and then shown Ed, hobbled and tied to the bedframe. Will explained the circumstances and the Doc stated he understood and said he would prepare some treatments. Will then mentioned that there were two more needing his attention and led the Doc into an empty room where Porter and Ansell were laid handcuffed, hobbled and hooded. When he removed the hoods, the Doc began to chuckle. Trigg had remained in the parlour to keep Edna company. "Strewth, it couldn't have happened to two more deserving galoots. Have they been trampled by stampeding cattle?" "You could say that, Doc, have a look at them, just in case." "In case of what?" As the Doc gave them a quick once-over, the law arrived. Trigg answered the door, and seeing the three stripes, gave them his personal card and invited them in. "Major T. R. Hemmyng, Cheyenne – you're a long way from home, sir." Sir, that was a good start – some of these lawmen were a wee bit ornery. "That's Doc Rawson's rig out there, ain't it, Sir?" "I think it is, Sergeant, he's having a look at Will Lawton's younger brother, he's not feeling too good, won't be long." "Will still in the army, Sir, saw him a year or two back when he was home. Will is well regarded round here, sir," Trigg was trying to assess these two lawmen, and they were sounding friendly, but how would they react when presented with Hogwash and Pumpy. Then the Doc appeared and much hilarity broke out. "Sergeant, get in here and feast yer eyes on these two; make yer day it will." Both lawmen were quick to follow the Doc into the room and more hilarity broke out as they clapped eyes on Porter and Ansell. Trigg took a deep breath as Will emerged from the room, then the sergeant was close behind him. "What's gone off here, Major? You bin having some fun and games?"

Trigg let Will explain the situation – the more Will said, the better he reckoned it would be. These fellers seemed to hold Will in good regard, so let him do the talking. "Trespassed, you say, walked straight in and threatened yer did they, armed and acting violent, were they, till you subdued em – like that word, subdued. I'll remember that. We've got em this time, Barny. I said we'd have em, only a matter of time. Judge Parker will be real pleased when I tell him later. Can you two gents be in the office at 10.00 hrs tomorrow morning to give yer statements?" Will confirmed they would be there. "See yer tomorrow, Will, Major. Been good meeting yer. Oh, have yer a wagon we can borrow, to cart them into the jail?" As the sergeant made his way out to the wagon Arthur appeared. "How yer doing, Arthur? Been having some fun and games, ain't yer." "I gid that Hogwash a good kicking. Would've gid him some more but that gennelman stopped me." "I bet yer did, Arthur, I wouldn't fancy tackling you." Trigg winked at the sergeant. That seemed to have gone to plan, but he was thinking the hard part was still to come. Trigg left Will doing all the talking with the sergeant and Doc. They were his folks and he had to know exactly what was being said. The fact that Thomas had paid these galoots ten grand, all his savings, was increasingly riling him, then the thought that these galoots' hosses were still hitched outside took over. "Arthur, do me a nice quiet favour. Go get the hosses that belong to Porter and and his croney and lead them away out of sight, anywhere, but out of sight. Then bring the rig to near the back door, and we'll hump them out through the kitchen. Be easier that way." While Arthur was doing that, Trigg closed the bedroom door, where Ed was lying snoring and moaning, eyes tight closed. Ed had not been mentioned to the lawmen yet. Then he went and led the lawmens hosses round to where Arthur was bringing the rig. Just the Doc's rig was out front and he had made noises that he was off. When he went back in, Will was still gabbing to the lawmen He overheard the sergeant saying that his brother was in Will's grade at school, and chitchat like that. The Doc came across and said he'd given Edna and Thomas a sleeping powder – best thing for them, a good long snooze. The Doc gave him his card and said he would call back in the morning. Trigg interrupted Will's gabbing. "The Doc wants to be gone, Will. We'd better get them galoots humped onto the rig afore he goes, so the Sgt can be witness that there were still alive when they left here." That raised a laugh all round, and the two galoots were dumped on to the rig and an old tarp thrown over them. That raised another laugh. Trigg explained. "We allus cover em in Wyoming; rains come that quick and the distances we have to go, stops em getting pneumonia and dying on yer, afore you've hung em." "I'll remember that as well, Major, good'n that one. Eh what was the other one?" "Subdued sergeant, it means to batter em senseless, in Wyoming." They hitched their conveniently located horses to the tailgate and headed for the jail, in obvious good humour. The galoots' hosses were brought into the stables and heigh-ho, $6,230 was found in a raggy old saddlebag, nothing else. Arthur was deputed to lead these horses close to where Porter lived and then give em a good smack; they would know where the Hogfarm was. "We'd better have a good think about Ed, Will. If we can keep him outa this fracas with Porter and his crony, we could stop him getting himself a criminal record. I reckon we leave him overnight and see what tomorrow brings. But it's yer pa that worries me the most, and the farm. If his back is real bad, Martin is gone, Ed might soften some, but will he want to carry on farming? Will yer pa want him here after that hiding he was getting off his son. When it gets that bad, even being family don't help." "Just what I was thinking, boss, it's bin bothering me since that letter arrived, but if we hadn't got here in the nick of time, it would have been a whole lot worse. That

Hogwash allus was talking he'd be a big man some day. Looks like he thought he had found a sucker in Ed and was taking him and Pa for the lot. With me over there in Cheyenne, he musta reckoned he had it made." They fed themselves, had a few beers and bedded down for the night. Trigg was awakened by a bed being dragged in the next room. Ed was trying to cut the strap tying his ankle to the bedframe. He reached for his Colt and waited, then he heard the door latch click open. Ed was up on his feet and getting away. Good, let him run, the further the better – Thomas would be safer. He laid quietly as the rig was walked slowly out of the barn and onto the track, then as it picked up to a trot, he watched as it disappeared up and over the crest. Could be good, could be bad, but for who? Did Hogwash have some more capable nasty sidekicks, and was Ed going their way? If he had, now was the time to find out, while they were over here, get it sorted. The law looked to be friendly. He had the coffee pot on as Arthur came in, surprised to see him up. "Arthur, does Porter have any tougher galoots with him, using him to do the dogging about work, while they pull the strings, call the play?" "Not as I knows, Major. He was just a fat man trying to be a big shot."

"Arthur, Ed got away in the night, took the rig; any idea where he would go?" "No, but there is a few of em talk big but only when they're pissed on rotgut. Ed was silly to get in with em, wouldn't listen to his pa, and just wanted a different life, I reckon." Can't live in his brother's shadow, but it was still Thomas that Trigg was concerned most about, and hopefully the Doc would have better news when he had inspected him later. "Why'd yer let him go, boss, I heard yer talking with Arthur. Was he fit enough to run?" "He was fit enough to cut himself free and get the rig ready, and creep out real quiet. I let him go cos I reckoned Thomas would be safer. I'm hoping he runs and keeps on running, as far as Wyoming maybe, and he gets his head right whilst he's running. He may decide to meet up with his big brother again, but only Ed can decide that, only him. Some of us get lucky first time, Will, others have to learn differently. Best of luck to him. I hope he sorts himself out, makes his peace with his ma and pa, but he has to want to." "That will do for me. When he's yer kid brother it ain't easy to see things clearly, but like you say, he has to want to." Doc Rawson arrived early, just as Thomas was awakening, but the Doc was not liking what he found. Allowing for some swelling he reckoned his back was severely damaged. Might get a lot better but he did not foresee it fully recovering. His age didn't help and a lifetime of heavy work would have caused problems of its own. They had to be prepared for hard times. Edna had awoken earlier but the news that Ed had gone on the run had her in the same state of mind that she was in the previous day. It was best to let them eat if they wanted to, but let them take another sleeping powder and be restful. Will had to take the stand in court and give his evidence. Judge Parker had the Major's written confirmation and that was good enough for him. Porter was given fifteen years' hard labour, Ansell got ten. The judge was busy: he had a whole list from last night's bust-up in the saloon to get through. They were done and dusted within the hour.

They went and settled up with the Doc, then mosied back to the farm, with Will giving him a rundown on the area as they passed the different properties. Most had seen better days, a few were boarded up, empty and were not finding buyers and some had been sold at 'fire' rates, and anything the buyer, or the inheritors could get. The war had been bad around here, not from the Confederate Army's looting and pillaging but the after-effects. Men and their sons had gone to war, but many had not returned, either in a box or of their own free will. Those who had were damaged, had lost limbs or were mentally damaged. Others had taken the bait and gone seeking the 'free' land out West, and others had taken their chance of a new start and simply abandoned their families, or taken to the outlaw life. The war had changed a lot of things. When they ambled back onto the farm, Edna was up and about trying to be busy but was more upset than unwell. Trigg had a bite to eat and saddled up. It might be better for Will to have some time alone with his ma; they had a lot to talk about. He saddled Will's horse as well and invited Arthur to join him – just a ramble around on a warm sunny day-old, son. They were gone for just over three hours. When they arrived back, Edna was in much better spirits and Thomas was well awake and had plenty to say – a good sign. Good time for a bit of banter. "You've got a good man there, Thomas, if he was ten years younger I'd be stealing him off yer and teaming him up with Scobie and his lads, riding the lines and nabbing the rustlers." Arthur asked who Scobie and his lads were. "Full-blown Shoshone redskins, Arthur. Me and Edna met em at Will's wedding – Fierce-looking hombres but they were very friendly, but I wouldn't want em chasing me." Arthur looked Thomas then at Will. "I can't ride fast like that, boss." "I know that Arthur, but yer fierce-looking." Arthur looked at Trigg, but the wink had him laughing as well. They were laughing – better than crying, anytime. But the big problem was still to be resolved: how were Thomas and Edna gonna get by? Will had that saddlebag under his bed, but they still had this farm to work.

The main point was that they owned the farm, he had the deeds in his desk, and no debt. The deeds were the most important item – keep them safe and do not let a bank get its hands on them. They set about adding the numbers up and working out what they needed, in money terms, to get by every week, including Arthur's wage. He could keep the dairy and the poultry going, giving them their own eggs, chickens, and milk, as well as his company and presence, to handle the horses if Thomas couldn't – chop the logs, grow a few vegetables, the simple items. It was a sobering thought, but that was the situation and it had to be sorted out, quick. He didn't want Will bothered about his folks wellbeing. He had more than enough to concern him as range boss. Sod's law always came into play when yer had two big problems; you ended up not sorting either one fully and you were in a bigger mess than when yer started. This one had to be sorted, and he only saw one solution. Thomas had to shut the farm down until he was fit enough to run it properly. They needed to agree how much Thomas and Edna needed to break even each month, with Arthur just doing the simple jobs. No mortgage, no debt, just break even until Thomas was able to work again. That was what Trigg put to Will, and if Will agreed, he would then have to agree it with his folks. To Trigg, there was no option, but it needed discussing and agreeing. Will was in agreement. If his Pa tried to work too soon, he could cripple himself, and then where would they be? A farm difficult to sell, and earning very little, and Thomas as good as knackered. Trigg saddled up again. He didn't want to be directly involved – it was for Will, Thomas and Edna to discuss and agree amongst themselves. He went for a ride around again in the early summer sun. He had other things on his mind. Sat on a horse and alone had always been a good place for him to think things out and he was the kind of feller that once he had been to a place, it was locked in his noddy. Second time round you always saw something new or different to when you first saw it, and the small clutch of low hills looked inviting, gave yer a better view of what he guessed were the six hundred acre or so farms in the valley bottom. Much of the land was now lying fallow – no point in sowing seed if yer couldn't harvest it. Scanning around with his glass, he picked out another farm barn that had burnt down and been scavenged. He heard the train whistle as it neared the road crossing. There were water mills aplenty. Then he spotted a land agent's sign swinging to and fro in the gentle breeze, and went for a look. Another farm for sale, 'no serious offer rejected'. What was a serious offer in these parts?

Then he saw hombres leaving the site of the burnt-out place with what looked a wagon loaded with looted wood siding, and he watched as it made the half-mile journey into another half-built ropey looking shack-stables place – the squatters were busy. As he neared Thomas's turn-in, he heard voices and the sound of timber being ripped off a roof on the other side of the hedge. He found a gap in the hedge, where, standing in the stirrups, he could see that the scavengers were busy. The place looked tidy. Being next door to Thomas's, he better tell him: could be good neighbours. Thomas had to be calmed down when he heard the bad news. Edna quickly explained that Mary was away seeing one of her daughters. Her place was for sale. She still lived there cos she feared the scavengers would wreck the place if it was left empty. Trigg passed a rifle to Will. They'd better get over there and run them off. He got his rifle out of the scabbard. They eased into the hedge keeping well hidden until they saw how many they were up against. Will called to them to get gone, but not seeing anyone, they paused for a few seconds then carried on ripping the timbers off the roof. The first shot took the galoot's old hat clean off his head, and the second hit the man's hands as he rammed the wrecking bar under the joists and sent him cartwheeling down the roof and thudding into the rose bushes below the verandah. Three more galoots appeared from over the ridge, obviously busy on the other side, and panic broke out. Still not being able to see where the shooter was, they were bamboozled. "Get off the roof and get flat on your bellies, or get shot – your choice." Trigg was wary – this was Indiana, not Wyoming, better be careful. Two of the galoots tried to get into the wagon, but a shot splattered the post that the horse was hitched to, spooked it and the tether failed and it took off down the field. They stretched out on the grass and all went quiet, apart from the galoot shot in the hands. "Leave your rifle, and go get the sergeant. I'll keep these galoots occupied. Go a few yards further down before yer go and let rip with the pistol, just in case there's another galoot trying to get a fix on where we are." As Will leapt onto Trigg's hoss and hightailed it for the sergeant, Trigg slammed another shot into the ground close to the nearest galoot – make em think, if they were thinking, that one had ridden off, but shots were still coming from two places; get em rattled. All was nice and quiet, then Arthur came hobbling across from the farm with the worn old shotgun.

"Be them damn squatters, Major, from down yonder. They're getting into any darned place that stands empty for week even."
"Keep yer head down, keep quiet and don't fire yer gun, yer just might hit em. I want these galoots alive and talking. Will's gone for the sergeant. We've just need to keep em pinned down and scared shitless." Arthur nodded and wriggled down into the long grass. Then another galoot appeared from behind the house, not seeming to know why his buddies were stretched out belly down on the grass. A shot smacked into the timber post he was holding onto, and he hit the hay rapidly. Trigg checked the magazines – and a dozen shots left in each one, should be enough unless reinforcements arrive for the galoots, but if some did arrive, he wouldn't be shooting to scare, it would be to survive. He had a quick squint up and down the track; it looked quiet, good. All he wanted to see coming down that track was Will and the sergeant, and his men, if he had any. But the time dragged on and on. He had to let rip some more shots to keep em down and call another warning that the law was coming, but where were they, where was Will? Maybe he would have to let these galoots sneak away after all. What was keeping Will? It took an hour and a half, and then only Will and the sergeant appeared, but the delay was soon explained. Ed, and two others, had robbed a storekeeper as the man opened up for his day's trading. Nobody had been shot. Another customer had been injured trying to flee the hold-up, but robbing a store in yer own town where everyone knew yer, necktie over yer face, why bother? Money had been stolen, a chase had ensued but they had got away and Will had got to the station just as they were returning. Reports had to be written, and wires sent to Indianapolis; time runs away fast when yer

busy. The sergeant went blustering in. Seeing the galoots were stretched out belly down and cowed, he was in quick, with two soldiers covering him – he didn't hesitate. It was his territory, so he and Will stood back and let him do it his way, and he did. Had em bound and hobbled in a jiffy. Arthur was sent to ready a wagon, a quick inspection of the damage done and they were carted back to his jail. The sergeant was having a busy morning, as Trigg saw it, maybe too busy for the sergeant's liking. More paperwork to be prepared. Trigg was requested to return later in the day, say three-ish, to make his statement, just for the record as they was caught red-handed and actually carrying out the crime. Trigg agreed, he understood.

Trigg was prompt, and composed his statement to the sergeant's satisfaction; just a local requirement he was assured. Then he wired off a message to Roger that all was well. He could assure Adalia and Mae that they would be returning within days, sound in wind and limb. He then called in to see the Doc. These fellers knew as much as anyone just what was going on, and had gone on, in these places. But this wise old owl was not for disclosing his knowledge to some johnny-come-lately soldier. A major he might be, but he had known a good few colonels he wouldn't trust, never mind a major. When Trigg mentioned that Will had just married a doctor's daughter in Cheyenne, called Mae Townley, the whole tone changed. "Father wasn't called Mark was he?" They had been fellow students but had gone their separate ways. He had heard that he had married Margaret Bates, and the last he had heard they were in Omaha. "Lots of the Bates family just north of here, all farmers as I know of, but I ain't been up there in years. Take my card and remember me to him. Good lad he was, always had a notion to go West he did, and he took that very pretty gal with him, did he?" "He did, and

he's got a very pretty daughter, now known as Dr Mae Lawton."
Trigg gave him $50, on account. Even doctors liked some money up front; it balanced out the money that took months to collect from folks who had been treated, but were a touch short. That was the Sergeant and the Doc in the fold, now you needed to get hombres on your side – friends in high places thinking; him and Will didn't need them but Thomas, Edna and Arthur just might. The only big problem now was where was Ed and his hoppo's? The law was after them but what if he decided to use the farm as a hideaway? Edna would not do anything to hurt him, she was his mother, and he was the babby of the family. Unless he threatened her or his pa again, he couldn't expect her to give him away, but anything that Will and himself were planning to do to help his folks would be frittered away on Ed. But what could they do, If the local law couldn't find him, what chance had they? Or did they ignore Ed, and sort out a budget for Thomas and Edna, and hope the law nabbed Ed? He related the morning's events to Will. They agreed that Trigg might as well get back home, and Will would stay on for a few days with his folks, just be around, in case.

They had agreed what they thought was the best plan for his folks. Will spelt it out, in no-nonsense terms. His pa was not to try and do any work at all, until he was fully fit and the Doc was agreeable. Try to get working too soon and he could cripple himself. He would get the budget money to them once a month, so they would not be in debt. Arthur could carry on working for them and keep things ticking over. Simple as that. It was the only chance he had of recovering his fitness. Thomas and Edna agreed, but it was a fait accompli – what were their options? With Ed on the run, Will had not told his folks that they had recovered the money out of Hogwash Porter's saddlebag. That cash could be lodged in a Cheyenne bank, where it was safe and out of any risk that Ed may get his hands on it. If his folks didn't know, they couldn't lie, and it could be taken that Hogwash had stashed it somewhere, if these other galoots running with Ed reckoned they were due some of it. Let Hogwash sort that out. Trigg called in to see Tom Benson in Omaha. He had to change trains, call in and see Tom, see how things were going. He related to Tom what they had been concerned with, a situation that Tom Benson was very familiar with. In his time on the train, an idea had started to form in his mind that could be a much better answer to Thomas and Edna's problem, and he could earn plenty out of it as well. But it needed a lot of sorting out. Who could he trust to do that? Then the possible answer came walking in. Enoch Pound – the feller seemed able to get where water couldn't. He talked with Tom as to where Enoch was born and raised. "Cincinnatti area or just west of there, I reckon I'll call him in." Tom had been right. His pa had died early, got drowned working the Ohio, and him and his ma had gone to live with his grandfolks in Bloomington. Trigg outlined what he was wanting information on. Didn't tell them why. "Not my kind of work, but I know who could do that for yer; cousin o'mine. I could have him in here in the morning." Trigg wanted to be home, but he was here, so why not? Trigg wired Roger: he was in Omaha, be home late tomorrow, Will was staying with his folks for a few days, would be home Saturday. Keep the women informed.

Hector Leibitz was introduced, and asked to state his work experience. Hector appeared to have the experience needed to manage – not that difficult a job. Trigg showed him his freehand sketch of the area, with the areas outlined in red that he was most interested in. Hector was sure he could do the job, and a fee was agreed, plus a travel and overnight stay budget. Get on with it, and report back to Capt. Benson when he had all the information requested. Armed with the sketch, Hector went to it. In his mind it was a doddle, just one item may be tricky, but he would get there and make his best endeavours to collect all the information. Back on the NY, everything was bobbing along nicely. Couple of small rustling attempts but they had been chased away before they got near the herd. Trigg related the events that had occurred to Thomas and Edna, and the local law had been cooperative, and the only possible problem of Ed remained. Will would get the budget money to his folks, giving Thomas time to recover fully, without incurring any debt. Adalia saw the sense in it all, with Martin having left to be with his wife, and Ed turning robber and on the run It was the best of a bad job. Roger agreed. He suggested sending the money to the Doc, letting the Doc deliver the cash to Thomas, under the guise of a visit to a patient. No need for the local bank to know, and no need for Arthur or Edna to have to collect money from the bank. "Excellent ploy, Roger. I'll write to the Doc and see if he will co-operate." Three days later Will arrived back with the recovered cash. It was deposited in the same bank that the NY used, but in its highest interest earning account for long term deposits. Trigg passed on Doc Rawson's card to his college buddy. You couldn't beat having these fellers talking to each other, professionally. It was up to Thomas now to do his part of the deal, not easy for a man used to being active and busy, and Mae said she would be asking Edna for a weekly progress report, so he was being coralled by the women as well. While he was away, Ragnar had taken Snufe and Hundy back down to where they had found the saddlebag and those precious stones. "Snufe and Hundy were moping, wanting summat to do, so me and Scobie took em for a run-out down there, and they had found another saddlebag, nowt much in it, and we found some more of those rubies and emeralds or whatever they are. Percy has em all in the office."

The following day, Chas came haring in – they had found some hosses grazing and was in for bridles. "Only eight of 'em boss. We'll take em straight into Sam." Sam inspected them and was straight into the office. "These are good hosses' boss, they ain't $40 mares, and they ain't been run hard. I reckon two are in foal, but I like these mares. Where they from?" Trigg went back with Sam, and was having the same thought: where have they appeared from? Scobie was told to get his lads out scouting around, to make some discreet enquiries in the Bluffs' livestock yard. "Have a good look at them afore yer go and a word with Sam; let him tell yer what he thinks." Scobie and his lads fanned out from the place of the grazing. Some oldish tracks were found but the only track they found that looked likely was coming out west from a new waterstop for the UP but was becoming known as Sidney. The UP was putting more waterstops and sidings in. More trains needed more sidings to lay up in, if a locomotive was having traction problems. Kept the main lines clear. Had some galoots opened the livestock wagons in a siding and driven the hosses out and away whilst the engineer topped up the water tanks. The hosses were coralled and the army notified, with a claim form registered in case no one proved ownership. The saddlebag retrieved by Ragnar and Scobie only contained $33 but some paperwork was of much interest to the fort. Bit by bit the story was unfolding on these Chicago Italians, and this latest batch of paperwork was very welcome to the Omaha Div.HQ officers. A short note was received commending the finders' good work. Ragnar nailed it up the office, next to the 'consolidation' banner. George Dobbs in Pine Bluffs had not heard of any incidents concerning stolen horses, so, sit tight and see what the morrow brought, if anything. Could be there had only been two robbers and some other ague had befallen them. Like stage and bank robberies, the robbery could be a spur of the moment idea, and then a change of heart, or cold feet, or what seemed a good idea was looking like being the death of them, so get riding and keep ongoing. Many galoots never survived the first attempted law-breaking effort, and others were around to pick up the bits left scattered about. What else could it be. Another eight good quality mares found some company on the NY.

Adalia had tucked the first few stones away, and the next few were added to them in her mother's hand-me-down jewel box. Hector did a very efficient and thorough job: names and addresses were listed and the feller's name in the State Capitol building was very fully described, as was his area of responsibility. It looked like Hector had identified the correct man. Trigg discussed his thinking and intention with Roger, who immediately began to share his liking for this development. Roger was sworn to secrecy; they were the only two who would be involved in developing this scheme. If it was found to be not viable, then so be it, they had tried, but they might have to look at other possibilities. This scheme was to establish another ranch centered on Thomas and Edna's spread and add three more adjacent, but vacant, farms, and the big piece of open land and hills that backed onto the farm fields. This land was open range, and had clearly been used as such in the past, but with the decline in the area's fortunes, was now just meadows and mostly low rolling hills. Too hilly for farming but cattle would manage it easy. Hector's enquiries had confirmed what Trigg had thought; this land was owned by the state. Now it was: what sort of deal could he agree to rent this land as one whole entity, hills included? The other clincher in this scheme was would the investor group be interested in him having this additional ranch, and would they stock it, like they were doing with the NY? That was the first hurdle for himself and Roger, to get their agreement, in principle. Without their agreement, it was not a viable proposition. The distance from the NY made it too difficult to manage. If they could put the deal together in its entirety, then it could be staffed accordingly, and operate on its own but report back to the NY. He would own the business. Thomas would obtain a rent for his farm, and a job if he was fit enough, and Will could have an interest in the new business, giving him a share of the profits, and an added involvement of controlling the ranch's range operations and staffing, if he wanted it. Roger would oversee the financial matters. That was the theory; now, could it be realised? After further consideration, it was decided that they ought to involve Roland and Jimmy in these negotiations to rent the two farms and the swathe of open land. Hector had listed the land agents handling the disposal of the farms, and all information pertinent to the state's staff regarding the land.

Jimmy undertook to sort out the two vacant farms, leaving Roland the more tricky business with the state officials. It would also keep their identity unknown until a deal looked to be on the cards. Edna's reports on Thomas's recovery were going well, until Ed made an early evening return to obtain some money, but Arthur spotted him, kept hidden, then when Ed went into the house, Arthur hightailed it for the sergeant, and Ed was arrested as he left the house. Fortunately Ed must have been suffering guilt pangs, or was being smarmy, but no violence had been threatened, just a spate of begging and promises to relinquish his law- breaking. 'Just loan me some money please.' But Thomas was not for forgiving and forgetting and refused point blank. The time taken in this begging and refusal had allowed the sergeant and his constable to get into place and nab him as he came out. It was a sad time, but Ed being under lock and key meant Thomas was now much safer. With the Doc having agreed to deliver the budget money, the situation was now as good as it could be, but things could crop up, nothing was ever perfect. The enquiry with the investor's group went to plan. They were always looking to improve the security of their livestock. As their experience with the NY was unblemished, and another operation like the NY would very welcome. Jimmy Hanson concluded two deals that were within the agreed budget, but the land deal was more complicated. They didn't know exactly what they owned, as this land had always been regarded as open range. It needed surveying and a proper plan of the area prepared. That would be better for all parties – an accurate record of what was to be involved in any agreed deal. No one could argue with that. Will mentioned that his ma, in her weekly letter to Mae, had related that there had been a shootout up on the hills between the state militia and some squatters. It had followed a confrontation between some surveyors and these squatters. Shots had been fired and the surveyors chased off, only for the state militia to be called out and rout the squatters, and chase them across the state border into Illinois, then the shacks had been fired. "Must have been mixed up with those we tangled with, boss." Trigg nodded in agreement. Hopefully the militia had been doing them a favour, but, as much as he wanted to let Will into the deal, he knew it would be wrong until the deal was done and agreed. With his folks still in a sad position, he didn't want to raise Will's hopes too far, then have to disappoint him. Better to let the budget scheme mosey along.

Harry and Joe had settled in well in their new situation and were using their soldiering experience to good effect. Tom Benson and Enoch had been able to use them on jobs where the hired-in detectives would normally stand off, just supply the evidence and let the client organise the recovery of the goods or money. Tom and Enoch had chosen well and numerous recoveries of stolen assets had been successfully carried out. But it was not a business that they wanted to develop, just a service that could be offered if it was deemed to be the only solution. It was another string to the BLA's repertoire, and they had proven they could operate that way. If the BLA wanted a galoot finding, they would hire a bounty hunter. It worked, but could be very messy. These bounty hunters were not too smart, just nasty hombres with short fuses, and often caused more trouble than they were worth. Many potential clients were aware of that, and did not want the bad publicity, or any publicity; they just wanted a nice clean service. Now the BLA could provide that level of anonymity, from detecting who was the thief to recovering of the goods. Trigg had foreseen that the BLA would get into the cattle detecting side of the business. Now the investors group people were gonna stock up this new venture, if and when it came into being, and had stated that they were always seeking more secure sites on which to locate their livestock, maybe now was the time to make them aware of the BLA and its services... or was it too soon? Their statement that they were always seeking more secure sites to locate their livestock on had him wondering just how many not too secure sites they had and just how much livestock went missing. The territorial governor and the colonel were busy forming a Livestock Growers Association. He knew there was a problem but two years on the Casements' construction train and another two years helping to get Cheyenne and then the NY up and running had maybe blurred his focus on the wider situation. His own problem with rustlers was due, he had assumed, to his ranch being where it was, just east of Cheyenne, and with the UPRR spewing trainloads of chancers into the area. Also, his connubial bliss and living well outa town didn't help either. It was what he wanted and enjoyed, but maybe he ought to get himself much better informed of the wider goings-on in the cattle business. Henri and Arnie Asmusson would be arriving shortly for a look-see at the NY. Another beef deal looked to be on offer – Henri was confident and he was marrying the boss's only child.

Arnie Asmusson liked the NY and the whole high plains area a lot. He rode the ranges, always accompanied by his personal guide GG. He also liked the description that Roger coined for him: 'Prime Steak, raised in the pure clean air of Wyoming.' Arnie liked a tag line. He could use that in his food shops. The photographs were taken of Arnie riding the range, herding the cattle and sharing a beer with the range boss and the cowboys outside the bunkhouse. Arnie was big on his publicity; he had personally been and seen for himself. Californians liked that type of image. "Its been a real good visit, Major. Allus wanted to cross them Rockies. See yer at the wedding." Roger and Henri had agreed the deal, and the start date. Roland received a draft of an agreement that the

Indiana state could accept. Tom Benson was instructed to keep Harry and Joe gainfully occupied. Trigg and Roger checked and rechecked the figures. Jimmy did a check. It all added up; the deal was viable. Ten years trading at the turnover predicted and it would be paid up, lock, stock and land . Will had the deal explained to him. The only bit not yet agreed was that Thomas would include his farm in the deal and that his spread would be central to the overall plan. It would allow the deal to become a viable undertaking. The new spread would have its own new name and be a self-supporting entity, reporting back to the NY. As such Will would not need to uproot his family, which Mae didn't wish to do, but he, as range boss, would be making periodic visits, so he would be seeing his folks more often than in the past. Will was fully in agreement, but it was his pa's farm. He would go over and explain the deal and let his pa make his own decision, but he could only envisage his folks being in full agreement. It was too good a deal to refuse: everyone was gaining. While Will was giving his folks their due respect, Trigg took Snufe and Hundy out on another rock-sampling exercise. This was to the place where Scobie and GG had tracked the hombre who had organised the stagecoach robberies. Both the hombres had been caught and jailed, but then when they had refused to cooperate with the inmates in the jail, had been found with their throats cut. No sharing of the loot. Adios amigo!. This area was real rough land, with a creek running through it; it had been worked over and searched by troopers three times, but nothing had ever been found.

Trigg brought the wagon to a halt. Scobie and GG rode up onto the high ground to keep watch, and he let the dogs loose – just let them run free and have a nosey around whereever the fancy took them. Ragnar stayed sat on the buckboard and he took out his rock-sampling toolbag and a hessian bag. He took out the lump hammer and steel chisel and chopped off a few samples. He inspected the freshly revealed rock face with his magnifying glass, then discarded them and chiselled a few more off, but all the time keeping a sharp eye on the dogs as they rooted about. Nothing interested them much, so he moved the wagon and began again. Two hours later still nothing, but now they were getting into the real craggy area. He sat and looked at the rock faces of this craggy area. A zagged crack ran down. It was an open crack for most of its length, but then it was full of earth and flowery weeds for a yard or so, about 5ft above the track. He could put his fingers right into the track, both above and below where the weeds were growing, so what was holding the earth above where the crack was open? Could be some stones had got wedged in and the weeds had taken hold, but, give it a thump and see what happens. The 4lb lump hammer shook the earth loose and the straggly weeds slid loose, and so did some more about 2ft across, and the lump of rock moved back. Another heavier thump and it sounded hollow; had he found a chamber? Only one way to find out, but hold on a minute, have a look round, just in case. He went back to the wagon for the small wrecking bar. It would be easier to lever it open. Breaking that lump of rock could cause it or something else to fall. No rush, it might be nothing. He called the dogs into the wagon with Ragnar. He levered the piece of rock out slowly, and slowly it became obvious that there was a small rough chamber behind, and it was not a natural hole in the rock. He levered the rock out and let it fall. Sure enough there was a chamber, but again, be careful, this was midget rattlesnake country, small but very poisonous, and very timid, but step back and let them scarper. He went back for some old leather gauntlets, then moved some rubble and heigh-ho. There was a small strong box pushed into the hole with an old cloth covered in dust, draped over it. He dragged the cloth off it using the lever bar, then hooked the claw over the box and pulled it steadily out onto the track. He lifted the smallish box – it wasn't empty, something rattled the sides as he took it back to the wagon. Then he went back and peered into the chamber, but it was empty, so he made good the opening and threw plenty of earth into the joints between the rocks. Lastly he cut a rough arrow into a rock 3ft away, just in case he wanted to be back there. Scobie and GG were called in and they made their way home. "Don't know what we've found, Pop, but that was an interesting little experience. That was the fourth time we've been looking in there, but the first time we've found anything, but there's more in there. I'm sure there is." The smallish steel strongbox had no markings on it at all. Wells Fargo and all the bigger security companies marked their strongboxes, sometimes only with a metal plate rivetted to the main box showing their name stamped into the plate, often with a box number as well, but this box had nothing. Herbie Brunner was still helping Jake out in the hardware shop. Being a skilled carpenter, Herbie could tell them what they needed to do the job, and exactly how to do it. When Herbie had suffered the robbery and beating, and then moved in with Jake and Beattie, the big job was boxing all his carpentry and joinery tools together. His personal bits and pieces went into a small bag, it was all his tools that took the moving, and they had been stored away in H&S's big barn. "You got any of them skeleton keys, Herbie? You carpenters are usually handy at getting locks opened when keys have been lost." "Sure have, Major, somewhere in me tool boxes. Ain't used em for a long time, but I'll root em out for yer." "Good man. I've a smallish strongbox that I can't find the key to. I'll bring it in." Herbie had a fiddle around with his skeleton key, and eased the lid open as the box lay on the workbench. Trigg opened the box and saw the dark green cotton bag. "I thought that's what was in there, thank you, Herbie." He then tied the box up tightly with some twine, just to make sure it didn't flip open unexpectedly.

"Have yer spotted anything worth bidding for in the next auction, Herbie?" "I have, Major, there's some big fireproof safes listed as Lot 7 – here, have a look." "Good make those, Herbie. Have a word with Roger. They could be very useful, at the right price, last forever they will, but make sure the keys and the codes are correct." The UPRR had started holding auctions to get rid of unclaimed goods and lost property. Herbie had taken to scrutinising the auction sheets, and then attending the sales. He had a notion that he could earn a dollar or two buying and selling some of these auction lots, especially if he could do a few deals in partnership with the Major and Roger. Trigg and Roger were very receptive to the proposition. Herbie had proved to be a good, honest friend to Trigg Hemmyng. All right, Trigg had saved his life, but he had also saved many others, all part of his job as a soldier, but Herbie, had somehow stuck around and been very useful for Trigg. They had becomes buddies, and anyway, legally of course, if Trigg could help Herbie, then he would, why not, and Roger was in full agreement. Herbie was always as busy as his damaged body would allow, no moaning or groaning, he just got on with his life, still liked a few beers, some banter and a friendly gamble, with a ready smile. A good old boy looking to earn an honest dollar. When the iron fireproof safes came up for auction, Roger made the winning bid. One was delivered into Jake and Beattie's office at the H&S, the other two were taken out to the NY and into the ranch office. One was for Roger and Percy's use, and the other went into the small armoury that could only be accessed through the main office. Its use was for the storage of ammunition and the small amount of dynamite that was kept in there. What better than an iron fireproof safe in a timber building? They weighed plenty, took some getting in, but they would be hard to rob or cart away. When Trigg was in the H&S office two days later, he had an unexpected visitor, Capt, John Rinker was wanting to see him. "I've resigned, Major, both my folks are unwell, so I'm going home to Idaho. I wanted to tell you personally, Major. I've enjoyed serving with you, just being in your company has been a real pleasure and you've taught me so much. Maybe not strictly textbook, but you kept me and a lot of troopers alive. I've met plenty who don't have your regard or

148|

concern for the safety of their men, more bothered about their own glory, but not you."

"Whoa Captain, you'll have me blubbering, steady on. I never did see much sense in getting good men shot up or worse. Best of luck, John Rinker, give your folks my honest congratulations on raising a fine son and an excellent soldier. Keep in touch; we ain't that far apart now, and you never know." They shook hands and bid each other adios. It was sad to see him leaving, but family came first, and being the only child, he was doing the right thing in caring for his folks. Then his thoughts turned to Sgt. Fred Stockham. He had paired them from that first day at Fort Laramie and they had proven to be a well-matched and a very effective duo.

Fred Stockham was an old buddy of Will's, they were privates together and both had earned promotions together, until Capt. Tom Benson had made Will up to sergeant and taken him across to Fort Laramie to join up with the then Major Dan Arnessen. What was Fred thinking of doing now? he ought to be talking to him. Will arrived back the following day. Thomas and Edna were very much in favour, the sooner the better. The deal was on and now the agreements had to be spelled out in plain English and written out for all concerned to agree on, and that was Roland's job. Trigg told Will of John Rinker's situation, and that Fred might just be looking for another situation outside of the army. Fred was the ideal man to look after this new venture. They knew him and trusted him. Will and Fred could call a spade a shovel and not fall out. "Go and talk to him, Will, he'll be working for you. If he's interested, bring him to see me and we'll see what deal we can agree." Fred was interested in a new venture much nearer his folks in Wisconsin. He had done his stint for the army and now seemed the ideal time to put some roots down, find a wife and settle, and who better to work for than those two? Count me in. A deal was soon agreed, and Fred also agreed, if he was asked, that he would be going back East to range-boss a new venture in Indiana. Again, Trigg wanted to maintain some anonymity, not be seen to be creaming off the fort's best men. They might not be bothered, but what the eyes don't see, the brain don't grieve about. Trigg took over as range boss on the NY leaving Will and Roger to get what was to be called The Roseberry Livestock Co. up and running. Will took the range hands he needed off the NY, there were plenty available to replace them, and Roger set up all the bookwork and ledgers that Thomas would need to keep the accounts in order and up to date. The telegraph was connected. The first 5,000 head ambled onto the Roseberry's range: it was working. The grazing range was much smaller than the NY's, but the grass was much better

The spread was more compact, easier to manage, and the quiet way it had been set up helped, but did not prevent the chancers thinking there were easy pickings to be had, but with the local lawmen well attuned to the situation, that situation was soon brought under control. Harry, Joe and Rowdy spent time over there, and some busted faces and battered ribs soon had the message well understood. Trigg kept well away. If the Roseberry was to succeed, it had to be Will and his team that did it. The herd was increased to 15,000, the limit that Trigg had imposed, but well within its potential. It was an all-year-round operation as well. Being at low altitude its climate was milder, more suitable, as the records proved, to allow farming and ranching to be a year round proposition, but nothing was guaranteed. "We need ten years' good trading' Will, then it will be a clear run. Let's get at it." Thomas was to receive a rent for his spread and a wage as the manager. Will and Thomas would get 20% of the annual trading profit, Fred, his wage and 10%, Roger 15%, the remaining 55% was his, for the risk and for being the guarantor of the whole deal. They could walk away anytime, he couldn't, unless he could find a buyer. After ten years of good trading, the deeds would be transferred into the Lawton family's ownership and Roger and himself would have to walk away. A month later, in the H&S, GG was in a hurry to see him. "One of those galoots who beat me near to death up at Fort Laramie has just walked out of the station, boss, and he was looking prosperous, real prosperous." One of Luke Bright's galoots – was he back in business? "Where'd he go GG? Which train did he get off?" "Scobie's tailing him. Don't know which train but there's only been an eastbound train through in the last hour." Luke Bright – another hombre who they arrested and transferred to Div. HQ, but then never heard of again. Was he back pedalling counterfeit money? Hopefully he was. "Take Harry with you and have a good look at him GG. Be sure its the same galoot, but don't let him see you." GG knew it was him – he'd bitten a lump out his nose in the fracas, before the other three had overpowered him. He'd never forgotten that face. "He's booked into the Bavarian, boss, and joined up with some more of his hoppos, they seem real pleased to see each other."

"Get his name and how long he's intending to stay in town, Harry, but be careful – the old ears and eyes routine Harry. GG, you and Scobie stay well clear, but well spotted, GG, well done." Harry was back two hours later with his name, and the other details entered into the register, likely to be all lies, and he was here for four days. He needed to get busy. If Luke Bright was back in the business of counter-feit money, then this was a peach of a job for the BLA. He knew the original details – GG had spotted this galoot that he was certain was one of Bright's hoppos. The only missing bit was where had Bright been since being carted back to Div.HQ, and where was he now? He sent for Tom Benson and Enoch to meet him in the H&S, and he put Harry to tailing this galoot in Cheyenne. He needed more men as Joe and Rowdy were booked to be over at the Roseberry. Roger needed a new feller to escort him around. Harry reckoned he knew one – a feller who helped out one night in Madge's Bar when he was elsewhere. "Bloody dynamite in both hands, and he reckons he's a good shot, and, believe this, he's English and from Nottingham." "Get him in here, Harry and quick." Andy Wood was not tall but built like a brick thunderbox. Trigg let Roger ask the questions, he would be working with him, and the answers were as Roger expected. He had only been in the US for a month, having served in the British Army. Roger nodded, and Trigg offered him a job subject to him being competent with a Colt and a Henry. He accepted and Harry took him out to the NY and put him to work on the practice range. Four hours later he was employed as Roger's escort, to take care of any threat to his wellbeing. Roger could maybe manage, he had become very capable, but with an extra pair of eyes and doubling the firepower, the odds were greatly more in his favour. Trigg had the Shoshone lads. Being fully involved on the NY, with these occasional visits to the H&S, he was well covered. One item solved, Tom and Enoch coming over on the train, and now the crux of this case – where had Bright been in the last five years? Had he, or was he still in jail, and was another hombre running this racket? The army should know, but who to ask, and keep it quiet? Could John Rinker find out, or was it better to contact Col.Dan Arnessen – go as high he could but would that take too much time? He didn't want to bother Col. Stratton, he knew he was very busy, as Martha had told Adalia that on her recent visit to see her godson

He went for broke and wired Dan Arnessen in Omaha, and got lucky. A wire came back stating the information would be wired, in code, to Fort DA Russell, immediately.

The only other option he had was for Tom Benson to make contact with Pinkerton's Chicago head office and try out this new cooperation deal he had recently agreed to. But that could wait a while, the information could be whistling along the wires as he pondered the case; now he needed to dig out his de-coding manual. The information arrived the following morning, and was decoded by John Rinker with the colonel in attendance. Everything was above board and legal. Bright was still incarcerated in Leavenworth, breaking rocks to pass his time away productively. So who was the galoot here in Cheyenne meeting, or was it one of his drinking buddies? Trigg and Harry were out of the fort and into the town as fast as it was possible to do so without looking like bank robbers. The galoot was located, he was still around, and now they had to find out who his hoppos were, keep them in sight until they were sure that the names were correct, and trail them until they knew where they worked from. It was, forget all about Bright. Had someone taken over the distribution, and could it be one of these hombres? GG's alertness had opened up potentially another very important bag of unlawful business. Tom and Enoch were due to arrive at 14.00 hours; it was crucial that they also got a good look at these hombres. It was soon established that all four of these suspects were staying in this same hotel. Had they all met up in Cheyenne because it was easy to get to. But where were they based? If they were staying for the four days, that meant they would be here until Friday, then they could be splitting up and going back to whereever they came from. Harry and this new feller, Andy, hung around keeping them observed, and Trigg went to meet Tom and Enoch off the train and explain the operation and how it had all come about. That completed, Enoch, who had met Harry before, wandered into the bar and took a seat close to Harry and some banter developed. Andy was given the nod, and he departed. Then Tom found his way into the Bar and sat nearby, quietly taking a good long look at the four galoots. Enoch, as was his cheek, even alerted one of the galoots that he had dropped some coins onto the floor, and was thanked for doing so.

Not to Trigg's amusement – he did not like them getting too good a look at his men, anonymity was his way of protecting his men from possible reprisals, but Enoch had his way of doing things and he had been very effective. Trigg liked to see that hessian bag go over a galoot's head. That stopped them seeing yer, gobbing chewbaccy and phlegm in yer face and biting. Also they had no idea of their whereabouts, and stopped em getting notions of making a getaway. With their senses blacked out, most galoots knew they were beat. Trigg had thought of trying to get into their rooms, but the name of the hotel made him think twice. The Bavarian. Bright's real name was Breitner; it was odds on that the hotel was German-owned and ran. One wrong word, or move, could scupper the whole operation. They had to be patient, let these galoots make the moves, and they had to be right behind them. The next day they did. Two boarded the train and headed east, with Tom and Enoch behind them. One, the galoot who GG had spotted, boarded a train heading west, with Harry and Andy behind him, and the other stayed put in the hotel. The plan for now was simply to locate where these galoots were based. They were dressed like fine upstanding businessmen so it was likely they were based in a town, not out in some pokey old isolated ranch house. Tom had other staff in Omaha he could call in, and Harry could send for Scobie and GG if the galoot heading west did make for the hills. Either himself or Roger would be in the H&S every day to respond to calls, but it was get on with it and see where it takes us, but don't get shot doing it. Any real threat, scarper and then we re-organise. He would be making discreet enquiries as to the owner of the hotel. They only had to get some good information on just one of these galoots, then Enoch could begin to work away in his proven style, to open up the whole can of worms. It might take months, but on the experience gained at Fort Laramie, these galoots were serious counterfeiters. Harry was first to report back. This galoot was located in Green River – little wifey glad to see him home, kiddie running around, they had his name and address. Tom and Enoch had one of the others located, but the other galoot had stayed on the train at Omaha, but Enoch had overheard them talking of meeting at his place in Des Moines, in a month's time. Tom and Enoch had felt it prudent to leave the train and get away from this last hombre. They had been on the same train for near on five hundred miles – could be getting their faces too familiar.

The other galoot had departed the train at Columbus and been greeted by a feller who Tom knew, he had dealt with him in his Jack Laidlaw days, and he watched as they greeted each other warmly. Then they had climbed into his coach and taken the Lincoln Road. Tom had known this feller to be a well-regarded, pillar of the Lincoln business community, and was a bit mystified by this meeting. He could be his son, nephew, even his son-in-law, but they would make the investigations. This could be another job for Hector – just his line of work, finding out who was friendly, or related to who. With Trigg receiving Tom's news, it was tally-ho, the chase was on. With Roger having no intention of travelling further than the H&S, Trigg left the new feller Andy to spend his time with Harry. Finding out about this galoot in the Bavarian, and who owned the place, could be a tidy little training job for him, and Harry knew how to do that. "Eh, boss, I'm a bit concerned with one of the mares that's foaling. With not knowing when she was served, ain't sure where she's at – ought to get the vet in, let him give us his opinion." "Sure, Sam, better safe than sorry. Is it the same mare you like a lot?" "It is, boss, lovely mare she is, strong, but real gentle. Make the ideal carriage horse for Adalia and your lad when she wants one." "I'll let her know, Sam, be expecting her. Thanks, Sam." Adalia liked the mare, and the mare liked Adalia, nuzzling her like it knew they were both of the maternal variety. It most likely did; some animals, just like The Dodger, could read people, whether by scent or some other sense. They could judge people in their own way, and this mare had taken a liking to Adalia. The mare was obviously a good judge. Trigg had settled easily into this full-time running of the NY, allowing Will to do whatever it took to have the Roseberry operating well. The alertness of GG had set the BLA into another potentially lucrative operation, but it had sidelined an operation that he was determined to fully resolve, the O'Hallerons. They had nabbed two of this family before the UP railroad operation had begun, but, reading through his own log from that time, there were six more, including the women, who looked to have inveigled themselves into positions from which they could influence illegal advantage to others, stooges, enabling themselves to be rid of any suspicion in the thefts, but reaping most of the loot. These O'Hallerons knew how to bully and frighten galoots into doing their dirty work, leaving them to remain undetected. This, initially, was another job for Hector. It was information and details that were required. Get those and then he could make a plan against each one. The outline spread of where they were located, given to him by Joseph the Jehu, meant that with the railroad, they might have spread even further. He had a message sent off to Tom instructing that as soon as Hector had completed his work for him, send him across to the NY, as he had another more involved job for him. Augustas and Alphonse he had already attended to. Augustas was the organiser of the army payroll robbery and he was carted in Div.HQ, but had the money ever been recovered? Alphonse was the cruel galoot in Kearney, and he had been carted into Fort DA Russell for the murder of Lt. Clabelle and the wounding of Sgt. Major Lawton. Alfredo was employed by Wells Fargo in Omaha, as what, Joseph was not sure, but he went to work well dressed. Alberto was employed by Union Pacific, in the freight and security section, and Aloyisius was employed by the same company, but out West somewhere, could be anywhere now. Aristotle was down in St Louis, also with a railroad company. Arrabella had married a feller in the Denver Bank HQ, and Annamaria had married another banker, this time in Lincoln. Hector would think he was being kidded but all Joseph's previous information had been good, and he had divulged it in a casual manner, it had not been dragged out of him under duress. With all these galoots, women included, they were in a position where they could learn plenty about which business was being done, and when – obviously very useful information on which to carry out robberies. Might not be every week, but over a period of time, a nice juicy job now and again would be easy to plan and very lucrative. These were the well-organised, very slick robberies carried out by hombres who looked like good reliable folks with regular jobs. Only Joseph blurting out these names of the other members of the O'Halleron clan, had alerted Trigg to the strong possibility that all the family were rogues, but had learnt that their father's business, rustling cattle down Kansas way, was a touch too dangerous for them and they had applied themselves to finding a less robust way of illegal profit earning. Hector sat transfixed as Trigg related his experience with two of this O'Halleron family. As he read down the list of other family members still to be investigated, he was rubbing his hands in expectation. This was just the type of hombre he liked to test himself against. The rough, tough six-gun-toting galoot was not his choice – too easy to get a good thumping, or worse. With these hombres he could dig and delve in his own way. He carried a four-shot Derringer, but this was only for the last resort, when all else had failed. They then discussed in which order to tackle them. It was agreed that initially Hector would accurately locate all these galoots, and try to ascertain the positions they now held in these companies. Being a wide-spread family, as soon as they had got the first one in queer street with their employer, the word would quickly spread to the others that somebody was out to cause them trouble, and the others would be doubly cautious in setting up any thefts or robberies. So that was the first move, to get an up-to-date assessment of each one, everything he could gain without the slightest hint to them that he was busy. Hector departed with a spring in his step on this information gathering operation. Tom Benson had used Scobie and GG on tracking and observing these other galoots that were suspected of moving counterfeit money around. Using one of the warwagons, Scobie and GG, together with Harry and Rowdy on the buckboard, and two saddle horses tethered to back had trundled around the area that Hector had located, and with their previous experience of this work, had quickly identified some likely galoots driving the wagons carrying the dodgy money. Whilst Harry or Rowdy took the reins, Scobie and GG were busy spying with their telescopes scanning the trails, then focussing on the suspects. These drivers were only the workmen moving goods about, more than likely they had no idea what was in the crates, just that the crates had to be delivered, so get on with it. Once some regular routes had been identified, they needed to 'acquire' one of the crates and see exactly what they contained. The only way was to way-lay one wagon and have a look-see. As the two drivers lit the kindling to heat the coffee pot, Harry eased his warwagon to a halt alongside their wagon and gained their permission to hang another kettle over the fire. The distraction was enough to allow Scobie and GG to sneak around the wagon and steal up behind the two drivers having some banter with the two strangers. Shod in their moccasins, the bags slid over the heads and the galoots were advised to sit nice and quiet and no harm would come their way. A crate was exchanged for one of the galoots. Just run of-the-mill ordinary wooden crates were used for this business; it was what was inside that differed.

When Harry heard the warwagon pull away, he sat quietly holding the reins to one of the saddle horses; then when it was well away, he climbed into the saddle, bid the two adios and rode away. The two drivers pulled off the hessian bags and watched him go, then scuttled round to the rear of their wagon to see what had been stolen, only to look a bit perplexed when nothing appeared to be missing. They saw the splinters of wood that they had heard as a crate was prised open, but there were four crates there, the same as before. The two drivers were trying to work out what had gone on, but agreed to say nothing. They had not loaded the crates in the first place; if anything was wrong, it must have been the galoots who did the loading. They brewed some more coffee, made sure all the splinters were cleared out of the wagon, then carried on as if nothing had happened. After all, they had been hired to deliver four crates and four crates would be delivered, like they always were. They would hand over this wagon and team, and take an empty wagon and team back to where they had started from. All in a day's work. The counterfeit money was lodged in Col.Arnessen's control in Omaha Div. HQ with the agreement that the army would not launch its own operation against these hombres. The reason being that loot of this nature had been recovered before, but only the workmen had been arrested. The main organisers and the printing press had never been located. The workmen were caught but all that meant was the main hombres skedaddled, lay low and then go back into business when everything had quietened down. Also, the army was continuing to lose officers and men, and continuity was crucial in nabbing these galoots. Trigg was then reminded by Adalia that Henri and Rosanna's wedding was only three weeks away; had he checked that his uniform fitted? As best man, she didn't want him looking like a trussed up turkey. Also, as Arnie personally invited GG, as a thank you for the care and attention given on his visit to the NY, had GG been measured for a suit yet? Trigg was a mite surprised that the time had sped by so quickly, but they had been busy; it was a timely reminder. His uniform still fitted all right, but convincing GG he had to buy a new suit was the hard bit, but fortunately, they found a ready-made one that only needed the legs shortening. A new shirt and tie, waistcoat and pocket watch and chain, and brown leather boots, and he looked the business. His sister, Scobie's wife Tina, even chivvied him into buying a new jacket and pants, for on the train and then after the wedding, and to save his suit until Roger's wedding later. Social occasions were not high on GG's order of things; he liked to be working unless there was some beer to be drunk. Will Lawson had also been reminded Arnie was keen to have a good turnout of cavalry soldiers on his daughter's wedding photographs. Several of Henri's fellow officers from Sacramento Div. HQ were on the guest list. With the NY in Roger's control, and the Roseberry and the BLA all busy and well-organised, they boarded the train and headed up into the Rockies. Ragnar had been added to the party, and Helen was travelling to assist Adalia – a special treat for all the care and attention since the little feller had been born. The little feller was not impressed by being on a train and took to getting plenty of shut-eye as the train rattled along on its way. On the following morning when they were high into the Rockies and the engine was working hard up a rise, Ragnar and GG were taking in the views as the track weaved its way around the mountains, through the tunnels, and over the trestle and girder bridges spanning the gullies. Trigg, with his lad struggling and wrestling in his arms, and Will were engaged in some banter with the conductor about the stories and reports of train robberies and hold-ups. The papers liked to embroider the events, talking to those closest to the incidents was Trigg's way of getting as close to the truth as was possible, and this conductor was content to talk of his experiences. The conductor was drawn away to other duties and Trigg and Will joined Ragnar and GG viewing these high passes, commenting on how difficult it must have been building these tracks at this altitude. "It's no wonder they needed thousands of Chinamen to blast and clear away the rock and the rubble, and that was before yer started laying track. A basketful a time to get the grades right, and working in snow tunnels during the winter, then building snow sheds to keep the tracks open after the work gangs moved on." "What they doing, boss, over there, look." The track swung right as it turned to follow the shape of the mountain, and you could see the locomotive as it nosed its way round the bend, spewing steam and smoke out as it battled its way up to a waterstop.

Trigg and Will eyed the riders as they eased off a trail and into a rocky area well covered in bushes. "Could be maintenance men Will, but they look mighty well-armed. Are there any renegade injuns around here that you know, of GG?" "They ain't injuns, boss, look more like train robbers to me, hoping this train pulls up for water at the cistern." As they watched, the light rain stopped, the clouds parted and the sun broke through, but the riders were nowhere to be seen; obviously they had taken cover and were judging whether the train would stop. Trigg looked at Will. They were in the First class, the coach that would be raided for the best return, both money and jewelry. "I reckon GG's got it right, but I only saw six of em, Will. One to cover the engineer, one to look after the hosses, and four to do the robbing, if the train stops, or they stop the train. GG, have you got yer pistol with yer?" GG opened his jacket to reveal the gun. "Ragnar, you go find the conductor. Don't panic him, just say Major Hemmyng wants to see him, urgently. Will, you stay with GG I'll get the women into the sleeping car and see yer back here. You're armed, aint yer?" Will nodded. A quick look out of the window and he guessed he had two minutes, no more, until the locomotive reached the cistern. "Get in the sleeping car, girls, quick; might be some trouble. Lock yerselves in and don't open up unless it's me or Will. Be as quiet as yer can." "The conductor's coming, but he don't know any Major Hemmyng." The train began to slow as it neared the cistern. It was obviously stopping, but was it for water or the engineer doing as he was ordered to? The Conductor appeared in a bit of a fluster. Trigg called him across, quickly introduced himself, then informed him his train might be about to be robbed. "Have a look from the landing and see what's going off up front. There are three of us armed and ready to down em. Go have a quiet look-see." The conductor having a look, if the robbers saw him, wouldn't be unexpected, and it would not spook them into thinking they had been spotted. The conducter saw that Lennie, the engineer, was stood, hands up, at the bottom of his ladder and four galoots were heading for the carriage. The Conductor was eased aside and Trigg waited until the galoots were near the front steps, then he took two down. The other two attempted to climb the front steps, but found they were staring straight at Will's colt.

One made a move and he was downed, then the other backed away calling to the galoot who had the engineer captured. Then panic took over – with three downed, it was get the hell out of here – but Trigg and Will weren't done.

GG had followed Trigg out onto trackside and as the three came galloping out from behind the bushes alongside the cistern, and headed back down the track, the hosses were downed, and the galoots went sprawling. Not nice but it sure stopped any galoots getting away. A few minutes, a dozen bullets and it was all over, barring trussing up those still alive. The saddlebags were the prize, but saddles and all the tack were stripped off the uninjured hosses and they were sent on their way with a smart smack on their rumps; they would find their way home. The injured and dead went into the conductor's store, and the coyotes and buzzards would see to the dead hosses. Thanks to GG's keen observation, the warning he had given them was the robbers' downfall. Trigg handed his card to the conductor for him to complete his report, with the request that any reward money on offer for the galoots, and UPRR appreciation money, be paid to Mr Roger Stead on the NY, and he would ensure it was paid into the Shoshone lads bank accounts that he held on their behalf. When the train pulled into Elko, the conductor had his store cleared out into the Station Manager's offices, notified him of the event, and then signalled the engineer to get the locomotive steamed up and moving. The conductor was intent on keeping his train running to the timetable. Being a touch early was all right, but arriving any place late had him spitting tacks. With nobody robbed, the passengers soon settled down to take in views of this much-vaunted region west of the Rockies

– California and Sacramento in particular. Henri had his coach waiting and they were whisked off to Arnie Asmusson's Hacienda – very sedate and traditional from the outside, but palatial internally and very cool in this hot Califonian late summer sun. The wedding was a very pretty Californian-Mexican affair, with oodles of beautiful flowers and guitar music – a very memorable day in an idyllic setting with Arnie and Susanna seeing their only child marrying a very handsome cavalry officer. "A mite different to ours liebling, but that's how it goes. Best of luck, good health and wealth to them both. I'm just happy we're both here to be part of it." "Soldier boy, let's hope they have plenty of what money can't buy."

A very pleasant surprise for Trigg at this wedding was Henri's mother. Henri had never discussed his folks apart from the reason that had forced him to leave home and head north to seek another life for himself. Like Trigg, he never thought that a war would be fought, but it had been. He knew his family home had been razed during the war and that his father had died fighting for the Confederacy, and his five brothers were either dead or had been reported as lost in battle. This description usually applied to soldiers blown to bits by cannonfire and explosions. Henri had paid an attorney to seek out his mother, and then he had brought her to California to live out the rest of her life in comfort. Meeting and becoming good buddies with Trigg at Carlisle barracks had led Henri to choose Fort Laramie as his choice of posting, there were no guarantees, but it was even further away from his home. Perhaps it was because none of the other would-be soldier boys had chosen this posting, but that's where they had started soldiering together. After all the celebrations had been enjoyed and Henri and Rosanna had been waved off on their honeymoon, and young Stiener was tucked up and fast asleep, Trigg and Adalia took the chance to talk with Mrs Otis Watson de Silva. She was not in the best of physical health in the aftermath of the Civil War and the deprivations of the carpetbaggers. It drove many to suicide. With all her menfolk gone, it must have been a horrendous time for Henri's mama. Now rescued from that dire situation, her character had shown through and she was now as sharp as a razor mentally. Arnie and Susanna joined them and plenty of the usual wedding day light-hearted banter took place, then, after being on the quiet side, Henri's ma made a comment that caused all eyes to focus on her. "You, Major Hemmyng' are a rascal at heart, in a nice way, but you are definitely a rascal by nature. It's no wonder you and Henri are good friends; Henri is the same, not at all like his brothers – they were so serious and determined." "Adalia, did you hear that? Me, a rascal at heart? I've been called many things in my time, usually a hard........." "It's why I married, well, one of the reasons I married you. We women don't marry just for love, Soldier boy. We can be a long time married and love don't pay the bills." "Oh, so it's to pay the bills, is it? We fellers have to earn the money, build the houses, plant the crops, buy and sell the cattle, reap the crops, mend the roof if it leaks, and sire the children."

"I'll wager you didn't need much persuading on that task Major Hemmyng." "Ah, now who's a rascal? Ma Otis, we have a saying where I come from – it takes one to know one – now we know who Henri inherited his from." He gave her a wink. It was good to see the lady trying to suppress a smile, but then failing. He thought of his Grandma Hannah Thom, a lady he had never met, but could be a similar age to Henri's ma. Both women had endured horrendous situations, his grandma still was, and hopefully she was still bearing up under all the sadness. It was likely he never would meet her now he was settled in Wyoming, but you never say never, it might come to be one day. "What's troubling you now Soldier boy? You look, as you often say, that you've lost a silver dollar and found a dime." "Just thinking of home, I'll tell yer later." Arnie was called to attend to a messenger who had just arrived with an important package for his personal attention. From being a relaxed father enjoying his daughter's wedding day, Arnie was now looking a very irate hombre, as Trigg caught a glimpse of him as he stormed into a nearby room. Susanna, his wife, had also noticed, maybe she was expecting it, but Trigg caught her eye as she excused herself from the gathering. Trigg sat tight. It could be anything connected to Arnie's business and he had enough employees to deal with that. Ragnar and GG appeared holding a hand apiece as young Stiener came toddling along as he practised his walking. "Another two weeks and he'll be chasing the dogs" was Ragnar's prediction. Arnie reappeared, nice and calm but still looking like a beetroot on legs, and apologised for his absence. Trigg eyed him; whatever was causing his discomfort was still there and he was fighting to contain himself, but that was business. "Damned counterfeit money, Major," was Arnie's quick aside to Trigg. Trigg quickly equated Arnie's predicament, a situation that had not occurred to him previously, but as Arnie's whole business in his spread of stores would be totally based on cash trading, counterfeit money was akin to poison. The NY, the Roseberry and the BLA were paid by money orders, only the H&S took more cash than cheques, and what paper money came into the H&S usually went back out fairly quickly as change or to pay the smaller cash suppliers; counterfeit money had never been noticed even. But in Arnie's case, it must be like his life blood. Trigg knew the law on counterfeit money; if you were given some, you should hand it over to the law and report the hombre passing it to you. All good and well in one-to-one deals, buying a horse or such, when you could recover yer goods, but with forty or more shops and busy, not easy, and you could scare other customers away as well. It was little wonder that Arnie was getting into the trade side of the food business and into hotels and the property business. "Do you get any trouble with the damned counterfeiters, Major?" "Not directly Arnie, but they are operating in our area. Me and Henri first came across them at Fort Laramie. We nabbed the, what I called 'workmen' doing the fetching and carrying, but we had to send all the galoots, recovered goods and information over to the Div. HQ. I was then moved to the UP operation, married, built the NY and then bought the BLA. Through GG's keen observation, we came across the counterfeiters again only a few weeks ago. As we speak, I have the BLA tracking these counterfeiters, not just the 'workmen', but the organisers and the printing press."

"You'll be looking a long way then. My information is that all this counterfeit money is printed over in China somewhere, Major." China. If it was true, then it was way beyond his and the BLA's reach, and maybe a waste of Enoch and Hector's time and effort trying to find the printing presses but there still had to be some organisation behind the distribution. The govenment had a schedule of compensation payments related to the amount of counterfeit money captured and delivered into their control and safekeeping, then probably burnt. So all was not lost; it just needed a tilt of the tiller. Get these 'workmen' nabbed and the loot registered and into the Div.HQ's stockhold. Enoch and Hector could identify as many of the distribution organisers as possible, then nab them, or simply notify the army of the names and addresses, and let the BLA claim on the basis of information supplied. He needed to discuss this point with Col.Arnessen, but the BLA could get straight into locating and nabbing the loot. Arnie Asmussen's simple comment that this counterfeiting was being printed in China could have saved him and the BLA a lot of wasted effort and money. He was in a hurry to get back to Cheyenne, the sooner the better. When this latest batch of counterfeit money began to cause Arnie to be involved in a full-time routine of daily checks in all the stores, Trigg took his chance and thanked Arnie and Susanna for their hospitality, and they were on the first train east. Trigg had related his thoughts and Amie's problem to Adalia, so she was fully aware of the situation and the haste to retum home. When they arrived back on the NY, the mare had foaled. "He's a rough, bad-tempered varmint, Major. Be real careful near him." Trigg eyed the colt though the corral fence, and the colt eyed him back and snorted some sort of threat at him. He climbed the fence and dropped down between the colt and the mare. The colt charged at him pushing Trigg off balance but he still managed to give the colt a sharp, hard smack on its nose. A stand-off developed which Trigg allowed the colt to win, by holding up his hands as if in surrender, then he turned and climbed back up the fence and sat on the top rail. The colt had been defending his ma, he could take that anyday of the week; it showed guts and courage. "How old is he Sam, a week?" "We birthed him day after you left for Henri's wedding, two week ago now." "Look after him, Sam, I like him – nothing wrong with having guts and courage." As he stood eyeing the colt and the colt eyeing him back, Adalia appeared to see her mare's progeny. The mare sidled up and began to nuzzle her, issued a quiet neigh and the colt came up close and did the same. "Look at him Sam, ladies' boy. We can't get near him, but he's all over Adalia, but he looks a good solid colt; we'll give him every chance." Trigg then got Scobie and GG together and talked about the counterfeiters. He had thought some more on Arnie Asmusson's comment about the dollar bills being printed in China. It could easily be the case – the Chinese were skilful artists and could also be just as skilful engravers – but what if the printers were in the US and this comment had been put about to try and mislead, detract, the authorities from persuing the printing presses here in the US. He stuck to his revised plan to nab every bit of counterfeit he could, along with the 'workmen', so Scobie could organise and instruct his lads accordingly. He then went to see Tom Benson and discussed his revised plan and the reasons why, but added the proviso that where Enoch or Hector saw a strong possibility that either the 'workmen' knew plenty more of the operation, beyond the distribution, or they saw further opportunities to learn more of the set-up behind the distribution, then pursue these chances.

He himself would meet with Dan Arnessen and discuss this point of China being the location of the printing presses and what the naval top brass was doing to stop the money entering the US. The whole situation reminded him of the old-time smugglers trying to evade the excise men in England. After further thought on what was becoming an increasingly complicated situation, too many people involved, too messy, he decided not to contact Dan Arnessen with regard to this matter. If Enoch or Hector found a situation worth further investigation, then fine, they could pursue it, or let the stuff simmer; they could always have another look later. Scobie and his lads worked steadily and found plenty. Although not legally able to arrest the 'workmen', they could detain them, under the self defence and being threatened aspect, and this they did – no one got away. If no fort was in the area, then they were carted into the nearest sheriff's jail, the sheriff shown the loot on the basis that this loot had to be carted into Omaha Div.HQ immediately, if not sooner, and booked in and registered, the sheriff being left the important job of jailing these galoots until an army detail arrived to collect them. The government wanted this counterfeit money in its control pronto; the galoots could wait awhile. The sheriff's log was signed, signifying his cooperation. Harry worked with Scobie, and Joe with GG. Having injuns subduing galoots was still risky, but the Shoshone lads did all the tracking and trailing, then the detaining, but sat nice and quiet and left either Harry or Joe to deal with the lawmen. No point in looking for trouble, they knew their wages would be paid on the dot, as usual. The only interesting situation that Enoch sniffed out turned up in Laramie City. The galoots who collected the crates off a train that had started in Sacramento, had, after being given a real good thumping to subdue them, named an address that turned out to be a Chinese laundry in Sacramento, close to the docks. The address was wired to Henri, and he notified his former army colleagues. They investigated, but found nothing, and the address was added to an ever-growing list that featured many similar establishments. As Henri had to admit, the inscrutable Chinese were everywhere and very mobile. Apart from sinking every boat that came across from China, it was like looking for the needle in a rice paddy. All the 'finds' were relatively small, probably only costing a few cents to produce and transport. How do you beat that? Nab one and there were six more waiting to take over.

The Central Pacific Railroad had used them to blast out and dig the railtrack over and through the Rockies and paid them peanuts. Were the little yellow men now reaping their rewards, their way? Trigg knew his plan was the only way he could earn money from recovering this counterfeit money operation. It was the least messy way of the three options; the other two involved getting in deeper with the army, or getting to grips with the Chinese in San Francisco or Sacramento and neither appealed. He would give all the information the BLA had gathered to Henri on some names they had learnt about in San Diego. Maybe he wanted to have a shot at the Chinese rather than sit back and get milked. He could even borrow Enoch and Hector for a while, but that was up to him, his choice. The BLA would taper down their pursuit, and fade away for a while. If previous experience was anything to go by, the distributors would ease up for a while, then start again when they reckoned the coast was clear to hire more wagon drivers and begin to distribute. They probably had stock squirrelled away to tide them over. The Chinese were inveterate gamblers; they would have all their options covered. Winning and losing was all part of the game to them. Back on the NY, the news that Adalia was expecting again smothered any other news in the Hemmyng household. Adalia had made no secret of her hope that she would like her children to be more closely aged. She had been an only child. If she was blessed with a larger family, she wanted her children to grow up together. Trigg was agreeable – if that was her preference, so be it, she had to bear them. His only hope was that both mother and baby were healthy and well. The baby was due to be born in late spring. After the euphoria of Adalia's great news, Trigg had to turn his mind back to this counterfeit operation. He himself had not made any progress on identifying the owner of the Bavarian Hotel in Cheyenne, but letting a week or two slip by was in the plan. Arnie's comment had altered the plan, but those four hombres still wanted investigating. If they were not connected to the dodgy money scheme, what were they connected to? It was time for Tom to have Enoch and Hector find out who the two hombres were who went East. He read through the notes he had made from the time GG had first raised their interest in these hombres. Harry had trailed the galoot who GG had spotted. to Green River. His address was known and his name could be genuine. Tom knew the feller who met the hombre who had departed the train at Columbus. The other hombre was believed to live in Des Moines. Harry had also learnt the name of the feller who had stayed on after the other three had departed. "Roger, does Beattie do business with the Bavarian Hotel?" "Yep, but only on a cash basis She takes the order and the cash and delivers the next day; she don't trust him. He's a big gambler and a nasty hombre." Trigg went for a chat with Jake. "Know much about the Bavarian Hotel? Beattie deals with them but cash only." "Only that it was sold sudden like last week and the owner scarpered fast." "Where'd he go, anyone know?" "Beattie'll tell yer better, but he left plenty not paid. I'll tell her yer want a word." So Trigg sent Harry and Andy to check that the hombre in Green River was still in residence and he hadn't scarpered, then wired Tom to get Enoch working to find the hombre in Des Moines. He wanted to give these hombres another once-over before he locked his notebook away in the new safe, for possible future use. "Strange galoot he was, charming one minute, angry as a bear the next minute; musta been some medical problem he had. Last anybody saw of him was driving a wagon up the Laramie City road, late at night, boss." "Up into the Laramie Hills, Beattie, anybody with him." "Not according to Aggie Sutton. He was having a smoke on his verandah; been getting his hen house mended when he saw him whacking his team." "So who owns the Bavarian now then, Beattie?" "Woman called Molly Leech, well thats who she says it is. She seems all right, nicely garbed, paying me in advance." "See what yer find out, Beattie, and ask that Aggie feller if he has any idea where that Jurgen Bloch is now." Harry and Andy were back quick. The galoot and his family were still in the same house, but he was now working as a labourer in the building business and not looking happy. The telegraph chattered into life. Roger took the message. "Hector is just leaving Laramie City. He wants to call in and see you later." Trigg nodded, Roger wired back a confirmation. Hector had been in Laramie City progressing the O'Halleron chase and that pleased Trigg greatly. Hopefully he would have some information that Harry and Andy could work on. "Just seen an interesting face boarding the same train I was getting off boss. I'd heard Moll Letterson had sold up in St Louis. Reckon she might be looking for a place here in Cheyenne, be right up her street here, wild and woolly." "Ain't heard that name mentioned afore, Hector, I take it this Moll Letterson is in the cathouse business." "She sure is, boss, and nasty with it – any galoot crossing her gets well seen to, but thats why I needed to see yer. Aloyisius O'Halleron is working in the UP freight yard in Laramie City, but calls himself Alwyn Haller. Yard foreman is Frank Evans, but Haller is the real gaffer, does what he wants to, and probably bungs Evans a few dollars to keep out of the way, be quiet. He's real nasty though. Feller I was talking to hated him. Been done over for not cooperating and can't work much now. Haller has a sidekick, big galoot called Logger, who is the ugliest galoot I ever seen – looks like he's been under some stampeding horses. I didn't hang around to find out where he lived, I was getting too many bad looks." "Well done, Hector, I'll sort this one out now, you stay well away. That cathouse madam's name – Moll Letterson was it?" "That's it, boss, big uddered boiler she is." "It takes all sorts to make world, Hector; be a boring old place if we was all the same. Her mother would have loved her." Harry and Andy were given the information on Haller. Their job was to find out where he lived and what he got up to out of working hours. "Beattie, have yer heard of a Moll Letterson looking to set up in Cheyenne?" "No, boss, what business is she in?" "Cathousing was stated, well-stacked madam I understand. A friend of mine saw her boarding an Eastbound train. Said he heard she's just sold up in St Louis, Could be she's re-locating." Beattie promised to keep alert, but the description fitted Molly Leech. They were continuing to get aggressive, bad behaviour from the colt, as he grew and strengthened, he was getting worse. Sam had nicknamed him The Varmint, and he was living up to his name. Truculent colts like him usually were gelded and it was getting close to that point with him when they had a fortunate meeting. Chas had come into swap his hoss when he saw Buddy having a bit of bother with the colt. Chas had mosied up and the colt took one look at him and stood there staring at him, but quiet and relaxed. Chas had begun to rub his face, tweak his ears, pat his neck hard, and The Varmint just stood and let him. Sam stared at Buddy, then at Charlie, then made to get near the colt, but that had him getting unsettled again, so Sam backed away and the colt settled again. "It must be cos they're the same colour, Sam, chestnut hide and a black mane." "I think you've got it there, Charlie, daft as it sounds, but look at him, never think he was same colt would yer?" They had tried pairing him with an older pony, gave him a pal to trot around with, but after trying him with six different-coloured ponies, he was only getting worse – it looked the only option was the knife and off with his bollocks. But the boss had said to look after him, so before gelding him, they had better get permission. Now Chas had appeared and The Varmint had taken to him, it was a different proposition. Sam had spent many hours talking with the boss and Roger of the horse racing that they remembered from their time working for the duke in England. Sam went and spoke with Adalia He needed to see the boss as soon as possible. "Like yer say, Sam, it seems a bit silly, but they are buddies, aint they, wouldn't have believed it if I hadn't seen it for myself. You take Chas onto your staff, I'll sort things out with Will and Scobie. Well done, Sam, the colt's looking real good." The Varmint was the best-looking colt out of the many that had been foaled on the NY. He was no particular judge of horse flesh but The Varmint had looked good from the first time he had set eyes on him. He reminded him of a foal he had seen back in England in the duke's stables, same colour, same smooth gait, and that foal had turned out to be over sixteen hands high and a stayer, could gallop flat out for miles, and had become the top horse in the stables, and then a stallion who had earned the duke a veritable fortune in stud fees. The Varmint might never race but he could make a good stallion. Plenty of fellers liked a good-looking, big stallion for a carriage horse – geld him and he might only end up pulling a wagon. His dam is a good mare – could be somebody had put a good stallion to her. Why not look after the colt and give him the chance to be the best he could be? Again, nothing ventured, nothing gained. Harry and Andy did not take long to locate where Al Haller resided and he was most obliging by visiting another spread down in the Snowies. This spread was occupied by an older couple, the feller being very similar to Logger, a good few sizes smaller in stature but facially very similar. The spread looked an ideal place to hide loot away. Harry and Andy observed from a distance through their telescopes, then stole quietly away before they were noticed. Trigg located the spread on his map. Now he had to present a tasty dish and see if it was detoured out of the railroad's freight yard and into Al Haller and Logger's possession. But that could wait awhile. Let any semblance of Hector's visit or presence fade well out of the memory. Trigg wired Hector in Omaha, requesting a full report on Moll Letterson. There were cathouses and cathouses. Most cathouse madams catered to every john that visited her establishment, but some were particular, only liked the big payers, and some of these big payers were wanting a certain type of service that only big money could buy. If this madam was relocating to Cheyenne, did she see an opportunity for her specialised services, or had she been drummed out of St Louis by others, either the city fathers or stronger competition. New Orleans was well versed in the cathouse business, but she was looking to Cheyenne to relocate. Let Hector pry a lot deeper. Beattie confirmed that this Molly Leech appeared to be Moll Letterson. She had overheard the heavy built saloon manager calling her Moll, and being reprimanded for not using the name Molly. Molly also matched the description too closely, and it had become known that a big extension was planned for the Bavarian, most of it bedrooms and high- quality gambling. Beattie's observations had convinced her that this lady was Moll Letterson, and that was what she informed the major and Roger. "That's good news, Beattie. A big plushy gambling and cathouse joint will need plenty of provisions; got to keep the customers happy and well fed ain't they? You keep Molly Leech happy and well supplied. But, I know you will, but keep her tight to her credit as well. The H&S is not gonner feed her customers, but well done, Beattie. Any problems, let us know."

When Beattie had departed, Trigg and Roger discussed this situation. "Big players can be real trouble, Roger. They play for big stakes, which means they lose big as well, and then look for a quick, easy payday to get back into the big stakes' games. They also have sidekicks to watch their backs from getting bushwhacked from behind whilst they're carrying their stake money, or their winnings. Other would-be big stakes gamblers are attracted to them, so there will be a lot of greedy, nasty galoots that will be around here, all on the make. Cheyenne will get busier and more dangerous." Ragnar and Scobie had taken the dogs out again to the gully located just off the NY's trail to Pine Bluffs. This was NY land. Trigg felt it was safe without himself and Harry being with them, and the dogs had located another leather bag containing $500 in $10 coins. It seemed that each of the galoots had stashed his own poke separately. Maybe they didn't trust each other, so there could be others still stashed. There were ten raiders, so Ragnar and Scobie could keep searching this gully. With it being on the NY land close to home, why not leave them to it. Trigg had another site he wanted to re-visit. They had chased some galoots out of this place, but when they had returned, nothing was found. It was time to let the dogs have a good nosey around. With the wagon loaded with the tools, Scobie and GG riding scout, and himself and Harry on the buckboard and Ragnar and the dogs in the wagon, they trundled out up into the Laramie Hills. This was rougher, tougher terrain. Nearer to Cheyenne but up towards an area the redskins called Vedauwoo. Trails led down to the UP railtrack, it had been a well used area, but this one place was of interest. The dogs soon were interested, but Scobie was in – there were some galoots heading towards them. Trigg hung the rock sampling sign on the side of the wagon and made sure the dogs and Ragnar were out of view in the back of the wagon, then he and Harry carried on chipping some samples of rock off and inspecting them with his magnifying glass, dropping the occasional one into the bag that Harry held. Scobie and G G secreted themselves in some rocks close by, Henrys cocked and ready. A tirade of obscenities greeted Trigg as the galoots spotted the wagon and came across to them. "Just collecting some rock samples, fellers, seeing what minerals are in these rocks. Could be of interest to the mining company that sent me here to find out." "You tell them nosey bastard miners to stay outa here or there'll be trouble." "It's open-range land, fellers, you'll have the army in here if you or your boss give them any trouble. The Fort's only a few miles away. Its only rocky scrub land, not worth the trouble is it. It certainly ain't worth getting shot for." "The boss don't like anyone in here, anytime; he'll be riled when he gets back tomorrow. You wannabe long gone, he gets real angry." "Thanks for the warning. Fellers, stay healthy." Trigg smiled at Harry as they watched them canter away. Scobie signalled as the galoots cantered over the hill and kept going down the plain. "Let's get busy. We've three spots to look at, then we'll get outa here." All three spots yielded finds that were quickly loaded into the wagon, and the spots were well covered over and left looking like they had never been disturbed. Then they left the area and trundled back to the NY. Trigg resolved to find out who the galoot was who seemed to think that the area belonged to him. With three finds on the first visit, this galoot just might need someone to 'persuade' him that he couldn't have his hoppos threatening fellers who ventured across open-range land. He wasn't in a hurry, but it would be attended to after this first visit had faded out of the hombre's memory somewhat. The report that Hector delivered on Moll Letterson's activities in the cathouse she had run in St. Louis was very detailed. Rumours and insinuations abounded on these sorts of establishments, usually spread by those who could not afford to frequent them, or had abused the facilities, either financially or personally. The activity that really rankled with him were the sad galoots who were only interested in abusing children. It might be a good idea to let Col. Stratton read this report. Trigg knew that if the colonel had sight of the report, it was highly likely that the territorial governor would be shown it. They might be aware of the situation, but why not make sure. His own conscience would rest easier. But these 'activities' came with power and privilege, fuelled by wealth. Like some hombres who had slain a man, they then had to scalp or mutilate them some other way as well. C'est la vie. But was Moll Letterson, the real power behind the throne, was she just the brash bawdy madam who took centre stage, whilst somebody else controlled the purse strings in the background, well out of sight, but pocketing all the profits?

Apart from the obvious, there was something irking him about this set-up, and his best bet was to let the colonel read Hector's report. He fully understood that the colonel could not do anything about the cathouse It was inside the city limits and therefore the mayor and his committee to administrate. The colonel could only get involved if the mayor requested the army's assistance. Let the colonel read the report, that was his best option. He met with the colonel the following day and let him borrow the report. The territorial governor was due back from Washington in the next few days. To get this niggle out of his head, he wrote again to Tom Benson asking him to send Hector to St Louis again, to see if he could discover who, if anybody, was financing Moll Letterson, and if he could unravel that information, who were they, what was the lowdown on them?

A big job but it could open up another nest of vipers. Cathouses and gambling were the fiefdom of greedy, nasty hombres. Hector would need to be extra careful.. Trigg went to see how the new arrangement for dealing with The Varmint was progressing and found everything was going well. The colt was still plenty truculent, but with Chas and now Sam, he was more settled. Sam now had the colt in a larger corral to give him more room to sprint about in, stretch his long spindly legs some more as he grew and strengthened, and now Chas was there, made him easier to catch. But he was still a varmint, still more than ready to fight when he felt like it, and that was sooner rather than later. Trigg and Sam watched as the colt worked off some of his excess energy, jigging and bucking his way around the corral, showing off as he noticed the two fellers watching him. "He's skinny, but he still looks strong, Sam. With all due respect, Sam, I'm gonner find someone who knows about thoroughbreds. Might be wasting my time, but I reckon he's worth it. You keep up the good work looking after him and I'm gonner contact the Brandt Brothers who we supply beef to; they are into horse racing, could be they'll know a feller who is a specialist in the business. Like I keep saying, nothing ventured, nothing gained and it won't be for the lack of asking." Trigg recalled the meeting with the Brandt Brothers, and their apology that their father Conrad was not present because he had gone off to buy himself a colt he had had his eye on, to add to his stable. They were the only people he knew who were keen on horse racing. He could start with them and see how things progressed. A letter was posted off.

A gang of rustlers mounted a very determined raid, but after a tough battle, they were beaten off without losing any stock but with three range hands injured, two after their horses were shot and took heavy falls, and Lakey, one of the new Shoshone lads, took a bullet in his shoulder. Five raiders were downed, two were dead, the other three with gunshot wounds. The other nine scarpered empty handed. Nothing of substance was found in the saddlebags, and the captured galoots were carted into the fort, their hosses were added to the remuda. Percy completed the report, claiming the hosses under the six-month rule. Two days later, Harry was sent to investigate some gunshot noise that Trigg had heard through the open upstairs office window. "I definitely heard gunshots, coming from up yonder, Harry, five, maybe six. Take Andy and be careful." Harry and Andy were soon back. "There's a shootout between two gangs over a gambling dispute, a deputy's been downed and the sheriff's backed off, too many of em to tackle, and the army's been sent for." Harry explained exactly where the shootout was taking place. "You and Andy go look after Madge's place, and me and Rowdy can go make sure Doc Townly and Mae are all right. Will's way out on the range somewhere. Joe can stay in here with Jake." As Trigg and Rowdy arrived at the surgery, a feller was in telling the Doc he was wanted up at the shootout. The Sheriff was demanding his assistance. "Is the shoot still going on, feller?" "It sure is, worse now than ever Major." "The Doc can't attend whilst the bullets are flying; what if he gets shot, what do we do then? You'll have to get the injured man out and carried back here." "I'll go tell the sheriff. He'll be mighty angry." "Well tell the sheriff to get them arrested and quick, or we'll all be angry. Go on, get and tell him to sort the job out, or is he waiting for the army to bale him out? Get gone."

The firing appeared to be lessening, so Trigg left Rowdy to keep the Doc's place safe and he mosied round the back of the houses to see for himself what the situation was. He had his shoulder holster on and a Henry rifle fully loaded, just in case. It was starting to rain and the clouds looked ominous. The scene looked deserted, as expected when anything that moved got peppered, but he had seen enough so he crept back to the Doc's. "It's a stand-off, Rowdy, the sheriff looks like he's waiting for the army to arrive before he gets big and brave. You stay here. I'm going back to the H&S to wire the fort. There might not be any cavalry available and they're sending an infantry troop." The infantry would be marching, could take em an hour to get there. Trigg swapped his good coat for an old, soft, leather riding coat and donned an old trail hat whilst Jake wired the fort to find out how the army was responding to the situation in Cheyenne. He had guessed right, an infantry troop had just left the fort. The rain had eased, but the wind had got up some. He collected another Colt and placed it in a bag, with some other items he thought might come in handy, then headed back to Doc Townly's. As he left the H&S, the gunfire increased noticeably. The stand-off had ceased by the sound of it, and it was a full on shootout again. Everything was nice and secure at the Doc's, but he noticed a growing glow in the sky above the houses. It looked like a building was on fire; some rain would be welcome. "It looks like a building's been fired, Rowdy, you stay here, I'll go have a look-see" A stray shot had shattered an oil lamp in the livery stables, and the straw had caught fire. Trigg noticed there were kegs of mineral oil stacked in there – stupid place to keep that, if the burning straw got to it, then there would be an almighty blaze. He kept in the shadows, the gunfire was still raging and he watched, but nobody was prepared to risk putting out the burning straw; must have been hoping the rain would dampen it all down. He gauged the wind; if the livery went up, the Bavarian was right in line for the wind to carry all the flames and burning embers straight at it. Nothing ventured, nothing gained. He took the pistol out of the bag and tucked it into his belt, then carefully surveyed all around him. Then he carefully lobbed the cloth bag and its contents into the livery close to the mineral oil kegs. Another quick look, and he stole away to Madge's Bar to see how Harry and Andy were coping. "Livery's alight, Harry and there's some mineral oil kegs stacked in there. Be a big blaze if that goes up."

"Lennie's been shot; they've just carried him down to the Doc's. Nobody will go in, scared of being shot trying to dowse the straw down, boss." Andy came into the bar with the news that the army was marching up Main Street. "Go and warn the sergeant, Harry, about the livery and the lamp oil." Harry knew the infantry sergeant well from his service time at the fort. "Make sure he knows about the kegs. I'm going back to Doc Townley's." Trigg wanted to be well away from the conflagration when it erupted. The rain was coming down heavier and the wind was strengthening as he arrived at Doc Townley's, just in time to help hold down Lennie Bell while the Doc dug a rifle bullet out of his back. "By, that mineral oil went up with one hell of a bang, boss. Never knew it was that lively." "Never heard a thing, Harry. Lennie was screaming the house down; had all on to keep him still. The bullet was close to his spine. Took me and Andy nearly all we had to hold him steady enough for the Doc to operate. No other properties caught fire, did they?"

"Only the Bavarian, straight down wind it was. The roof

burnt off quick, then the whole place was saturated by the downpour. It's had to close until the new roof is fixed." "Who were the galoots who caused the shoot out, anybody know'em Harry." "The Army's got them, Lodgie reckoned that one gang were from up the Salt Lake Road area, the Laramie City road to us, but who the others are aint known yet Boss, but the only good thing about all this is that Lennie had sold the livery stable to the company that owns the Bavarian last week, and been paid in cash. Sally was telling Madge when the shoot out began, she said they wanted the land to extend the hotel." "Good, so Lennie won't be having to worry about working too soon, no pushing and pulling them hosses around, he'll be able to rest up and recover." That was good news. He had thought about Lennie's position during this situation and what could have been a bad problem for him, even to buying the burnt-out shell for its land value, but these hombres from St Louis had got in first. The livery burning down might help them, but who had stored all that lamp oil in there and why? Time will tell, it would be interesting to see what Hector discovered.

A wire arrived at the H&S. Conrad Brandt was on his way to see the colt. He was due at noon on Friday at Cheyenne station. He's coming to buy The Varmint, or so he thinks. Trigg could read between the lines as regards this hombre. He liked his sons, good fellers to deal with, but the feeling he had of the father was that he liked getting his own way and had the money to do it. Why else was he travelling so far to meet someone he didn't know, over a colt he'd never seen?

It made for a lively meeting, one ex-Army infantry major negotiating with an ex-army cavalry major. But he was on the train and heading his way – be real interesting. Trigg had Harry meet him off the train. He didn't take much identifying. Harry had met and served under infantry majors and he could spot them a mile off in the dark, and this one was no different. "Climb aboard Major, we're only round the corner, had a good ride?"

"Yes sergeant, two can play that game. I'm disappointed with the welcome, sergeant, I thought I rated a Shoshone at least, not just a run of the mill sergeant."

Harry clammed up. This Major was not the haughty high-falutin type, he could dish it out any way that suited, and this kind of officer would respect that. Harry fancied being a fly on the wall when these two got to negotiating.

The introductions were quickly concluded and Trigg spelt out in no uncertain terms that he was seeking good advice on whether the colt had the potential that warranted him being sent to a good racing stable to be schooled correctly. He had written to his son simply requesting a name or two that he could contact. "I've been looking for a good colt for years, Major. Where is he? Let me have a good look at him. I'll give a good price." "You're welcome to have a look at him, but he ain't for sale sir, not at any price. I like him, but he don't like me and he won't like you, so don't get too close or he might bite a lump outa yer, or give yer a good kick. He's a real tough varmint, Major. The only feller he likes is one of my Shoshone lads, but he's a lady's man, nuzzles em like a baby he does. He's out on the ranch. My wife will be in soon – she's visiting her friend, a lady doctor – so while they are visiting, we'll use the coach to get out there and let you have a look-see, but he ain't for sale. Is that acceptable to you, Major?" "I've come all this way; might as well have a look at him while I'm here." The small coach he had for the ladies' visits into Cheyenne came trundling in with Joe on the reins and Scobie and GG riding scout. Major Brandt humped his case into the coach and clambered in after it. "Where I go, it goes." Trigg guessed he had brought a bundle of cash with him. "So these are your Shoshone lads are they? Just got the two of em?" "No, we have eight, Scobie yonder is the gaffer, used to be my chief scout, and the other is GG, his brother-in-law. I met up with them at Fort Laramie in '60 and they've been with me ever since; real good, honest reliable fellers they are and top fellers at their job." The coach ride out gave them the time to find some common ground, and by the time they arrived on the NY, the talk was more the cattle business from both their angles. Trigg introduced Sam to the major, then asked where The Varmint was. "He's down in the bottom, trying to get into a fight with a gelding in the other corrall, you know what he's like. Chas has gone down with a cornbucket; only thing he likes more than fighting is eating. He'll be up here soon." Sam was right. Chas was bareback on a gelding and the corn rattling in the bucket was enough to get The Varmint's attention. Chas galloped away and The Varmint was after him, and quickly trying to get his nose into the bucket. When he caught sight of the two hombres watching him, The Varmint detoured and came snorting at them as he dug his front legs into the turf, then glared wild-eyed at them and sped away to where Chas was sat on the gelding. "He's all trouble, but he moves smooth and powerful, don't he, sir?" "He sure does. how old is he exactly?" Sam told him. "If you do decide to sell him, can I have first refusal? He is trouble, but gelded, he could win races. If you get fed up with his antics, let me have the first bid, please. The best man I reckon for you is a feller called Sylvester Knowles. He don't train horses, but he knows plenty that do. If anyone can find the right trainer for a trucculent hoss like him it's Sylvester. I used Sylvester as an horse agent, buying for the army during the war. He's been a bit of a lad, but he's mellowed now, and his daughter, Geraldine, keeps a check on him. He'll want to be your racing & breeding agent, taking a percentage of the winnings or the stud fees. He knows his way around and he's honest and straight. I'll write him and give him your details, but if you decide not to send the colt into training, promise me first refusal. Like you, I like him, I really do, Major Hemmyng." They shook on the promise.

The man had been straight and honest, and the more he was in his company, the more he liked him. Trigg offered to accommodate him for the evening, and was accepted. The coach was sent to collect Adalia and Nancy, and Trigg led the major into the ranch office where he was introduced to Roger and Percy. An increasingly interesting discussion developed regarding the cattle and livestock business, but a sudden arrival in the office of Charlie, the range foreman, brought things to a stop. Some rustlers were trying to run off some livestock, and gunfire was being exchanged up on the range. Charlie was in to make them aware in case other rustlers came on from another direction – the feint to distract the defenders away from the main prize. Trigg's first thought was, where was Adalia and Nancy? He sent Rowdy and a range hand to join up with Harry and GG who had taken the coach to collect the women from Cheyenne, and if the H&S was nearer, to stay there. Ragnar and Helen, with young Stiener, were brought into the bunkhouse, the 'castle' when danger threatened. Percy and Roger rounded up the other women and kids, and the shotguns were loaded, and readied. "Here's a Yellow boy, major, stick close to me. Charlie, get back out there and see what's going on, then get back, and we'll take it from there." Scobie was already up in the big barn, scanning the surrounding plains.

"We hunker everybody down until we know the situation, major, then we can get organised." Scobie shouted down that Lakey was galloping in. "Will's downed two, boss, and three more are pinned down in some rocks, the others have scarpered east with our boys after em." "Were there any more, Lakey?" "Two of the lads are looking but Will don't reckon so, boss." "Well done, Lakey, Go back and see if Will needs any help. We'll sit tight here and be ready if yer need us." Sam, Buddy and Chas were in from the remuda corrals; they were ready if more men were needed. "Darned bastard rustlers won't leave us alone, Major. Ne'er a day goes by without some galoots trying to help themselves. Sorry about all this." "Don't apologise, Major, I'm more than ready to riddle one or two of the thieving bastards, just let me at em." Then the coach came trundling in; the women were back safe and sound.

Plenty of wives had been taken hostage in other raids. Having them back rid this situation of a nasty possibility. Chas saddled up and went out to help. He still had that raw aggression bubbling away just below the surface, but if his buddies were in a scrap, he wanted to help out. "No point in holding him down, is there Major? Let him find his own way of keeping his temper in check. He's a good lad, just needs to be more calm and pick his moment." When they brought the two dead and the three captured men in, it put the incident into another light. These galoots did not look like rustlers, but had been quick to open fire on Will's range hands without reason. They had been confronted like many others had, but only the quick warning from the Shoshone lads that there were other riflemen hiding in the rocks enabled Will and his rangehands to drop flat into the grass. It was like an ambush but they had been thwarted. The two packhorses found hidden in a gully were searched and some surprising items were revealed, especially the specialist sporting rifles with the telescopic sights. Who were these galoots hunting? Trigg had Percy list all the items found, then both packhorses and the galoots were carted up to the fort. The other galoots had made off with the loose horses, so no saddlebags were recovered.

Once well off NY land, Will's range hands had given up the chase; they had no jurisdiction to capture riders on the open range, and horses could only go so far after a day's work. You had to be careful not to overwork or injure them. It could be a long walk back. Major Brandt had the same question as Trigg, what or who were these telescopic sighted rifles intended to be used on? In a good shooter's hands, they were capable of taking a man down from 700 yards, the victim would not even hear the rifle being fired, but although no saddlebags were recovered, the army had the three captured galoots to question. The report of the incident and a claim against any reward money for these three and any subsequent galoots proven to be involved, were lodged. Also the rifles were claimed as they were recovered on NY land. A week after Major Brandt's visit to the NY, Trigg received a letter from the feller who had been recommended as the man who could assess The Varmint's potential. Three alternative dates were offered for his visit. Trigg immediately replied and nominated the date, but clearly stated that the colt had not yet been broken in the usual way. He could be ridden, but only bareback by his 'buddy', a Shoshone brave. A letter confirming the date of the visit was received, with the comment added that as long as he could be ridden, it made no matter if it was by a snowman, as long as the colt ran in a straight line and and the rider could put the colt through a few straight forward exercises. Trigg was wary of what these exercises might consist, but after talking with Sam and Chas, he was placated somewhat. Chas was talking of how the colt was getting stronger by the day. As the date for the visit was not for another month and the colt looked to be in a fine state of fitness, he was settled in his mind; after all, if he did not like what the colt was asked to do, he would veto the request. He saw no sense in pushing the colt too hard, too soon. Trigg was ready to have a crack at this All Haller located in the Laramie City railroad freight yard. He had some crates manufactured with a polished hardwood finish. They looked very smart, were totally different in appearance to ordinary run-of-the mill crates, but were loaded with rubble to the same weight as other crates. A small copper plate was screwed on stating that these crates were the property of the St Petersburg Fine Art Co, and care was needed in their handling and transportation. The plan was for these three crates to be put aboard a train at Pine Bluffs for delivery to Laramie City freight yard, from where they would be collected. To highlight these crates being delivered, Herbie Brunner had been recruited as the collector, and he was to visit the freight yard prior to the expected delivery, enquiring as to whether his crates had been received. Herbie was asked to play the concerned gent, keen to collect his special delivery. Herbie was more happy to act out this role as the major and Roger had just agreed to purchase an upcoming lot in the UP auction that was beyond his price range. The deal had been agreed for Herbie and his brother Gordi to take over this purchase and pay off the purchase price plus a small interest cost, as they sold off the material. At the same time as these fancy crates were being carefully loaded at Pine Bluffs, Herbie was in the Laramie freight yard enquiring about his fancy crates; where were they, when would they arrive, when could he collect them? Herbie acted out his role with much gusto, the whole yard knew he was asking, then he bid them adieu, promising to be back two days later.

His acting worked: Al Haller got curious. When the fancy hardwood crates came in later that day, he became even more curious. When he read the name on the brass plate he decided he was having these crates and whatever was in them. Harry and Andy were in position to see the crates offloaded into the Laramie freight yard. When Herbie trundled in to collect the crates a day later, Harry and Andy, with Scobie and GG were sat quietly in a war-wagon with a full view of the yard. The crates were loaded onto his wagon and he made his way out of Laramie and up past Pole Mountain. Harry trundled along well behind and Scobie and GG took to the saddle horses and rode off to keep a watch on Herbie's wagon. Two miles out of town, Herbie was accosted by three riders, and his wagon was taken from him, leaving him sat on a rock by the roadside. Scobie watched through his telescope as the wagon was turned round and headed back into town. He sent GG to alert Harry, who then watched as Herbie's wagon came past heading back into town. He urged the wagon into a trot and was soon picking Herbie up. Then one of the horses was taken out of the forks, a saddle came out of the wagon, and he took off to catch up with Scobie and GG to trail Herbie's wagon. Andy and Herbie trundled off back towards Cheyenne and home. Their expectation that the stolen wagon would be taken to the spread up in the Snowies was spot on. The three of them took it in turns to trail the wagon whilst the other two ensured no one was watching and likely to bushwhack them. When the wagon moved off the track and onto what they believed to be the Loggers folks' spread, Harry turned and high tailed it back into Laramie and wired the H&S with the news. As Andy and Herbie trundled on, they detoured into Fort Sandars and reported the theft of the wagon and the crates. Trigg took the wire and then rode up to the fort, not knowing who was available, but taking pot luck. The colonel wired Fort Sandars with the info as to the robbery. A lieutenant led a detail out to the Snowies' spread and the fancy crates were soon located. Logger and his folks were arrested and carted into Fort Sandars. Another detail went looking for Al Haller, found him, and he was escorted into the fort but kept well isolated from Logger and his folks. An infantry unit was sent to occupy the spread. With the main suspects arrested and the spread under military control, the situation was allowed to sit and stew for an hour or two. When the colonel informed Trigg of the situation, Trigg wired back requesting permission for the BLA personnel, as originators of the information that led to this illegal operation, be allowed to enter and inspect the premises with regard to a possible connection to other unlawful operations that the BLA was currently investigating. Col.Stratton wired his agreement, and then sent a written confirmation straight down to the H&S office. The commanding officer at Fort Sandars was notified of this agreement, enabling him to notify his staff. Trigg wired Tom Benson of the situation, then he took Harry and Joe with him and hightailed it across there. He presented the lieutenant with his BLA business card, and introduced ex-Sgts Harry Pickering and Joe Kennedy, and then enquired of the lieutenant as to the extent of this spread, and it had been fully searched. "No, Major Hemmyng. I have been instructed to secure the stolen crates only, as evidence of the robbery, and that is all. Nobody has been allowed onto or off this spread since I arrived here yesterday. The owners and the hombres who were here have been arrested and are now detained in Fort Sandars." "So you are not aware of any other entrances or exits on this spread? Can I suggest lieutenant that you form a detail to patrol this area, just in case other miscreants are trying to enter using other adits or tunnels. These mines lieutenant, can contain a warren of tunnels." "I will Sir, thank you for that information." "Here is my written permission from Col.Stratton to allow the BLA entry to this site. We will go about our business now knowing that you will have this whole site bottled up as tight as a drum. Thank you for your cooperation, lieutenant." "Now we can have a good look-see at this place; no need to rush, let's give it a good inspection." There were other adits – some had bushes and shrubs covering the opening, and all of them contained crates in various states of being. Some were unopened, others had a side ripped off, and there were scores of bagged materials. The place looked unused as a mine, probably since the time that Haller had met up with Logger and introduced him to a life of theft to earn a living. They didn't venture very far into the tunnels, they didn't need to, and the odours and liquids dripping down were enough to keep you out. Were they acids and gases of different compositions, all of which were reputed to be dangerous to a member of the human race? Those and the creaking pit props were more than enough to keep them out of venturing more than a few yards in. It needed an experienced mining engineer to negotiate his way safely around in there. He needed to locate one.

Tom Benson registered the BLA claim to any reward monies outstanding against the information leading to, or the arrest of, these thieves. Trigg was happy to the use of the name All Haller. He did not want the O'Halleron name becoming associated with this hombre just yet; there were others of that ilk to be dealt with yet. If Aloyisius O'Halleron wanted to be known as All Haller, so be it, but he knew better. No point in complicating the situation just yet, but another O'Halleron had been nabbed. The job now was evaluating the loot in that mine, and if there were other hombres associated with Haller in Laramie. Had the galoots who threw Herbie off his wagon been nabbed? Granted, no real violence had been used but Herbie knew the ruse and was expecting to be robbed, and cooperated, knowing help was not far away. Had there been other robberies with a more serious result? Hector was sent to make enquiries at the local Laramie news-sheet, to see what had been featured in the local rag, and maybe have a chat with the resident law man. The more stones yer turned over, the more shady galoots you uncovered. Roland Simons was on the lookout for a mining engineer, off the record of course, no names, no pack drill. Just point me in the feller's tracks and I'll make his acquaintance. Roger opened another file, entitled, The Snowies Case. The UP auction was scheduled for the following Tuesday and Trigg wanted to discuss this deal again with Herbie. He had agreed to do his bit in this deal, for Herbie's sake, but the more he thought about it, the more it looked very close to sharp practice, if not plain theft. Gordie Brunner was working for this builder in Green River as a foreman carpenter. He had been promised many bonus payments for jobs completed quickly and profitably, but never received any of these payments even though the jobs were completed to the budget that had been agreed. The contractor always came up with other costs that he reckoned made the bonus payments null and void, although these other costs were nothing to do with the carpentry aspects of the jobs. Gordie was well brassed off with this repeated swizzling him out of his bonus payments and had seen an opportunity to get his own back, with some interest included. This contractor and his buddy always took a few weeks' vacation and went on whoring and gambling jaunts, having told the wives they were going hunting. To make matters even worse, Gordie was left to keep the works ticking over along with the lady bookkeeper. This year Gordie had overheard them talking of their upcoming trip to San Francisco. The only game left there was all in the casinos. It was his best chance to put into operation the ruse he had discussed with his brother Herbie. Pull this one off and they could set up in the lumber business in Cheyenne. Gordie had put the first big timber shed up in the Red Flat Desert. These sheds were designed so all the timbers were bolted together so they could easily be taken down and re-erected at a different location. The first one had been constructed, now another one had to be erected. The crux to this deal was the price Gordie had negotiated with the lumber company. The lumber would delivered to an isolated rail siding out on the Red Flat and then paid for in full a week later. Gordie had to get this lumber unloaded quick because the UP wanted their wagons out of the siding and back into use – all part of the UP's conditions of carriage. If the wagons weren't unloaded and free to collect within three days of delivery, the UP area freight manager would impose severe costs on the lumber company or even distraint of goods. Gordie knew that this area freight manager was not to be crossed; they had only just avoided trouble with him on the first shed. Gordie watched as the two hombres boarded the train heading west, then put his plan into operation. He ordered the lumber, all 10 x 2's 16ft long sugar pine joists for delivery as previously agreed. He then confirmed with the bookkeeper that a cheque could be collected in two days' time by the lumber company's 'drummer' who lived in Green River and who the bookkeeper lusted after. Then he wrote his notice to end his employment, due to his brother's failing health. He had to go look after him urgently. The letter went into the boss's pigeonhole. The drummer arrived with the delivery docket, and collected the cheque, had a bit of banter, as drummers do, then he was gone, his job done. Gordie waited two days then packed his bags. He sent a note to the bookkeeper that his brother was ill and he had gone to care for him, and might be back in a week or two. He settled his rent up to date and then caught an eastbound train early the following morning. As the train passed the siding, there it was, a whole load of lumber waiting to be unloaded. Win or lose on this deal, Cheyenne looked a better bet anyway. Trigg had pondered this deal and his agreement to it. If Gordie had set the clock ticking, then it must be too late to reconsider. What were his options? If he gave Herbie the money to buy the lumber himself, then if these hombres got nasty and came over to take some revenge, Herbie, after all his previous injuries, might not survive. How would he get his money back then? Maybe his best bet was to buy with a cheque on the BLA account. He had other options but that seemed his most sensible one. The trick would be to keep an eye on these Green River hombres and dissuade them from any violence. He sent for Herbie. He was only down below working in the hardware shop. When both Herbie and Gordie appeared, he knew the clock was ticking. "Are the auction sheets out yet?" "No, boss, will be on Friday morning, when all the lots are decided, and folks have the weekend to browse them." "What was the trade price of the lumber, Gordie, and how much do you reckon it will fetch at the auction?" "$2,800, Major. How much it fetches depends on how they auction it – if its in several smaller lots, or if it's just one lot. Be cheaper if it's only one lot; won't be many can afford it in one lump." "How much are you prepared to pay for it? You two will have to sell it. I will buy it, but it's yours to sell. You pay me back as you sell it, that's the deal, remember." "$1,500, no more." "So that is Roger's limit. He does the bidding. Where will it be stored?" "I've agreed to rent some ground in the railyard, if we need it. We'll stack it in there and cover it in tarps, till we get to selling it." Trigg was still pondering his options as he stared at Herbie, but then all hell broke loose down in the shop. An old-timer who often called in to chew the fat with Jake came bustling in with some urgent news. "Beattie's been robbed doing her rounds and Abe's been shot dead." Jake was going rabid as he grabbed a Henry and began to load some shells in, but Trigg was quick down the stairs and questioning the old-timer. "Beattie had just gone into Fullers when some scraggy galoots shot Abe, then dragged him off his seat and emptied Beattie's seat box and scarpered." "Is Beattie hurt?" "No, she was in Fullers, but she's real angry, giving the deputy a real telling she was when I came to let you know." "Steady on, Jake, don't lose your rag, we'll sort things out. Which direction did the robbers scarper, old son?" "Straight out east, scraggy old nags they had, they won't run too far." Trigg sent Harry to help Beattie, and see what the deputy was doing about it just as Roger got back from his meeting with Jimmy Hanson. When he learned of the situation, he went with Harry as well, more concerned for Beattie than her paperwork. When they arrived, Beattie was still berating the deputy about his lack of action. Abe always sat on the passenger seat, under which Beattie had her paperwork box. As she collected the cash accounts, she would attach the receipt and the next week's order. Abe would move over, the seat was tipped up, the paperwork and cash went in the box, down went the seat and Abe sat back down, guarding the box. Abe was not a vicious dog, but had a nasty looking snarl if anyone got too close to Beattie's rig. The locals knew and jessed him; he'd never been any trouble but now he was no more. The deputy was not overly bothered, a dog had been shot. He had other more important jobs to follow up after last night's brawling and knifin' in the Last Chance Saloon. Roger comforted Beattie, Harry assured the deputy that if he was too busy, then All right, you see to your troubles, we'll see to ours. "If those galoots have scarpered east, we'll get them George, and we'll bring em back for you and the Sheriff to deal with." Trigg was thinking exactly the same as Harry. If those galoots were on scraggy old horses, and they were moving east, that was ideal to him. They were obviously newcomers to the area, and didn't know what they were heading towards. Scobie would have his lads out tonight looking for a campfire. No need to arrest them, just locate them and keep them observed overnight, spook em a few times in the night just for the hell of it, then Will, Rowdy and a few of the lads could subdue them and cart them back into the sheriff. The robbery had taken place in town, within the city limits. It was for the mayor and his officials to deal with, so be it. The NY would act in accordance. The galoots only just managed to hobble onto NY land. After a strange night of wolves' howling and rocks landing on their campfire sending burning embers in all directions the galoots seemed happy to be rounded up and bound and hooded. It was a slow walk back into Cheyenne the following morning. Will was determined to make sure those scraggy old nags didnt expire on NY land. They had probably been stolen as well. The saddlebags still held all Beattie's paperwork. Let the sheriff see it as proof, then Beattie could have it back and carry on with her job. C'est la vie. The big loser was Sherman; he never did get over losing his best buddy and brother. As much as they brought Snufe and Hundy to jostle him around, the sadness never ever did leave his eyes. Herbie adopted an easy-going attitude when he collected the auctioneer's details early on the Friday morning, but his nerves were buzzing. Lot No. seven, and it was being offered en masse. His excitement mounted; he felt certain they were gonner get this lumber as he delivered a copy of the schedule to Roger. They had decided on a policy of Gordie keeping out of sight, lying low until after the auction, just in case some nosey hombre from Green River clapped eyes on him. Out of sight, out of mind, take no chances was the thinking. Herbie went to visit his brother in his room and gave him the good news. Auction day dawned wet and got steadily worse. Herbie's excitement grew. Even the weather was helping; only them like himself would be at the opening of the auction in these conditions. The Auctioneer reacted accordingly and knocked down the opening lots in quick time. Lot 7 was knocked down for a $1,050 to Mr Stead of the BLA.

Herbie went and organised the previously arranged gang of

labourers. The lumber was unloaded from the box vans and stacked and totally wrapped and roped under tarpaulins in the corner of the railyard that Herbie had agreed to rent. So far, so good, now all they had to do to realise a small fortune was sell it. With both being skilled carpenters, energy and expertise coupled with much deal making quickly had the lumber moving out of the yard. Gordie also found a few supply and fix deals, leaving Herbie to stay put in their new yard and look after the money earnt in the sales of the lumber. They had another stroke of good fortune when Gordie overheard the two Green River contractors bemoaning their misfortune. These galoots had followed the trail of these UPRR distraint goods back to Cheyenne, but when they learnt it had been purchased fair and square at auction by a company located in Omaha, that had been the final straw. A session of hard drinking ensued, followed by a brawl caused by each man accusing the other of this debacle. They were arrested, fined for public disorder and placed in a box van due for transit to Green River. Herbie and Gordie watched the box van disappear up the rise westward, then went back with renewed vigour to their new-found business. Major Trigg Hemmyng had other things occupying his mind. Sylvestor and Geraldine Knowles had visited the NY and assessed The Varmint. They liked him, and were keen to become involved with the training of the colt. The situation now was that Syl, as he was usually known by his friends, or Sly, by his competitors, was of the opinion that the best man to handle and train a hoss as truculent as the Varmint was located down in the state of Kentucky. Harry Clayson had been a sergeant in the Confederate Army, had fought throughout the war and lost three of his sons, his wife dying of a broken heart over their loss after having to bury them, their father and eldest brother being still away fighting. "Now Harry, and his surviving son Henry, have left all that carnage behind them, hard as it has been, its all in the sorry past to them. But there are lot of the old monied families carrying the dream that the Confederacy will rise again. Some of these families were near on ruined, but others survived the war surprisingly well, how, nobody really knows, but it is these hornery critters that will become your competition, even your enemies. Many are very keen on horse racing, and crave the intention to own the best colt, that might then prove to be the top stallion. They are not slow to spend big sums to breed or acquire the horse that will give them this reputation, and the competition is fierce." These statements only reflected the same situation that existed in England -big wagers were made between competing owners, and Trigg knew that well from his time in the duke's employment. "Now, we add in the fact that your colt could do very well. He is quick, very strong, and there is still more growth in him. In the right hands he could, with a dollop of good luck, be very successful. If we can keep him out of the public eye, away from being known about by these competing critters, he could be the surprise horse of the season. Even you do not know his pedigree, so who is he? There are six big races; win five and he will be worth a fortune as a stallion. Win the first two and all the intention will be on him, then the trouble off the course will begin. These big spenders will, if they can't buy him, will try to stop him, by any means they deem necessary. There aint any good old competition rules like, let the best horse win, no sirree, too much money and glory at stake, and you being an ex-Union Army officer will only inflame the situation. In their eyes, the Confederacy will rise again." It was this sort of situation that Syl left Trigg to ponder on. Syl and Geraldine were travelling on to Sacramento to meet up with an old buddy of his. The visit to the NY had just fitted in very conveniently, never having been so far west before. The plan was for Trigg to ponder on this situation, then Syl and Geraldine would stop off on their return and discuss the situation again. Trigg had found Syl a likeable feller. Adalia and Geraldine being of similar age, had struck up a likely friendship, and like Major Brandt had said, Syl had been a bit of a lad which clearly showed in his knowledge, he obviously knew the horse racing business from both sides. Having made that journey over the Rockies not many months ago, and knowing that Syl did not know any other folks in California, Trigg gave him a short letter of introduction to Henri, just as a stand-by if they experienced any problems in Sacramento. Geraldine had placed the letter in her valise, thanking him for the kindness. Being the type not to be cowed or scared off by these possibilities of roughness and maybe injury to The Varmint, Trigg and Adalia agreed on a plan to be discussed when Syl returned from California. Firstly, the horse would be registered and raced in her name to lessen Trigg's military experience being questioned. Secondly, the horse could be sent to Harry Clayson's Stable for its training, and if deemed good enough, raced in the first two races of Syl's choosing. Then, based on the situation after these two races, they could re-assess the situation. Trigg's forethought on Syl and Geraldine's visit to Sacramento was well founded – the train was stopped and robbed somewhere up in the Rockies. The robbers cleaned out the first class carriage, only leaving Geraldine with her small valise. When Geraldine showed the letter of introduction to the station manager in Sacramento, their troubles evaporated. "If Captain de Silva honours this letter, Miss Knowles, your troubles are over." A runner was sent to inform Henri and twenty minutes later, Geraldine was being introduced to the most handsome gent she had ever seen. Syl had gone stomping off in a temper when his buddy was not at the station to meet them, but was soon placated when, comfortably ensconced in Henri's coach and heading for a hotel owned by the Asmussen group, he was thanking Henri for his kindness. "So how are you involved with the Viking, Mr Knowles?" Syl explained how they had become involved, but was curious as to why Henri had referred to Major Hemmyng as the Viking." "That's who the family is descended from Sylvester, a long time ago, but seeing him, its easy to see the lineage, ain't it. Stay involved with him, you'll soon learn." During their short stay on the NY, Syl had sensed a frisson of toughness in Major Hemmyng. Granted he was very alert like good soldiers always were, with that ability to snap into action at the first sign of any danger. He'd met many like that in his time acquiring horses for the Union Army during the war, they were men not to be trifled with and their word was their bond; agree a deal and they honoured it. Nothing in writing, the deal sealed with a handshake, and they never forgot any part of the deal, especially the money. And this one was of Viking stock, was he? This comment by Henri tied all these instincts he felt about Major Trigg Hemmyng together. He needed to keep them sharply in mind when he returned to Cheyenne, and that letter of introduction was in keeping with that kind of man – foreseeing a problem and having the answer. They would have been in a very awkward situation in Sacramento. His buddy was found to be in a hospital somewhere in San Francisco, having been badly injured in an incident aboard a boat, and his lady friend was set to look after him. Not being bosom buddies, Syl curtailed his visit to Sacramento and headed back to Cheyenne. His first taste of California had not been good; he wanted to be heading East again. When they met on the NY, Syl was in full agreement with the plan to place the colt with Harry Clayson and begin to school him for the racing business, then after the first two races, reassess the situation and make a new plan. Trigg had discussed with Chas that he could travel with the colt, subject to Mr Clayson's approval, and Chas was agreeable. Syl thought it an excellent deal; truculent horses needed a friendly handler and Chas was certainly that. The next problem was how to get the colt down to Kentucky. Would he accept the train? if not they would have to trail him down there, tethered to a wagon. Following Henri's comment, Syl and Geraldine discussed their deal with Major and Mrs Hemmyng, as the registered owners, in fine detail. The gist of which was that the owner would be responsible for all Mr

Clayson's bills and expenses, and Syl would take a 10% cut of all the colt's winnings, and future stallion fees, if any. Geraldine was to put all this on paper so that there were no misunderstandings.

Syl then proposed that Major and Mrs Hemmyng visit Mr Clayson's establishment and satisfy themselves that the man and his son were fully capable of schooling the colt and that the stables and gallops were adequate for the purpose. Trigg agreed, arrange the date, we will meet you there. Hector had been nosying around in St Louis, and had learnt a lot that did not make very pleasant reading if you were a religious feller. Moll Letterson had backers for sure, and they were all so-called, fine, upstanding pillars of the local community. The names meant nothing to Trigg at this time, but he could start finding out himself what other aspects of the local community interested them. There were more than a few military types on the list, with Syl's recent statement of the old monied families being very supportive of the campaign to allow the Confederacy to rise again. This visit to meet Mr Harry Clayson and inspect his establishment could be very useful; he would use his ears and eyes carefully. When Syl and Gerald met them off the train, Trigg and Adalia had agreed an even more quiet visit. "Just introduce us as Trigg and Adalia Hemmyng, cattle ranchers from up in Wyoming, and if you think my accent will cause any comment, explain that I'm English." Fortunately, Syl had not given Harry and Henry the full details of this potential client. He was still slightly hesitant over the deal, and had only agreed the stabling and the training costs subject to this visit and the client deciding to proceed. He had talked at length about his assessment of the potential in the colt. So this visit was conducted on a meet and greet and see how it all went, type of visit. Syl was more than happy to proceed on this basis, taking it one step at a time suited him fine. With young Steiner trying his best to run wild, it looked a very sociable type of visit. Knowing the spread intimately, Syl had the coach run straight into where Harry had his office located, only to run headlong into a serious dispute between Harry and Henry Clayson and a fierce-looking older hombre. The appearance of the coach caused the shouting to cease but the anger in the faces was still there, with Henry waving and ushering this still mouthy hombre off the spread. "Sorry about that, Harry, shouldn't have come blundering straight in like that, I hope it was not too severe an argument."

"Don't worry yerself Syl, it weren't anything really, but he is an hornery bastard, won't let me get on with me life – I've had a belly full of soldiering, so has Henry." Syl introduced Trigg and Adalia, and young Stiener who Harry took a real liking to, adding that they were ranching up in Wyoming Territory. Henry immediately asked how he had found a potential race hoss up in Wyoming. Trigg explained exactly how they had come to own the mare that was already in foal when it came into his possession. The story amused them greatly. "Never heard a story like that afore – hope for all our sakes the colt is as good as Syl rates him, but he's a truculent lad I hear." "He is that, but we've never tried to break him; I've just let Chas, one of our Soshone lads ride him injun style, and its worked so far." A general discussion followed as they wandered around the stables and then were taken on a gig ride around the exercise and gallop areas. Trigg had no objections; the yard was clean and well kept, even though it was very busy with horses being exercised and then groomed, and all the stock looked in good condition. Harry had a book listing all his successes on the track and there were plenty of rosettes pinned to the walls. He had asked the questions, followed up the answers, met up with Syl, and now Harry, and he had no objections. If he did not make a decision soon, it could be too late for The Varmint – he was at the age that he needed him to decide – the longer he delayed, the less schooling time there was for him to be ready for the racing season. Trigg had a quiet word with Adalia. Was she happy with what she had seen and heard? She was – that was good enough for Trigg, they would give it a go, nothing ventured, nothing gained. If it didn't work, at least they had tried. That evening they agreed the deal with Syl and Geraldine. The Varmint boarded the train,without blinking an eyelid, on his trial run from Pine Bluffs to Julesberg, and behaved impeccably during the run there and back. It was like he was taking the rise out of them and behaving himself.

Trigg had Chas and Sam take him down to Kentucky, and he was delivered into Harry Clayson's yard without incident. Harry had a head lad called Jackie Sime, a very experienced, retired jocky who had the reputation of being able to ride anything, camels, llamas, elephants, but when he went too close to The Varmint, the horse turned on him and tried to bite him viciously. Not a little nip. It was a full-blooded nasty attempt to take a lump out of him. Jackie Sime took a hard look at Chas, then sent for a groom called Ruben. Chas and Sam had calmed The Varmint when Ruben appeared, a negro lad with a big curly mop of hair and a face seemingly set in a beaming smile, who was introduced to Chas. The Varmint stared at the pair of them, then uttered a little grunt. "Ruben, pat the horse down." Ruben eyed The Varmint, then just walked up to the horse and patted him slowly and easily, talking to him as he did. Not a flicker came from The Varmint. "You help Chas from now on, Ruben." Jackie Sime's experience had worked, and Sam breathed a sigh of relief. The Varmint was taking a lot of notice of his new surroundings, but Jackie Sime was not in a hurrying mind it was a slowly slowly routine – let the colt take it all in real steady, but it still didn't stop him wanting to fight. "He's a big'un and aggressive, but we'll get it out of him through exercise and hard work. You two lads are gonner be real busy." Sam had been told to stay down there until he was satisfied that The Varmint showed signs of settling into the stables. Having been there when the hoss was birthed, it was a thrill for Sam to be allowed to stay down at the stables and watch how things were done in a proper racing stable. It was an even bigger thrill when he saw the looks of delight on Harry,

Henry, and Syl's faces when they let Chas loose on The Varmint and checked their stopwatches. Sam had been staying with Syl, and it was a high old time that evening when Harry and Henry joined them for dinner. Sam had only good things to tell the boss when he got back to the NY.

The dispute that Trigg had witnessed when they were at the stables had started to interest him. Harry's comment that the ornery bastard wouldn't let him get on with his life,and both Harry and Henry had done with soldiering. So what was being asked of them that had caused Henry to as good as throw the hombre off their spread, and had caused a real hard argument to take place? He would let it stew for a while, not appear to be too interested. The winter had been its usual mix of sleeting rain, snow, followed by hard frost but had arrived early and gone early. Stiener's second birthday was a month away and their second child was due anytime soon. It was spring 71 and they were busy. Horse sales were very good, beef prices were still holding well, mutton was even better, the investors were still busy and trade was good for both the NY and the Roseberry. Roger had married and life was moving along nicely. In the breaks in the winter weather, he had made three outings with the rock sampling department that had been well worth the trouble, and the BLA had gained a clutch of contracts that were keeping them very busy. Geraldine had registered Adalia's racing colours and Syl was discussing with Harry a schedule of races in which to enter The Varmint, now officially called Theo the Varmint. The 'Theo' being added by Adalia because of how they had come to own the mare. Adalia saw it as a gift from God, – hence Theo, and it made a good name. This schedule of races had a few facets to it that Syl wanted to discuss in some detail; a meeting was needed to explain the ifs and buts involved in deciding things. With Adalia in no condition to travel, Trigg took Harry with him to Kentucky. Trigg was keen for both Harry and Joe to become familiar with the situation down there, and when better to learn the lay of the land and the fellers involved than a casual-type visit there. Adalia was very comfortably attended to by Helen, with Ragnar ready to be the errand boy, should he be required. How long he could keep this facade going, as just being a rancher, was difficult to assess; maybe it would be better to come clean and inform Harry and Henry, and watch their reaction closely. Having met them and spent time with them, he gauged it would not be big deal, and if he told them, all the better than them learning about his Union Army service from elsewhere. That could raise any number of problems.

Syl met them off he train and coached them round to his place. "We're dining out tonight, fellers, Geraldine's away visiting a cousin." Trigg introduced Harry, explaining their past military service together and why he was here. Trigg reckoned he needed someone down here to trust, and Syl could be that man, was he interested? Syl nodded agreement. He would not be involved in any rough stuff or gunplay, but the more important aspects like gathering information, the names and the addresses of the galoots, and being able to identify them and ensure that the likes of Harry had these galoots pointed out. Sylvester Knowles was beginning to study what he was getting into, but if that was what was required, then so be it – this rancher had saved him and his daughter from what could have been a very awkward situation in California. If anyone ever cribbed his dealings with this feller, he was simply managing his horse racing business, he had it in writing, didn't he? And this extra business added a tingle of excitement to his life, but he did not want Geraldine involved, be better if she concentrated on the racing, and hopefully any stud business, if this horse proved an attractive proposition. Syl talked all this through with Trigg and Harry to make sure they were all singing from the same hymn sheet. Syl led them just around the corner from his place to a recently-established Italian eatery that was proving very popular, and it was handy. Syl and Geraldine were already regular customers. Harry and Henry

Clayson arrived on time. Harry Pickering was introduced and Trigg made the Claysons aware of his military service and that he also owned a private detection business located in Omaha, that traded mainly in large company robbery and recovery of goods. His Union Army service had been up in Wyoming, dealing with the Sioux and the Cheyenne on the Oregon Trail, and then on the construction of the UP railroad from Omaha to Cheyenne, as was sergeant Harry Pickering's. Harry Clayson took a long hard look at this Englishman, then shrugged his shoulders and relaxed. He had felt there was something else about this feller, but he had come clean and he could take that. To Harry it was the future that concerned him. What was gone was gone. He was trying to get a good business developed for his son's future and this feller had just trusted him with the care of the best darned colt he had seen for years. If this colt produced his potential on the track, it could lift his and Henry's reputations sky high and be the making of them. There were many good trainers looking for that 'dream' colt, and they might just have been brought one, from of all places, the Wyoming territory. Harry Clayson stood up and offered Trigg his hand, looked him in the eye and smiled. "You'll do for me Major. You've been straight with us. We'll be straight with you." Syl relaxed; now there were no secrets they could talk more freely. "Let's enjoy our dinner, then we ought to go back to my place to discuss the racing matters that we are to resolve. It's too public here, too easy to be overheard." No sooner had Syl uttered the words than a group of women, a mother and her three daughters, it looked like, came hurrying into the eatery looking worried. "Did he see us? Have we dodged him, Meryl?" asked the mother. "He's coming this way, but he's looking around, we might have dodged him, Ma." Trigg and the fellers sat quietly watching but trying not to seem too concerned. Then the door burst open and this galoot roared with laughter when he espied the women. "You'll not shake me off that easy, Bonnie Patrick. I need some answers and quick, You ain't getting away this time."

The woman said she didn't have answers, she didn't know, never had known; go away and leave us alone in peace. But the galoot was not content and started demanding she tell him what he was sure she knew. The women and her daughters were looking very distressed when a feller appeared from the kitchen area and asked the man to quieten down and leave the eatery. The galoot turned and made to thump the man, but the man pulled a knife and stood prepared to fight the galoot. "Whoa, fellers, steady on," called Trigg as he and his sergeant stood up and drew their Colts. "I trust you are the owner? Do you want the galoot ejecting from your premises?" "Yes please, before I carve him, and get arrested for doing so." "You heard the owner, feller, get on yer way or get carried out – your choice." With two fellers levelling two Colts at him, the galoot knew he was beat, but he hurled some abuse and threats at the women as he beat a retreat. The owner feller followed him out and watched as he walked across the street and into a bar, then returned to them.

"Thank you, gents, what would you like to drink?" Then the mother came over and thanked them for their kind and gallant action. "We just beat these fellers from doing the same, lady. Anything for four pretty Ladies – hopefully we can now enjoy our dinners in peace." Some more people entered the eatery; their dinners arrived, and very tasty they were. Then they returned to Syl's place to resolve the racing schedule. "There's a lot of tactics involved, Major. There are six owner-breeders who compete fiercely for the distinction of owning the best colt. The first two races set the scene and depending on which colts win, this then brings the tactics into being. If the first two races are won by different colts, with different owners, the pot starts to boil. The target is to win as many races as possible, but not get beat by any of the other winners, so these owners then have to judge in which races their colts run or don't run in. It might be the owner thinks his colt won't handle a particular track, maybe the the bends are too tight, or the going gets too heavy or too fast or the straights are too long. Now, an owner who ain't bothered about all this malarky could run his horse and take what comes, but if his horse wins the first three races, one or more of the other owners might try to buy this colt and run his other colt against it knowing his colt will win, i.e. fix the race. If they can't buy the owner out, the colt just might suffer an injury, or worse, Its a no holds barred situation. They are determined to win." "So what yer saying, Syl, is that if The Varmint were to win the first two races, then either sell him to the highest bidder and take the profit, or I've got trouble. Unless I play their game and comply, I could end up with an injured horse, or worse." "Very possible, or if The Varmint did win the first races, we then ship him back to Wyoming and bring him back for the last race: the decider. All the other winners would likely be running, and if he wins that, he's then unbeaten. Run three times, won three times, it's how they think. He's unbeaten and could have beaten all the other contenders as well, it just depends on how these hombres decide to run their colts. The stud attraction is massive. Folks want their good fillies served by the top stallion. Might get a colt from the mating, thats when you really start to profit from the hoss"

"Syl, I appreciate the lecture on the possibilities, but first things first, Harry and Henry have to get him in tip-top condition. Jackie Sime has to school Chas in the black arts of what jockies will do to get a hoss and his jockey into trouble. I'm paying the bills, you make sure your things are being done. Any trouble you can't handle, wire me at the H&S. Your talk about these other owner-breeders was very interesting. I take it you know who these hombres are?" "Yes, we do, you saw one when you came down to view the stables, and he was one of the more pleasant of them, if you could call him pleasant The others think they own everything they touch, and are quick to you let yer know your place." Henry Clayson did not mince his words, and his father was not happy at his son's unexpected contribution.

Trigg liked that – the son had some spirit and his own opinion of these hombres. Trigg had also noticed that Henry was half out of his seat when the bit of trouble occurred earlier, only his father's hand on his shoulder kept him down. "So, Syl, we'll agree that we go for the first two races all out, then we'll meet again and see what the situation is then. As I've said before, I ain't selling The Varmint, so if you get any offers to buy the colt, don't dismiss them, say you'll discuss them with the owner. We ain't gonner be disrespectful or rude are we? Let's see who makes the offer. We will conduct ourselves correctly and not give any reason for them to be angered in any way. We are gonner be the good guys. If the refusal angers them, then that is their problem, not ours. A list of these owner-breeders would be useful, Syl. They might choose to approach the owner directly, so as I usually say, forewarned is forearmed. "Are we all agreed gents? Any one want to discuss any other matters? No, well I think we ought to drink a toast to The Varmint, and another one to a successful and rewarding horse racing association." They all raised their glasses, well topped up with Syl's finest French brandy. The following morning was spent at the stables, giving Harry a look at where it was located and how the establishment was laid out. They had a chat with Jackie Sime and were introduced to Ruben. Henry basically ran the stables with his pa doing a skipper's job of deciding the route and keeping the boat on course. Henry's energy and his pa's experience.

As they were about to leave, a hansom came hurrying in carrying the four women who had been in the eatery the night before. "I'm wanting to buy a filly and Mr Clayson was recommended to me as a very good dealer and trainer, so here we are." "Well, Mr Clayson's son Henry is over there, and this gent is Mr Sylvester Knowles; he could be your racing manager." "Is he any good? I wasn't given his name." "I hope so, I've just signed up with him to be mine." Mrs Bonnie Patrick and her three daughters were in a much pleasanter mood than had been the case last night. "I was so upset and frightened last night, I don't think I thanked you enough for your gallant assistance." "Don't give it another thought, ma'am. You go and buy yourself a filly. We may meet up again at a race meeting sometime. Good luck with your choosing." Trigg and Harry's bags were on Syl's rig. They were cutting it close with the train times, and he had put Syl in line for another client. Then he saw the hansom was still waiting. "Syl, we'll use the hansom, you look after the lady. I'll be in touch." Trigg and Harry used bags that accommodated a Henry rifle. They were soon transferred and it was a quick handshake and away they went. "Be interesting, Harry, when The Varmint starts racing. It's a whole different carry-on down there compared to Cheyenne, ain't it. Hopefully we can sit tight and enjoy the ride." "There ain't nothing as strange as folk, is there? Joe will be itching to get down there and have a look-see. I wonder if that Rubin ever stops smiling; probably the same when he's fast asleep and snoring. Ain't surprising that The Varmint took to him, is it, boss?" "Bit of good luck that. Makes it a lot easier for Chas, having someone the hoss seems to like; real handy that will be." Syl sent the letter containing the other owner-breeders names. Trigg made a copy and sent it to Tom Benson, requesting that Hector go have a mosey around down there and see what he could learn. Trigg had nothing but good news for Adalia. The colt had settled in well, had a new groom that he liked, a Negro who never stopped smiling, Chas was being schooled in the art of being a good jockey, and in the black arts of the business, that rogue jockies employed to interfere with other jockies or the running of a horse. It was not unknown for these rogues to kick a jockey off a horse, lash his whip across a hoss's face and eyes, or another jockey's face. Jackie Sime, the head lad and a very experienced racing jockey was teaching Chas what he could expect. Henry Clayson had up lined a good few rides for Chas, to get him well acquainted to racetrack riding and he was confident that Chas had the determination and the physical toughness to do well as a jockey. The only remaining uncertainty was The Varmint himself. He was still showing that desire to fight other horses. It was only occasionally now he was being exercised more often and harder, but it was still there. The hope was that with the same jockey, who knew him well, and Jackie Sime's experience with pre-race routines, they could keep him away from the other runners, shelter him from any attempt to unsettle him before the flag dropped, then it was up to him and Chas to negotiate the race. All they could do now was carry on with their normal business and wait for The Varmint's first race. Trigg read the information that Hector had gleaned in Laramie City with great admiration. This feller was very, very competent. Even on the descriptions that Herbie had given on the two galoots who had robbed him of the wagon. Hector had found out who they were; two brothers in fact who were now scratting around for work since Al Haller had been arrested. Whilst Hector was in Laramie City, and Trigg and Harry had been down in Kentucky, Trigg had told Joe and Andy to return to Logger's family spread that the army still had under its control. His thinking was that once the initial hoo-ha had died down, others that may be connected might come looking, knowing that there could be some loot for the taking. The lieutenant had taken notice of Trigg's advice and kept his soldiers well out of sight so that any looters would not be alerted, and they'd come onto the spread thinking it had now been vacated. Three more gangs had come looking and been arrested as they tried to break into the adits, and others had arrived but when nobody could be found, had moved off, and the lieutenant had been smart enough to let them go and not break his cover. The lieutenant had readily given Joe the names of these galoots, and even a look at the last gang that he had arrested and bound and gagged awaiting armed transfer into Fort Sandars. There had been more visitors than expected to this spread and its mining tunnels. Trigg contacted the mining engineer who Roland Simons had become aware of through his personal contacts. After a preliminary meeting and discussion in the H&S office, Trigg and Mr Sven Diereson had found enough common ground to create a suitable basis for a working relationship. The mining business was a very widely scattered and haphazard industry, with anything from a one-man-band to a large conglomerate group, and all were ornery, obstinate and determined galoots to do deals with. Trigg had learnt that it needed a knowledgeable miner's experience just to get them listening, never mind talking, and his experience of dealing with these galoots told him that he would be much better off having a creditable mining associate. Like this Logger's family spread situation, you could nab the robbers, but then the hard part began, rooting about looking for the loot in these old mining tunnels. With his dogs, he was becoming very handy at finding loot stashed in open bad land and such, but as already experienced, there were plenty of these old, worked-out adits that were used to secrete stolen goods. Now starting with Logger's family spread, he was determined to investigate these worked out mines more thoroughly. Sven Diereson had spent all his life mining, but was now feeling the effects of all that hard work and struggle; this was a deal that appealed to him – his mining experience and Major Trigg Hemmyng's experience in detecting which old mines were being used to hide the loot away. The clincher for Sven Diereson was that this Major had the men with the ability to ensure that the recovered loot was kept safe and secure. They had agreed a trial run, to see if this sort of association would work, and this Logger's family spread was to be the test. The army would leave a four-man squad of Infantry troops to guard the place, and Sven Diereson could take a team into the mine and assess the state of the tunnel propping and look for, and if found, excavate any signs of buried loot. The deal between Trigg and Sven was a fifty-fifty split after all the expenditure had been covered. There would be bits and pieces to agree, this was the trial run, but the only way to find out if such an association was viable was to get one done, and then decide. Sven Diereson arrived at the H&S offices with his three-man team of miners. Trigg placed Joe Kennedy in charge of this operation and all the tackle and tools needed were loaded into a wagon. A quick meeting ensued at which the operation was discussed and agreed and Joe, assisted by Andy, guided the miners across to the Logger's spread and the investigation of the tunnels was began.

Two days later Adalia gave birth to another son. Mother and baby were both healthy and well. Trigg had another son, to be called Bernard Auguste, after his maternal grandfather. A week later he received Syl's letter stating the dates and venues of The Varmint's first two races; the first was not for a month. Should be just enough time for Adalia to rest and recover and be ready for the travel down to Kentucky. Chas would be having a steady schedule of other rides in lesser races to get him into the feel of competitive racing. This horse racing business was slotting nicely into place, but Trigg was very aware that this could be the calm before the storm. Syl's warning of the lengths to which some of these other owner-breeders could go was still very much in his memory, but all that would only depend on The Varmint being good enough to win these first two races. A lot of things had to go right for that to become a reality, but nothing had gone wrong yet; would their good fortune hold steady? In eight weeks' time they would know. Sven Diereson and his miners found plenty of well-hidden loot. This first trial for the new association had got off to a very profitable start. Trigg had a long list of mines reaching back into his time at Fort Laramie, where they suspected illegal ventures were being based, or operated from, but the neccessity to pursue other more urgent operations had meant they had had to move on - orders were orders, reports had to be investigated but now that was not the case. Some of these old workings could be revisited, and now he had an associate who knew how to investigate these often perilous tunnels in some safety. Just as important, the growth in new mines was gearing up; other opportunities would present themselves as some of these new mines failed and other galoots used them for secreting their ill-gotten gains. It was a business in which he was very interested as it could be operated on a similar routine to the rock sampling jaunts. Being self-financing and not requiring any large outlay, it could simply mosey along to suit Sven and his miners. Trigg would nominate the mines to be investigated, and then Sven would carry out the work. A nice steady routine. If any more urgent investigations needed carrying out, he would just re-organise the schedule accordingly. The NY and the Roseberry were running sweetly under Roger and Will's steady control, and Jake had the H&S bubbling along nicely. Ragnar was entrusted with the kitty that had been gathered for the wager to be placed on The Varmint to win his race.

The ornery critter had become the talk of the ranch and the H&S, even Herbie and Gordie Brunner had wopped their $10 apiece into the kitty, such was the interest in how the colt would run. It was not would he win, it was by how much. Race day dawned damp and got wetter. Chas was instructed to keep out of any bunching, keep wide with plenty of room for The Varmint to stretch his long legs when it came to the final dash. Trigg viewed the race through his telescope and Chas had the colt positioned exactly as instructed, but coming round the bend into the final straight two other colts hugging the rails appeared to collide and push across causing a barging match to take place. Trigg could see the whips being flailed in the melee, but the pink and light blue striped colours came steadily on and on and on, as smooth as the silk shirt, the ornery critter got his head in front and refused to be beat. Trigg had let the telescope drop as he looked at Ragnar then at Adalia then back, as The Varmint breasted the tape a length ahead of the field. That darned ornery critter had gone and won. All the speculating, all the hopes and he had gone and done it, and by the way he was conducting himself now, he had done it for himself. The crowd were cheering and he was snorting back at them, which made them cheer even louder, then he reared up and threw his front legs at them causing them to cheer even louder. The critter was showing off and the crowd were screaming encouragement. Then he adopted a posture that seemed to say, who did yer think would win? And all the time Chas was sat tight on him, enjoying all the cheering, and why not, he had ridden exactly as instructed. Ruben had slipped the bridle on and was patting him down. A groom had a pail of water ready for him to drink, but The Varmint was still posturing to the crowd when Henry Clayson arrived to get the colt back into the paddock, and unsaddled. Trigg stood back and let Adalia accept all the congratulations, with Geraldine making the introductions of the new lady owner to the more regular patrons. He had one eye on Harry Clayson and Syl as they had their heads together in a delighted way but also looking like a shade of concern. One race won. Not a runaway victory, but The Varmint had won, and those other owners' highly valued colts had been beaten. The fact that their colts may have been more severely baulked by the interference that had occurred would not matter, they had been beaten. The result had been declared and the wagers were being honoured.

Trigg stayed close to Adalia and smiled a lot as Geraldine led them into the unsaddling enclosure, then hoisted young Stiener up in his arms as The Varmint was led into much applause. He stood back as Adalia received the winner's trophy and rosette, then as Harry received the trainer's trophy, and Chas the jockey's prize, all the while the pair of them clapping vigorously as the awards were announced. Ragnar, being the cagey old dog he was, had spread the kitty money about, and was now busy collecting the winnings and bringing each wedge of money for safekeeping to his grandson – so things were a shade hectic, to say the least, but it was a hell of an hour before the situation had settled down again. Trigg had retained responsibility for his ever-energetic son, but he noticed that the young lady who had been very prominent in the party, making the presentation awards, was now closely in attendance with Geraldine and Adalia as many of the more sedate older race patrons were still being introduced to Adalia, this new unknown lady owner. Harry and Henry had done a very efficient job in keeping The Varmint's profile low key, only saying that the colt had talent but were not sure how he would react on the course when the time came, and the jockey the same. But now, it was not so much that the colt had won in a unsatisfactorily run race, but that the colt had wowed the crowd as well. Maybe next time he could be totally the opposite; truculent horses could be like that, good one day, not interested the next time they ran. That was the line of answers Harry and Henry gave to the newspaper reporters. The NY and the H&S were buzzing when Ragnar shared out the winnings, and although Trigg was well pleased for them all, his natural reserve began to rankle him. He did not like publicity, knew it was nonsense really, but that's how he was. All this 'hiding your light under a bushel' type of talk made sense to him; he reckoned it gave him the advantage when he wanted to do something. It was his business and nobody else's. Maybe getting into this horse racing business had been a wrong move and if any of these Jonny Rebs made him a good offer for the Varmint, could be a better deal if he sold out. Take a quick profit and stick to what he knew. But the training fees and the entry fees for this second race had been paid, so see the deal through that had been agreed. Adalia really liked the colt, but she had another baby as her priority, and being the excellent mother she was, a bag full of dollars was likely to easily offset the sale of the colt.

One thing led to another with Sven Diereson's finds on Logger's spread that resulted in the army issuing arrest-reward notices for six hombres. Trigg had these passed on to the BLA; it was work that Enoch and Hector were very effective in. With this work and the now routine work with rustlers on the NY, the time was on them quickly for the train ride down to Kentucky for The Varmint's second race. Adalia chose not to attend; she was not feeling up to the journey and preferred to stay at home with the boys. This turned out to be a fortuitous decision as the situation that greeted Trigg when he stepped off the train was, from a racing situation, very disagreeable. Syl had obtained the entry list for The Varmint's race and it was very plain to any experienced racegoer that mischief was afoot. Harry Clayson was livid. There were four entries in the race that were simply being used to provoke a deliberate attempt at foul tactics. It was not the horses. It was the jockeys being employed to ride these horses. Each one of these jockeys had been guilty of actions causing other jockeys or horses to be baulked, blocked or the jockeys unsaddled during a race, causing disqualification. Harry had raged at the race stewards for allowing these jockeys to be allowed to ride, but these jockeys had all served their suspensions and were now free to be employed to ride. It was very obvious that following the first race, tactics would be employed that were intended to stop the winner of the first race winning the next race. Syl's assessment of the tactics was being proven true, but a race earlier than even he thought. A discussion with Syl and Harry and Henry Clayson was quickly entered into as to what could be done, legally, to negate this tactic. The outcome was that very little, legally, was able to be done. There was no proof that any foul tactics were intended, no regulations had been breached, but experience of other similar occurrences strongly indicated that dirty deeds were being planned. Syl and Harry were adamant, someone was out to prevent The Varmint winning this race, any way they could, and this tactic was the only obvious sign; there may be other less visible attempts as well. Harry Clayson was already making arrangements to transfer The Varmint to another stable nearer to the next racetrack under cover of darkness this evening, where they could mount a twenty four-hour guard. Trigg arriving early, with Scobie and GG was more than welcome. With Adalia not travelling, Trigg, Harry, Sam, Scobie and GG had travelled overnight, a fortunate decision as it now gave them most of Friday to do something about this intended mischief, but what plan could they devise? GG muttered something in Shoshone to Scobie, that had Scobie beaming brightly. "Boss, a trick we Shoshone lads were learnt was that when the Sioux and the Cheyenne came stealing from us, it was our job to daub their ponies' balls and arseholes with a lotion that caused them great irritation and made them unrideable for half an hour or so, until the lotion had been washed off. We used the same paste that we use for curing bad cuts, but we mixed some nettle sting and crab rash flower seed into it and it don't half make a strong stinging paste; yer can't see it, but it's real strong." Now Trigg was beaming – four rogue jockeys, get their hosses lathered up in this lotion and they wouldn't be running far. If this was the only mischief they were planning, they now had an answer. "Can you get some of this lotion made up down here, Scobie?" "I reckon so. We'll have a scout round in the woods and see what we can find." "You go and get busy, I've an idea how we can get it applied." There were plenty of little wooded areas on the racing stables' land so Scobie and GG were on private property and not likely to cause any consternation among the locals. Whilst they were busy finding the wild flowers and weeds and seeds that were the ingredients required, Trigg took Sam and Harry Pickering to one side to discuss his plan to get these hosses well pasted up. Harry and Henry Clayson had been excused from this discussion. As the official owners of this racing stables it might be prudent that they were not party to his plan. If there were repercussions, then they were in the clear. What they didn't know, they couldn't lie about, and anyway, they would be nowhere near when the plan was put into operation. Trigg's plan was that this irritating paste needed to be applied close to the start of the race, but a diversion tactic was needed to give the paste time to take effect. Some of those Chinese jumping crackers would be needed to cause some mayhem at the start – might even spook a horse or two into galloping off and having to be retrieved. As there were twenty two colts in this race, and colts weren't the most docile of hosses, were they, if one or two did get spooked, so what? The simple plan was that as the colts arrived at the starting post, a few Chinese jumping crackers would be set off, in a bag, and then dropped around the start line to cause some nuisance.

Whilst this was going on, him and Scobie, knowing the numbers of the hosses carrying the four rogue jockeys, would offer assistance to the jockeys in calming their mounts. Trigg would engage the jockey whilst Scobie applied the colourless paste at the rear. A good handful liberally applied and then quickly move on to the next one. It was a simple plan that needed a swift, determined swoop and be gone. They weren't hurting the horse, nothing would be visible, just that the hosses would not be interested in racing. Harry Pickering and Sam were all in favour, one bad intention would be negated by a simple ruse. Now they needed some jumping crackers and two leather bags. Jackie Sime, Chas and Ruben were told of the ruse so that they understood and knew why it was being done, as they would be close by. Friday was spent acquiring the materials and refining the plan. At 19.00 hrs that evening the wind started blowing hard, and the local prediction was that it would be worse the following day, even thunder was likely. The more diversions the better, as long as they could get to those four horses, that was all he needed. The following morning, he told Syl of his intended ruse. It would be prudent to let Syl in on the plan as he would be near to Harry Clayson and could keep him and Henry in check if any ruptions were created up near the finishing line. Also, he needed Syl and Geraldine to be ready to collect the trophy, if The Varmint were to win again. With this new situation, he wanted to stay out of the paddock area; the longer he was anonymous, the safer and stronger he felt. He wanted to get this race over and done with, win or lose, but he wasn't gonner be cheated out of the win, so stay obscure and he felt stronger. Syl was in full agreement with his plan and very ready to act as a shield to ensure that neither of the Claysons did or said anything that might cause them trouble. "You give them a belting, Major, I'll keep the Clayson's out of trouble. It looks like today is going to be very eventful, even the weather seems to be looking for a fight." The borrowed wagon was anchored up just beyond the start line well before the racing started. Trigg and his men snuck down in the back nice and cosy out of the winds and the intermittent rain that came slanting down. They were interested in only one race. Scobie mixed his paste, adding some extra nettle-pus in for good measure. The weather kept many away but there were still plenty to watch the start as Harry and Sam made their way out and mingled with the watchers as the starter arrived and began to bark his orders as the horses and jockeys and their handlers arrived.

Dressed in their borrowed stable coats, Trigg and Scobie pulled the old battered trail hats hard down and stepped off the buckboard. That was the signal for Harry and Sam to mosey around and start slipping a few lit crackers on to the ground then move on sharpish before the crackers erupted into action. As they began, the wind brought a tree bough crashing down, causing extra consternation, and the desired effect on the colts. Jackie Sime had kept The Varmint well back knowing what was coming, then he watched as Major Hemmyng and Scobie flitted about in between the horses. Then he heard the starter hollering for the hosses to be brought into line, quick, he weren't telling em again – but all of a sudden two hosses began trying to buck their jockeys off, and he saw the starter looking wild-eyed and raging. He knew this starter was a stickler to get his races started bang on time. Then the flag started to fall; the race was on. "Get gone, Chas, keep him wide." and he smacked The Varmint's rump good and hard. Jackie Sime stood and grinned as he saw two jockeys bucked off and sprawled out on the turf. "Couldn't happen to two more deserving galoots." Then his eyes caught sight of two more hosses crashing through the running rail and heading for the fishing hole in the creek down the hill. "Get in here, you two, it's gonner hail it down soon." Jackie Sime and Ruben were given a pull up into the wagon and handed a bottle of beer, then they settled down and joined in with the belly laugh that was being enjoyed by the others, as Sam trundled the wagon away from the race track. Jackie Sime had given The Varmint a flyer and he was never headed – nearly was, but he fought his way up the rise and held two colts off to win by a length, again. Harry Clayson stared in disbelief at his son and Syl scratched his head in bewilderment. All three had been resigned to not winning, maybe even not finishing, but now Syl and Geraldine were having to collect the silverware. The crowd were hootin' and a hollering his name, but there were some very grim-faced hombres drowning their sorrows. Syl collected the trophy, and he saw the hatred in their eyes, and knew this involvement was just beginning, or already over, and only one man could decide which it was. And where was he now? Syl was beginning to remember his conversation with Capt. Henri Watson de Silva, and that comment that was made about him being a Viking, stay involved and you'll learn.

When Syl and Geraldine boarded the train for the one-hour journey home, the Major, Harry and Sam were already aboard. They had been coached to the station back and boarded the train there. "We did our work and high-tailed it, Syl, nothing more we could do and I didn't see any point in hanging around. We heard the crowd roaring his name; good race was it?" "He refused to be beat, again, just dug in and battled his way over the line first." Having been able to get loaded up quickly and back to his stables, they were away from the hullaballoo of the speculation of what had caused the ruptions that was going on back at the racetrack. Harry Clayson was well pleased to be back on his spread, and even more delighted with the day's results and Syl's explanation of how these rogue jockeys had been thwarted. The horses back in the stables, they all went out for dinner again in Syl and Geraldine's favourite eatery and celebrated The Varmint's second victory and the ruse that had been worked to ease the colt's run. But Harry and Syl knew that those who planned for those four rogue jockeys to be employed, and had been thwarted, would be making more plans to get even, or worse. It was a case of enjoy tonight and be ready for the next attempt at stopping the Varmint from winning again, and next time it could be real nasty. "Two races, two wins. It is getting darned serious now, and those galoots will be fuming and very determined, and to hell with the consequences. They know the right people in power, to deflect any suspicion from themselves and set up some scapegoat to take the blame, and they won't hesitate to try and impose some revenge on us, irrespective of whether or not we are to blame. The Varmint is in our control and they want him stopped from winning again." Harry Clayson had thoroughly enjoyed the day, and knew it was a party pooper of a comment, but he knew it was true and wanted everybody present to fully realise what they were facing. "You won't sell the Varmint, so we will have a big fight on our hands. Where do we go from here, Major? Any more good suggestions? That last ruse was a belter." "Not yet, Harry, but I agree. That ruse was only good fun really, nobody got really hurt, not even the hosses, and that will annoy them even more. We'll have to agree a plan. Do we run The Varmint again soon, or let him rest up a while?"

My preference is to run again soon, while he is fit and raring to go. If he wins again, then we get him well away, back to Wyoming if necessary, and keep him off the track and see how the other races turn out. It could be that after this next race, if The Varmint wins again, he will have beat all the other more fancied colts, and we won't need to run him anymore. He's beaten them all, ain't he?" One more race. " If we put out rumours he is being rested, then we can enter him at the latest possible time in his next race. Syl and Harry can decide which race it is. I will take him back up to the NY out of harm's way, and out of Harry and Henry's responsibility." This strategy soon proved to be fully justified as the Claysons' stables were attacked and a stableblock was fired. One arsonist was shot dead, another wounded, and both were known to be in the employ of Hank Johnson Jones. The pot was beginning to boil over, these Confederacy 'will rise again jokers' had broken cover. Not surprisingly, no further action was taken by the local lawmen. Insufficient evidence was stated as the official reason. But Major Trigg Hemmyng knew now exactly what he was up against, and was even more determined to overcome this situation and see The Varmint prove his ability. And he didn't wait long. While this arson attack was still very fresh in everyone's memory, he instructed Syl to enter The Varmint in the next counting race, making the entry at the last possible moment, as planned. He had read the situation spot on as regards these other owners. They had obviously convinced themselves that The Varmint would not contest this next race, and had entered their colts thinking that one of their colts would win this race. Then, when the hullabaloo over the arson attempt had died down, they would try again to dispose of this interloper's colt once and forever, and to hell with what anyone thought, as no evidence would be connected to them next time. They could then 'arrange' the last two counting races, divvy up the winnings and stud fees, and everyone else could like or lump it, they were sure they could placate, or buy out, any serious complaints. The late entry flat-footed them. The Varmint was snook in, extremely well guarded and the Happening Man's good fortune worked again. The race was run on a bone hard track, two horses collided and went down as they rounded the final bend, leaving the Varmint, being ridden in his usual wide line, to gallop in and win easing up.

The horse was quickly through the unsaddling and post-race niceties and away from the track. One bullet was all it would have taken but it never came. The bullet for The Varmint never came but plenty of other threats and 'promises' were made in the succeeding days. Trigg Hemmyng knew his luck could change, but that was life, and if they were that determined they would have to look for him on his turf, not on theirs. He couldn't stop them trying, but they would pay dearly. This whole 'Confederacy will rise again' malarkey was fascinating him more and more. He had read the newspaper articles and the numerous privately printed reports on the situation that had unfolded after the Civil War had ended. Then his involvement with the BLA and its contracts down in the south had all whetted his curiousity even more. Now this business with the horse racing had brought it all a lot closer. Maybe there was a lot more truth in the allegations than at first it appeared. Maybe, just maybe, there were stashes of gold and other precious metals, and coins. Hector and Enoch had beavered away down there and found plenty of material that was worthy of investigating further, but first, as was his original intention in getting into the horse racing business, was the stud value of The Varmint. That would be his first intention, the other interest could be investigated later. Major Trigg Hemmyng talked long and hard to himself over this situation that he was now in with the Varmint. He was loathe to cut and run but he convinced himself that was his only safe option. If he persisted in stabling the horse, with the Claysons and another attempt was made to injure the critter, maybe cripple him or worse, then he would only have himself to blame. The horse's ability had opened up a whole nest of vipers, and his best option for all concerned was to remove the focus of this contention and have a re-think, and at least he would still have The Varmint safe and well. Trigg met with Syl and the Claysons and stated his reasons for withdrawing the horse. He stood firm and, although appreciating their arguments for continuing, he was not for attracting any more trouble to the stables or to Harry and Henry. They had a business to run and many other clients to maintain.

Even though the Claysons had 'lost' the horse from their yard, they were still big supporters of the horse and willingly gave their honest advice for his future development.

Trigg had a separate discussion with Syl. He reiterated his reluctance to withdraw the horse, but confided in Syl that his decision was tied in with his other business interests that were steadily increasing in this area. It was Syl who then suggested that Conrad Brandt could be more than useful in any future use of The Varmint in a breeding programme, with his extensive spread of contacts amongst the racing fraternity. Conrad Brandt! Maybe Syl had identified the answer to Trigg's dilemma, that of how to get The Varmint involved in a worthwhile stud programme. When they met, Conrad Brandt expressed little surprise at the situation that Trigg had become embroiled in. He had kept himself well informed of the situation in Kentucky and had been close to contacting Major Hemmyng to offer his advice, having already met him previously and knowing Major Hemmyng was new to the horse racing business. Also, he knew that Major Hemmyng, having spent his military service in the Northern Territory, had no experience in Confederate politics and sympathies, a situation that he shared with most of the US Congress, but that was another story. Yes, he could locate owners interested in having their talented fillies covered by a proven race winner. A deal between the two-ex soldiers was not difficult to agree. Trigg wanted The Varmint looked after correctly and Conrad Brandt's main interest in life now was horse racing and breeding. He had a good stable set up, erected for when he found a promising colt, and where he would have stabled The Varmint if he had been successful in his efforts to buy him the first time the two of them had met. Now circumstances had brought them back together in a deal that was very suitable to both parties.

There was nothing in writing, only each other's verbal agreement and a handshake. Trigg had The Varmint transported to Conrad Brandt's stables, and Chas and Ruben moved in as well. Having his regular groom and exercise rider was considered vital with a horse as potentially truculent as The Varmint was. This deal was mainly based on a stud programme, but more racing had not been ruled out with The Varmint being so fit and capable of competing at distances from a mile and a quarter upwards. Big, fit horses like him often turned into 'stayers' as they matured, and being successful at these distances also lifted his stud value.

The whole reason for this change was well understood and accepted, and it only spurred people on to ensure that no stone was left unturned in the battle to overcome the creators of this situation. With The Varmint's wellbeing resolved very satisfactorily, Trigg now took to his intention to find out more about these 'old money families' that seemed to hold power in these southern states. He had cut and run to give the impression that they had scared him away, but the opposite was the real reason. He wanted anything of his well away from them and out of harm's way. True, nothing was totally safe, but when he was ready to get back at them, then he would have very much more of a free rein and be flexible. Hector and Enoch had nosied around and found plenty of interest that the BLA could use. That would be his official business interest. His unofficial personal interest could be intertwined but kept well obscure from any prying eyes. But like he always preferred, that could wait awhile, just let the situation fade from folks' memories. The Varmint was now in good hands and would be enjoying a stud career, not even a ornery critter like him could complain, but he just might! When Trigg next met with Roger, all the talk was of the Wyoming Stock Growers' Association coming into being. As he had previously stated, having such an association made plenty of sense, if one was able to be made to work at all. There were a lot of political and practical problems to resolve, and his army experience told him that self-made ranchers, usually from the profits of rustling, were not too keen on having to comply with regulations of any sort, even ones they may have been involved in drawing up in the first place. What might have seemed a good idea six months ago, could be just the opposite in practice and they would not be slow in ignoring the regulations if it suited them. Ranchers only liked what suited them. "Like I said before, Roger, you are in for some very lively meetings, the minutes of which, if there are any, will make compulsive reading. Please make sure I see any copies." The other very interesting point of intent that he was made aware of by one of his former army colleagues was that George Armstrong Custer, nobody was quite sure of his army rank now, since he had been thrown out of the army in disgrace, was rumoured to be attached to a scientific survey of the Black Hills of Dakota, sacred homeland of the Lakota, known commonly as the Sioux Indian Nation and main ally of the Cheyenne Indian Nation. It was now the summer of '73 and the survey was scheduled for the spring of '74. "If Custer is involved, it will be an army-led survey first and foremost, and if the Redskins take offence, there will be real trouble. If the redskins stay hidden and choose not to confront the survey, then depending on what is found, it will have a big outcome on what happens after. Needless to say, if gold is found, then it will be chaos, army or no army. Most people thought the same – finding gold would cause a stampede of miners that would swamp any attempt to control it. It had been that way in the other gold finds and in this one the Union Pacific Railroad would pour gold prospectors in even faster than before. That was its business but it would only make the whole situation a lot worse. Trigg Hemmyng knew that whatever resulted out of this scientific survey, he would have to make the best of it; nothing he could do would have any effect and he would have enough on looking after what he already had. And he would not be found wanting. Gold was 'discovered' in the Black Hills and the expected stampede of miners, prospectors, and all the associated jumble of saloon-keepers, gamblers, and whorehouse operators, descended on a place that became known as Deadwood. Such was the rapidity of its development that the city of Cheyenne and the Territorial Legislature combined to construct a stagecoach route of over three hundred miles in length to ensure that Cheyenne became the stopping point on the Union Pacific Railroad for all the traffic both to and from the Deadwood goldfields. Trigg Hemmyng rubbed his hands in glee. Every cloud had a silver lining, maybe even a golden lining in this case. He foresaw a multitude of stage and wagon robberies, just the business that would provide him with a host of 'rock-sampling' opportunities.

Some men drank and gambled, others went fishing or hunting, even whoring. His favourite past-time was 'rock sampling', and the more he practised the better him and his team became.

But that was sometime in the not too distant future, and there were plenty of other 'finds' to be made in the near future

The NY and the Roseberry were continuing to enjoy good business with the investors' group. The BLA was also making good progress and the H&S thriving, business was good. The only disappointment had been the situation concerning The Varmint. True, it could have been much worse, but given a fair crack of the whip, it could have been much better, but those nasty old Johnny Rebs were not for giving folks a fair run.

Another aspect of the racing scene that had taken his interest was that of how the womenfolk had come together and become very friendly. Seemingly with no regard to their social backgrounds. They had, by the correspondence that Adalia had received following his sudden withdrawal of the Varmint, had become genuinely friendly. Having read these letters, Trigg had no doubt that matters other than racing and race horses formed a bigger part of their interest.

Geraldine, with her fuller involvement with her pa, had been the original focal point for making these introductions and she had obviously been very lucky or had been very astute in her choices. Racing, being like it was, was very much a man's business, but these ladies had put the racing to one side and had talked plenty on the subjects that were of more interest to themselves.

The letter that really intrigued Trigg was from the lady that he had never actually been introduced to, but he had learned from Syl, was the daughter of the hombre who they had witnessed having a very serious, near-on fisticuffs dispute with Harry and Henry Clayson in their stables that time. He had seen her many times, always seemingly on her own, apart from the time she spent with the other women whilst the races were run and in the subsequent period when racing matters were attended to. Adalia's additional information regarding this lady's personal situation only caused him to ponder her situation more.

Her father was an avid supporter of the 'Confederacy will rise again' and didn't care who knew it. His three sons had perished in the war and the many choices of a suitable would-be husband had been presented to her – all sons of other supporters of the cause – but she had refused them all point blank. The man she had wanted to marry had gone missing shortly after her father had been informed. Only the care of her ailing mother kept her from running away from home, a threat her father had replied to by vowing to find her and dispose of any man that was with her. It was a bleak situation but one that she had tolerated by choosing to accompany her father to the races, a sport she enjoyed and which allowed her to meet similar like minded people, although always under her father or one of his croney's, unrelenting scrutiny.

"It's no wonder she enjoys her days at the races if she is mired in a situation like that in her home life. We have to count our blessings' ain't we, Leibling?"

Three days later, a letter arrived from Syl describing how

Mrs Bonnie Patrick and her three daughters had been subjected to another, more serious, physical assault by the same galoot who had threatened them in the Italian eatery the night himself and Harry Pickering had intervened in the dispute.

Mrs Patrick had bought two fillies and Syl was now acting as her racing adviser along with Harry and Henry Clayson as her trainers. Syl, knowing Trigg had the BLA, had written to him, without her knowledge, on the off-chance that he might be able to assist these women, whom Syl rated as very decent and pleasant folk but in a nasty situation.

The problem that was causing the trouble for Mrs Bonnie Patrick had originated around the time just before the Confederates had surrendered. It involved missing Confederate money that the rough galoot was convinced Mrs Patrick knew the whereabouts of – where her late husband, Clancy Patrick, an army captain, had secreted the loot. Syl was of the opinion that she was telling the truth when she swore she had no idea of where the loot was, but the galoot was having none of that. The local law had investigated this latest assault but it seemed to be a stand-off, no-one had been brought to book and the situation was still the same. Until someone had made a decisive move one way or the other, further assaults or even worse were very likely.

With these two situations arising very close together, Trigg decided to let Hector and Enoch have another mosey around, just the usual eyes and ears, read the local papers and hang about in the local saloons, where everybody had an opinion.

Tom Benson had other business ongoing in the area that could more than likely be useful to this operation, and no effort would be spared in making use of any information that came to light. Tom's contacts in the Pinkerton Detective Agency could also be utilised, and any galoots known to be on its record system would be fair game. These galoots were not really aware of these records being kept, but the BLA were enthusiastic supporters of this system. Tom Benson was not the fittest of fellas, but he was very adept at working the telegraph and then having the information acted upon by his detectives.

Trigg Hemmyng had the BLA working very well, the bank statements were testament to that. His intention to move into the cattle detection business was still alive and kicking in his mind. He had left it to simmer until he had the right man to run this more specialised and decidedly more dangerous operation.

Rustlers were often very callous galoots, the worst of the lot in Trigg's experience and understandly so, bearing in mind the huge rewards. One good night of thieving could set a hombre up for life. It was a fact and many 'ranchers' were not slow to give a long easy grin when it was alluded to, but that was it, just the grin, never a comment that might incriminate them. Trigg Hemmyng had a fella lined up to run this operation for him but until the time was right for both of them, the only thing that needed to be done was to keep well abreast of who was coming into the cattle business, where they were located and who was suspected of being the rustlers. With cattle being regarded as a simple way of earning big money, there were plenty of new operations being reputedly organised. He and Roger could keep themselves informed of these developments, and he would keep in close contact with his 'prospect' so that the most opportune time could be agreed upon for them to hit the ground galloping.

Wyoming, and the West in general, was still growing quickly. Opportunities were opening up all the time and being in the right place at the right time made it much easier.

Trigg Hemmyng was determined to ensure that him and his men collected as much of this loot as was possible. It would not be from a lack of effort on their part, and if others had to be eased aside, so as to speak, so be it. The past had been for honing his ability, the future would be for capitalising his talents and his confidence was high.

Available soon:

Era 3 of *The Happening Man*

who gets involved with some of the Wild West's more famous and notorious Outlaws and Con men as the story moves into this fabled era of notoriety.